Dead Folks

Also by Jon A. Jackson

Deadman
Hit on the House
The Diehard
The Blind Pig
Grootka

Dead Folks
Jon A. Jackson

THE ATLANTIC MONTHLY PRESS
NEW YORK

The author would like to acknowledge the assistance of the Salt Lake City Police Department and the Utah State Medical Examiner's Office.

Published simultaneously in Canada
Printed in the United States of America

First edition

Library of Congress Cataloging-in-Publication Data
Jackson, Jon A.
    Dead Folks / Jon A. Jackson. — 1st ed.
      p.   cm.
    ISBN 0-87113-638-4
    1. Mulheisen, Detective Sergeant (Fictitious character)—Fiction.
  2. Police—Michigan—Detroit—Fiction. 3. Salt Lake City (Utah)—
Fiction. I. Title.
PS3560.A216D39   1996
813'.54—dc20

                                              96-2289

Design by Laura Hammond Hough

The Atlantic Monthly Press
841 Broadway
New York, NY 10003

10 9 8 7 6 5 4 3 2 1

For David Morrell, creator of Rambo,
the most widely recognized literary character since Sherlock.
My thanks to a wise and generous teacher.

Prologue:
Talking Horse

Mulheisen was sitting in Pinky's restaurant, staring at a remarkable picture of a naked woman. Pinky's was one of his favorite places in Detroit. It was basically just an old frame house, located near the MacArthur Bridge, on Jefferson Avenue. The house had legendary associations for Mulheisen since, in his childhood, every time they passed the house in his father's car, his father or his mother would point it out as the place "where they caught those Nazis." The "Nazis" were said to be spies who had assisted a Luftwaffe pilot, a prisoner of war who had escaped from a Canadian prison camp. This was not exactly the case, as Mulheisen eventually learned.

Mulheisen's father had been for many years the water commissioner, responsible for, among other things, the municipal waterworks in Detroit. One of the principal installations of these works was located in Waterworks Park, just a few blocks farther out Jefferson Avenue from Pinky's. During World War II, it was feared that the waterworks might be sabotaged by Nazis, or Nazi sympathizers—"fifth columnists" in the slang of the day—which tremendously enhanced the glamour of the tale of the escaped Luftwaffe pilot in little Mul's mind. The fact that the naval armory was nearby also helped in building this legend. Wow! Nazis! Actual Nazis, here in ordinary old Detroit! The mind reeled.

That Mulheisen later bothered to find out the known facts about this legend says something about his character. He had become a policeman, ultimately a detective, a career choice that greatly startled his parents. What he learned was that Pinky's was not the house where the escaped Luftwaffe pilot (a magical phrase that rang in little Mul's imagination like a golden bell) had been arrested. It was in the neighborhood, though, and the pilot had been briefly harbored by an amiable middle-aged couple who were not Nazis or even Nazi sympathizers, but merely Germans who had immigrated to Detroit at least twenty years earlier . . . innocent people, themselves victims of war.

The Luftwaffe pilot had escaped from a prisoner-of-war camp in northern Ontario in company with a Wehrmacht captain who was a cousin of the wife in the couple. The Wehrmacht officer was recaptured quite early, but the Luftwaffe pilot made his way to Detroit, where he took the chance that the couple might assist him. They did, out of compassion for a fellow German who was in danger and despair, and perhaps out of fear—they may have simply wanted to move the escapee on down the road, so that he did not imperil their already troubled circumstances.

It wasn't easy being a German immigrant with a noticeable accent in Detroit in 1944; one kept a low profile. The American public did not distinguish between ordinary Germans and Nazi Party members. For that matter, one didn't even have to be a German to be harassed as a sympathizer, as in the case of a suburban family who found their house surrounded by angry neighbors one night because a baby-sitter had told her parents, who told other neighbors, that there was a well-read copy of *Mein Kampf* in the house. (The husband, something of a self-styled intellectual, convinced his neighbors, after a long harangue on the porch, that he was "just trying to find out what the hell all this danged Hitler fuss was about.")

As it happened, the pilot was never caught, Mulheisen learned. He managed to get to New Orleans and thence onto a freighter that took him to South America. He didn't make it to Germany before the war ended, so one could say that he failed in his duty, but he had certainly tried and he had been brave and nearly successful. The German-American couple, however, was nabbed by the FBI and sent to prison for a good long time, their lives utterly ruined. Perhaps they were lucky not to have been hung, or shot, which surely would have been the fate of their counterparts in Nazi Germany.

Mulheisen was aware, of course, that his own family was of German origin, having immigrated to America in the mid–nineteenth century. But they made very little of their German heritage, perhaps because of the two world wars, in which their new homeland took sides against the fatherland. There were times when Müllers changed their names to Miller, and towns once called Berlin overnight became Lincoln City. He didn't even really know where in Germany the Mulheisens had come from, although he had a vague idea it was in the central region, perhaps around Erfurt. He wondered if his parents' interest in this episode had been enhanced by their own Germanness and if they had somehow, perhaps unconsciously, communicated their heightened interest to their child.

Legends aside, the reason Mulheisen had first come to Pinky's, years ago, was because he had heard that it served an excellent calf's liver. He had since decided that he didn't like calf's liver; indeed, he wondered how he could *ever* have liked calf's liver. But he still went to Pinky's because it was a comfortable place with an ambience that appealed to him, of homeyness overlaid with a modest and confident elegance. As for the alleged Nazi association, it was interesting to him that even after he had discovered the evident facts about the case, Pinky's still gleamed in his imagination with a mysterious, if dimmed, glamour.

Pinky's was rather empty today, the post-Christmas lull, perhaps. Mulheisen and his old friend Vito Belk had scooched their chairs together at one of the tables so that they could both look at some pictures that Vito had brought. These pictures looked like photographic prints but were actually computer generated. They were mostly black-and-white, about eight inches square, but some were in color and some looked like infrared. They were aerial shots. Some were of a mountainous terrain seen from several hundred feet, but most were much closer.

"These pictures are tremendously magnified," Vito said, "so details tend to be a little fuzzy. She's not fuzzy, though." Vito was a heavy man, a fuzzy man, with a beard that covered almost his whole face; when he smiled his teeth sparkled through the hedge.

Mulheisen smiled back at Vito's joke, but his smile didn't exactly sparkle. He was an almost homely man, with a longish face and longish teeth that were slightly separated. This feature had given him the nickname "Sergeant Fang" on the Street.

Vito's joke was that the woman in the picture was floating on her back in a pool, her arms and legs outspread, and while she had a great mane of black hair drifting about her head, she had no other hair visible on her body. She was gazing upward, seemingly in a state of bliss, as if looking directly into the camera. She was a small woman, slim and almost boyish, except for the mane of black hair. Almost no breasts, no hips. Very pretty face, with large eyes and full lips. The faint line of the vagina was visible.

"What altitude was this camera?" Mulheisen asked.

Vito wasn't sure. He looked at the back of the picture and then at the others. There was nothing on the back. "They're from different satellites," he said. "I'm not, uh . . . I can't say which sat-

4

ellites. You understand. But most of them are about two hundred miles, I think."

Mulheisen wasn't interested in which satellites had taken the pictures. He was just interested in what was in them. Each picture had a date-and-time line printed on it, such as "8 September, 1801:05 GMT," or "18 December, 2145:27 GMT." This was the instant, in Greenwich Mean Time, when the picture was taken, Vito explained. "Not that it's a snapshot, or something. There's no film involved, just transmitted bits of electronic information that get stored in a computer." He didn't say where, but Mulheisen could guess.

"This is a great shot," Vito said, tapping the one of the naked woman floating on her back. It wasn't clear if he meant that the picture had come out well or that he liked the subject—perhaps both. It seemed to have been taken from a distance of about ten feet above the water. Three accompanying shots of the same instant—the same shot, actually, at different magnifications: say from a hundred feet, five hundred feet, a thousand feet—revealed that the pool was a hot springs on a mountainside, surrounded by mature evergreen trees.

The woman in the picture was known to Mulheisen as Helen Sedlacek, and he believed that she had murdered a Detroit crime boss named Dante "Carmine" Busoni. He believed that she did it with the assistance of a man known in the crime world as Joe Service but known in the Butte, Montana, area as Joseph Humann. He believed that Helen had killed Carmine because the latter had ordered the killing of her father, a charming crook known as Big Sid. This hot springs was located on Joseph Humann's property, some forty miles south of Butte.

"Now here's the same scene about twenty minutes later," Vito said, regretfully putting aside the nude shot and picking up a new one. "This was taken by a different satellite, coming from a different direction. It doesn't have quite the capability of the first, so we didn't get it down to three meters, but you can see that this is not the girl in the first shot."

This one was in color, and while Vito's criticism of the camera's capabilities was accurate, Mulheisen could see that this naked body was not a female at all. This was a dead man with long-ish hair, lying on his back at nearly the opposite end of the hot springs pool, a flaccid penis clearly visible. He could tell the man was dead, or infer it at least, because of dark spotlike smudges on the chest, which seemed connected to a pinkish cloudiness as of blood around the body, and the disposition of the body: this was not a living person trying to keep afloat. This was a guy who had been shot at least four times. The head lay back and submerged, with the mouth open. The face wasn't very visible.

Mulheisen looked at it for a long time, then said, "This is as close as you can get it?"

Vito shrugged. "Maybe one of our guys could get it a little better."

"That'd be good," Mulheisen said. "The face isn't identifi-able at this angle, but the disposition of the bullet wounds could be matched to the body we have. If this is who I think it is, and if we can establish that these shots were taken twenty minutes apart, as it indicates . . . "

Vito shook his head. "I don't think so, Mul. I mean, I can get you—maybe—a better shot of this guy, but if you're thinking you can use this as evidence or something, forget it. These pix don't exist. In fact, if my boss knew that you were looking at them, not only would my job be history, I might become part of the history of Leavenworth."

Mulheisen looked at his old high school buddy wistfully. They had shared a bench in chemistry lab and their hall lockers had been across from each other's. They had smoked cigarettes together in the loft above the stage, when both were on stage crew. He wasn't real sure where Vito worked now, but he had an idea. It was either a federal agency or it was under exclusive contract to that agency and, either way, it meant that Vito wasn't supposed to show around pictures that were taken by satellites, at least not without some higher authority. Mulheisen now asked if that authority could be obtained.

"Possibly," Vito said. "It depends on the satellite involved. Some of these, maybe this one"—he pointed to the picture of the dead man—"are just geographical survey satellites, mapping. But others have more, ah, *special* missions. If a need, a greatly pressing need to know could be established. . . . The problem is, even for the public-domain-type pictures, somebody asks 'How did you find out about this?' So first, we have to agree that these pix don't exist— yet—and I didn't show them to you. Okay? Okay. Then I have to go to the boss and say something like, 'I was talking to a buddy of mine the other day, a cop, and he was asking me about satellites and I admitted that yeah, there are a lot of satellites and at any given time there might be a chance that one is flying right over where you are standing and if it is mapping or whatever its function, yeah, you could probably retrieve that data somewhere and maybe, just maybe, you might be able to see what was happening at that moment.' So then my boss would probably ask me why I was blabbing this crap all over town, and then I might convince him that it was essentially harmless and besides, it might be of value to the police and we should always cooperate with the police, et cetera, et cetera. But whether he'd go along with that, I don't know. I kind of doubt it." He picked up his coffee and sipped it, but he made a face when he realized it was cold, and he set it down. He signaled the bartender and asked for a cognac.

Mulheisen nodded. "Well, at least I can look now and if it turns out that it would be useful evidence we can worry about that later. But Vito, I would never tell anyone how I got hold of this."

"Or even that you got hold of it, is better," Vito said.

"So what else do we have?" Mulheisen asked.

They turned to the other folders, other pictures. A series of scenes of a cabin in the mountains, in December, in snow. Then a picture of that same cabin, or what had been that cabin, lying in a black, smoky ruin amidst the snow. This had been the property of Joseph Humann, a.k.a. Joe Service. It lay approximately two hundred yards over the ridge from the hot springs.

There were several shots between the first one, of the pristine snow, no tracks leading up to the cabin or the nearby shed/garage, and the later shot of the burnt-out cabin. These intermediate pictures were murky, obscured for the most part by falling snow or partial cloud cover. But they did show an automobile in the yard, near the shed. And another one showed a female human figure walking through the snow, carrying an armful of firewood. And finally, a shot of two women, one holding wood and another bending over, perhaps to pick up wood to place in the other's arms.

This was of great interest to Mulheisen because he knew, from the time line on the pictures of the two women, that they were taken at a time when Joseph Humann, otherwise known as Joe Service, was supposed to be in the cabin, attended by his nurse, Cathleen Yoder. Mr. Humann had nearly been killed by a would-be assassin three months earlier, at approximately the time of the pictures of the hot springs, in fact. Humann had made a remarkable recovery. So remarkable that by the time of this picture, just three months later, he had been able to leave the hospital for a day or so, a kind of holiday, to visit his cabin.

What was interesting in these pictures for Mulheisen was the presence of *two* women. The pictures were not good. The visibility was bad and this camera hadn't been able to get the resolution to within three meters, as the best of them did, but you could distinguish the one woman from the other. Mulheisen had seen Ms. Yoder, the nurse, before. She was the smaller woman, the one with blond hair cascading from under the woolen hat, whose arms were being loaded with wood. But the other one, that tall one, he didn't know her.

This was significant because within a few hours the cabin would burn, the propane tank would blow up, and everybody in the building, except for one man, would be killed. But there was no body of Joseph Humann or Cate Yoder or any other woman in that burnt-out hulk. And Yoder's car, the one he could see in the satellite shot, was gone. At the time of the explosion there had been two other cars present, one of them rented by Helen Sedlacek and the other belonging to a local crime figure. So Mulheisen and the other authorities had reasonably concluded that Humann and his nurse had left before the arrival, probably separately, of Helen Sedlacek and six men, known crime figures, five of whose bodies were found there, plus the one who survived. Helen had been apprehended by Mulheisen shortly afterward and was presently in a Butte jail. But there was no sign of any second woman who had been present with Humann and Yoder. Except in this satellite picture. It was definitely not Helen; she was smaller than Yoder.

Mulheisen was truly puzzled, because he had thought that he had pretty much figured out this whole scenario. Humann and Yoder go to the cabin, then they leave; Helen Sedlacek comes to the cabin, but she flees into the woods on foot when the killers arrive; the killers arrive, invade the empty cabin, a fire starts, the cabin blows up, killing all but one of them; Mulheisen and the other cops arrive; Helen is arrested.

The cabin pictures were not of much interest, except for the presence of the unknown woman. Mulheisen was almost sorry he had asked Vito to obtain them—he'd been so sure of his interpretation of events. It was practically a closed case, except for the disappearance of Joe Service. But now . . . an unforeseen element had muddied the water. By contrast, the hot springs pictures had clarified that situation. They weren't exactly witnesses to a crime, but they certainly placed Helen on a remote scene within minutes of a homicide.

Mulheisen considered that what he had really been looking for in the cabin shots was a picture of Joe Service. He'd seen Joe Service when he was in the hospital, but he hadn't been able to talk to him at the time. A picture of Joe Service was of no particular value. He would no doubt be all bundled up, assisted by the nurse and, perhaps, the other woman. But Mulheisen longed to see him. He had no strong evidence against Joe Service for any crime, not enough to obtain a warrant for his arrest, anyway. But he had enough to hold him for questioning, if he could find him, and more evidence could be found . . . *would* be found.

The simple truth was that Joe Service had so plagued his investigations over the years that Mulheisen felt an almost physical need to see him, to touch him, to know where he was. And he felt that he would achieve this.

"Can I keep these?" Mulheisen asked.

Belk looked pained, but then he sighed and said, "All right, Mul. But for chrissake, don't show 'em to anybody else. Don't even talk about 'em. Okay?"

Mulheisen nodded agreeably. He shuffled through the pictures again, musing on their very existence. An event occurs, he thought, and it is witnessed. But for various reasons the witnesses will not, or cannot, or at least they do not, tell you what happened. Unless you can get them to tell you, the event is lost to history. Only imagination can recover it. He thought of the famous poem of Auden's about paintings of the Old Masters. In one of the paintings the poet notices a murderer's horse, innocently scratching his butt on a tree while the deed is done. If only the horse could talk! Well, what he had here was a talking horse. He almost shivered.

Mulheisen put all the pictures in a large envelope. He leaned toward Vito and said, with a nod toward the bar, "You know about this place? About the escaped Luftwaffe pilot?"

Vito didn't know the story. Mulheisen was surprised. It had been an important thing in his life, but suddenly he saw that it was just a minor drama. He recounted it briefly.

"So they never caught the guy?" Vito said.

Mulheisen was staring into the middle distance, thinking. "He got away." He paused. "Sometimes they get away."

1

New Kid in Town

The Avarris car rental agency in Salt Lake City is just a little metal building in a parking lot next to the airport lot. The clerk was a not-quite-handsome young man, about six feet and two inches tall, with blond hair and blue eyes. His jaw was too big, and as much as the eye tried to deny it, he had hips. He wore a gold company blazer that needed dry cleaning and his name tag said Eldon Twigg. Joe Service reckoned Mr. Twigg was about twenty years old. Joe himself was a relatively short man, about thirty, with new black hair that had lately grown back in after being shaved for surgery and had acquired an alarming number of silvery strands. He also had a beard, which he had never worn before, and it, too, had silver in it. Normally Joe's energetic, vivacious nature more than compensated for stature, but Joe had been shot in the head not too long ago and he had just ridden all night through a winter storm in Montana and Idaho, so he wasn't in top form. Nonetheless, he was a determined man, so he put on his best face and said he'd like to rent a car, the best car Avarris had, a Cadillac or a Continental, something like that.

Avarris had a Cadillac, a practically brand-new Coupe de Ville. "Expensive, though," young Mr. Twigg said. Joe waved his hand contemptuously. Price was no object. Twigg eyed Joe's drawn, bearded, not very clean face and rumpled clothes—jeans, a sweater, a not-recently-cleaned ski jacket. Twigg wasn't sure that this client was really a Cadillac client. But you never knew these days. Multimillionaire actors and sports stars flew around the country unshaven and wearing jeans busted out at the knee. This client had something of that look, the arrogance, the slightly dangerous don't-fuck-with-me look. Twigg asked for the credit card.

"I don't use credit cards," Joe said.

"You have to have a credit card," Twigg said, his jaw wagging ponderously. He decided that the client didn't have the scruffy actor look.

"I have a deal with Avarris," Joe said. "You can check on your computer. It'll be under Joseph Humann, Tinstar, Montana."

Tinstar, Montana, Twigg thought. Joe Humann? Not a movie star, not even a famous director. "Uh, how are we spelling that, Mr. Humann? Two 'ens'?" Stifling a smirk, Twigg punched the information into the computer and stood looking at the screen, skeptically. After a moment he frowned slightly and said, "Well, you have a listing under our cash/credit program, Mr. Humann, but you haven't used the program in more than six months. That means your credit has to be reviewed."

"Reviewed," Joe said. He smiled, but it wasn't a pleasant smile. "I give these"—he hesitated, then spat out the word "people," clearly choosing this innocuous word over a more rude usage, a choice as effective in its way as a violent curse—"cash so they'll let me give them cash instead of a piece of plastic! I'm paying them to allow me to pay them in cash!" His voice was rising in anger, but he suddenly reined it in. "How long does this review take?" he asked quietly.

Eldon Twigg was scared. Something in Mr. Humann's voice and manner had sent a thrill of terror deep into his scrotum. His voice was a little shaky as he replied, in a near whisper, "Not long, sir. A half hour maybe. I'll request the review, shall I?"

Joe nodded. "I have to go out to my, ah, friend's car," he said. "I'll be right back."

"I'll start getting the papers ready," Twigg said. He watched as Joe turned away and shuffled out the door, stumbling over the threshold. Twigg could see a young-looking blond woman sitting behind the wheel of a road-splattered Ford. Humann opened the back door of the car and got in.

The driver was a very pretty young woman, but neither was she looking her best. She'd driven all night after a harrowing time in a remote cabin in Montana, a half hour of terror followed by confusion, flight, and not nearly enough in the way of clarification and explanation from Joe. She was a nurse named Cathleen Yoder. Everybody called her Cateyo, as if it were "Katie-o." She was twenty-six years old and unmarried, an improbable virgin in these promiscuous times.

She watched quietly while Joe opened a cardboard box that he'd thrown in the back last night, before they'd fled the cabin. She had no idea what was in the box but she became alarmed when Joe began to mutter and fling handfuls of old letters and bills all over the back seat of the car. He looked up at last, his face more drawn than ever, and staring right at her said, "Stupid!"

Cateyo recoiled. Never had Joe used a word of abuse toward her, never, nor even a mild reproach. He smiled then and said, "Not you, babe. Me. I'm a dummy. A goddamn dummy." Then he slumped back on the seat. He looked so tired, so defeated, that her heart ached, literally ached for him.

"What's wrong, Joe?" she said softly.

He sighed and tried to pull himself up, but it seemed too much effort for him. He sank back. "I'm stupid," he said. "I'm also flat broke."

This was a new experience for Joe Service. He couldn't recall ever being broke. But then, his memory wasn't what it should be. A bullet in the head can erase memory, in theory. There are other theories, however, that claim that memory is not simply stored in a single location in the brain, as in a filing cabinet, but is parceled out all over the brain and anyway is not so much a quantity as a process. Joe wasn't conversant with these theories. But he knew he wasn't remembering everything he should. He wasn't thinking about that now, though. He was grasping at another shadowy memory that suggested, vaguely hinted anyway, that he really had a lot of money in many different places, if he could just remember where and how to get at it.

He struggled with this one, gazing blankly at Cateyo's concerned face. "What?" he said, finally, realizing that she had spoken.

"I said, I have some money," Cateyo replied.

Joe dismissed this with an abrupt movement of his head. No, no, he couldn't take her money. He couldn't be dependent on this . . . this, well not *dumb* broad, but at least a naive, trusting, simple, and, mmmm, very attractive young woman.

"Why not?" she demanded. "We're in this together, aren't we, Joe?"

"In what together? We're not *in* anything," he said irritably. "You're just *with* me." He regretted saying that as soon as it was uttered. Her face fell, but she was not a marshmallow. Her expression hardened.

"I've done a lot for you, Joe. I've taken care of you, I came with you. I've given up my life for you. You can't just throw it back at me."

"Given up what?" he sneered. "Your life? What the hell are you talking about? You haven't given up anything. Go back. Go back, now. What, you forgot to call in, or something? The hospital won't make a big deal of it. You're a good nurse. The hospital might be annoyed, but that's all. Go on. Get out of here."

He started to open the door, but she grabbed his hand on the back of the front seat. "Don't, Joe," she warned him and he stopped. "You can't do this to me. Without me you'd still be back there in that cabin and who knows what that means? God knows, I don't. I came with you because you needed me. Without me you wouldn't be here."

Joe started to retort to this, but then he realized that she was right. She had helped him, he did need her. "I'm sorry, babe," he said, "I wasn't thinking. I . . . I'm not all here . . . yet." He patted her hand and let her take his hand in hers. She gripped it tightly, lovingly.

When she was convinced that he meant it, she smiled and took a chance on humor. She said, "Besides, back there on the pass you said we'd get married."

"What pass? Monida Pass? I didn't say we'd get married," Joe said, but he didn't withdraw his hand. He grimaced, half smiling at her, a look of mock reproach. "I said . . . I *think* I said it was an *idea*. A good idea, a bad idea . . . it's something to think about. Hey, c'mon, lighten up. Umm, how much money have you got?"

"Well, I've got about two hundred dollars in cash, and I've got a Visa and a MasterCard—"

At this moment they were interrupted by a rap on the rear window. Young Mr. Twigg was leaning down, smiling, showing a lot of teeth. When Joe turned to look at him, he said, "Mr. Humann? It's all right."

Joe lowered the window. "What's all right?"

"Your credit," Twigg said. "The head office called right back. Your credit is fine. You won't even need to make a deposit. They'll just bill your bank, as before. Anything you want, they said." He brandished some papers. "I've got it all made out. Just sign here, by the X." He thrust the papers through the window.

Joe took the papers and gestured for a pen. Twigg handed him a ballpoint. Joe read the form. It said that Avarris would bill his

Salt Lake City bank, Zion National Bank. He signed and gave the papers back. "I'll bring the car right up," Twigg said, and vanished into the little office.

Joe turned back to Cateyo. He shrugged and lifted his hands and his eybrows comically. "No prob," he said. He got out of the car and closed the door.

"Joe!" Cateyo called after him in panic.

He leaned down and looked in the open back window. "What?"

"You're not . . . ," she faltered.

"Hey, relax. I'm not taking off." He limped around the car to where she sat and when she rolled down the window he leaned in and kissed her lightly on the lips. His tongue flickered across her lips and she shivered. "Let's go to a hotel," he said. "Follow me."

The kid brought the Cadillac up, a very shiny metallic maroon Coupe de Ville. He hopped out and handed the keys to Joe. "Here you are, Mr. Humann. Have a good day."

"Thank you, Mr. Twigg. I appreciate your patience and . . . and your kindness. Do I return the car here?"

"Oh, no. You can return it anywhere we have an office. There's a list in the glove compartment. We're not as widespread as some, but where we don't have an office you can return it at any Nationwide or Mountainwest agency . . . we have agreements with them. There'll just be a slight additional fee."

Joe thanked him and got in. It took him a moment or two to orient himself. The car felt good and rich. It was softly comfortable but radiated an aura of power. It had many indicators buried in the leather-bound dash. He took a good long time to stare at them, but they were largely incomprehensible. He had to adjust the seat, ponder the mechanical arrangements, but finally, though somewhat mystified, he decided to just go ahead and turn the key. The idea that the key could be turned had just occurred to him. He was confident that it would all come back to him, although he hadn't driven a car in over three months. And he was right. He did everything automatically. He drove out of the parking lot, with Cateyo following. But before he got very far he pulled over and got out to talk to her.

"I might be a little confused here," he said. "Why don't you just lead the way back into town and I'll follow you."

"Where are we going?"

"To a hotel."

"What hotel?"

"Any hotel. Any good hotel," he corrected. "The one with the fanciest-dressed doorman. You've got your cards, right? Let's go to the biggest, most expensive hotel. I'll make it up to you."

Cateyo looked mystified, but she made an expression that seemed to say, Okay, whatever you say. She maneuvered out onto the freeway and headed back in to Salt Lake City. After cruising around downtown for a few minutes, she pulled into the sweeping entry of a very large hotel, with Joe Service right behind her. A doorman in a long coat and a fancy hat hurried to open her door. Another opened Joe's door.

Joe told the desk that their bags would catch up to them. A few minutes later they were ushered into the best suite, at the top of the hotel. The bellboy opened the long traversing drapes, revealing a splendid view of the Wasatch Front, the mountains looking craggy and etched with newly fallen snow like a steel engraving in the midmorning sun. "Give the man a five, honey," Joe said to Cateyo.

When the bellboy had gone he turned to her. She stood there, a little rumpled looking, tired, but young and pretty. He could see she was scared. It occurred to him that she may never have been alone in a hotel room with a man. He took her by the arm and drew her over to the window and they gazed out over the snow-dusted city at the mountains. He hugged her with one arm and gave her a little kiss on the cheek. She responded with a shy squeeze around his waist.

Joe broke away from her, peeling off his ski jacket. "I'm starving," he said, "but I'm also beat. And I feel grungy. I'm going to take a shower."

"You'd better take your medications, first," Cateyo said. While Joe unabashedly shucked off his clothes she laid out various pills. He gulped them down with water, then walked into the huge, luxurious shower. It was beautifully tiled and had a built-in seat. He turned the water on full blast and hot.

As he had hoped, Cateyo joined him a few minutes later. His body was something she was quite familiar with. She had washed him countless times in the hospital in Butte. It was a great body, somewhat softened by a prolonged hospital stay, but still well muscled. Joe had actually seen Cateyo naked only the night before, but this was his first opportunity to lay hands on those tender breasts, to hold the resilient flesh of those buttocks. Weariness vanished in the steam and lather of aromatic soap. These two young, finely constructed people responded to each other's caresses in a timeless way: halfway through the soaping, they lost patience and rinsed themselves as quickly as they could before partially toweling off and rushing to the enormous bed. They threw themselves on top of the satiny spread and Joe crouched before those eagerly opened thighs, gazing down at her pink vaginal lips, peeping through the damp blond fur.

Perhaps no creature on the planet is as sexually volatile as a female human about twenty-six years old, especially a virgin. Joe was frankly priapic. Cateyo lay with her knees up and wide apart. When Joe reached out and cupped her vulva she jumped galvanically. She was hot and ready.

Cateyo trembled with anticipation as Joe lowered himself toward her. She lay partially supported on her elbows, not sure what to do. She was not a prudish young woman. She was a practiced nurse and had often thought about this moment. Here in this splendid room, with the mountain light flooding in the tall window, she felt rather exposed, a little fearful, but definitely ready for what she expected would be a great, great watershed moment in her life.

Joe leaned forward to slide his hands up along her flanks, reveling in the subtle weight of her breasts against the haft of his thumbs. The large, helmetlike head of his cock prodded the curtains of her vagina, found a partable aperture, and nosed into her slightly before meeting an unexpected resistance. Her vagina was very dry. He reached down with his hand and maneuvered his cock, prying open the lips slightly. He thrust, then again, and was gratified by a little flush of moisture. But now he met another resistance, not just dryness. He looked into her blue eyes with his own in surprise. It had not occurred to him that she was a virgin.

"Do it," she urged him, huskily. She braced her heels on the bedspread instinctively and gave a little gasp as he thrust into her, harder. Then he stopped. He looked down in amazement. For the first time in his life he was stymied at sex. His cock had softened.

"What the hell," he said, annoyed. Then he sat back on his calves, shocked. His penis had completely wilted. His fingers fumbled at the limp organ, shaking it impatiently, as if to waken it.

"Here," Cateyo said, eagerly reaching down to take hold of him. Many times, in the night stretches of her care for him at the hospital, she had manipulated him into great involuntary erections and finally eruptions, sometimes when he was not conscious. She had even taken him in her mouth before, an act of such daring and incredible depravity in her mind that she still could hardly believe she had done it. Her hand aroused him slightly, now, and quickly she swooped down again to suck at him. She was frenzied, dying to have him in her at last, and she was pleased to find him quickly stiffened and ready again. She lay back and once again she waited for the great moment.

Just as eagerly, Joe leaned into her. His now moistened cock entered her more readily, but once again, when it met resistance, it crumpled and went dead on him.

Joe was horrified, humiliated. He jumped back, off the bed, and stood there, staring first at his useless penis, then at her sprawled and waiting body. Nothing could be more simple: a beautiful woman, an eager man, two young lovers anxious to enact life's essential act. . . . But it was clear to him that it was no go. He felt almost no sensation in his heretofore ever-ready organ.

"I can't believe it," he groaned. He felt frustrated beyond imagining. He had heard of such things. Who hadn't? But it was something that afflicted old men, the slobs, the drunkards . . . not active, lean, virile young men like himself. "What's wrong?" he said, plaintively.

"You're tired," Cateyo said, quickly. She came to him, hugged him, pressing her lively breasts into his flat, smoothly muscled chest. "You're exhausted. Don't worry about it." It killed her to say it, she wanted him so desperately, but she sensed, as a woman, as a nurse, that it was just an unfortunate moment. They would get past this. They need only wait a bit; perhaps later.

"Let's eat," she said. "You'll feel better, stronger. You need rest." She turned back the heavy comforter, peeled back the sheets, and helped him between them.

"Yeah, yeah," he said, his anger and puzzlement making him resistant at first, but then very quickly lapsing into a passive patient mode, readily submitting to her nursing, her comforting. "I'll feel better. Call room service. Get some breakfast up here. Coffee, eggs . . ." He lay back with a groan. He felt wiped out.

Cateyo went to the bathroom and donned one of the heavy terry cloth robes with the hotel name on it. Then she called room service and ordered. She lay down on the cover, next to Joe, and held him. By the time the food arrived he was unconscious. Ravenous herself, she drew the little serving cart over to the window and sat there to eat both breakfasts. She drank both glasses of orange juice and two cups of coffee while looking out at the mountains. It was very beautiful. She had never in her life stayed in such a fancy place.

She looked over at the huge bed, where Joe was curled up like a street kid, his black hair peeping over the comforter. He slept like a child. She wondered at all this. She stood in the sunlight by the window and daringly opened her robe. They were on the top floor, or near the top, she knew. She ran her hands over her body. She wanted him.

What on earth was happening to her? How had she gotten here? She was twenty-six years old, an intelligent, competent nurse, a farm girl from Montana whose mother had died when she was ten. Her father had been a cranky, ultrareligious man who had died a few years after she went away to nursing school, of a heart attack while feeding cattle in the field. She had never understood him very well. Later, she herself had developed religious notions. And then along came Joe. He was a mysterious man found shot and nearly dead on the highway outside Butte. From the first she had realized he was special, even while he lay in a coma for many days. She had thought of him as an avatar, an angel perhaps, someone sent to her by God. He was a new man. A reborn man, a man yanked back from the dead, she'd imagined. For a long time, when he couldn't talk, couldn't tell them who he was, she had called him Paul, a playful name, as in Paul Newman, or like St. Paul. She hadn't meant it all that seriously, but the idea had gripped her for a good long time. Now she knew he wasn't an angel, not an avatar, not some new man sent by God, but it no longer mattered. She knew he was deeply involved in some criminal activity—that had been made clear to her by a police detective who had come out to Butte from Detroit, a Sergeant Mulheisen. They had no particular evidence against Joe, apparently—they hadn't arrested him—but she brushed aside these concerns as irrelevant. She was deeply in love with him. Right now, as she ran her hand over her smooth belly, she wanted him so badly it was painful.

She looked across the room and tried out a word she had never actually spoken aloud. She didn't say it very loudly, just whispered under her breath: "Fuck." Then, "Fuck me." It sounded odd in the still hotel room air. A brutal word, in a way, but somehow essential and vital. She whispered it again. "Fuck me, darling," she said.

Then she lay down on the cover next to him, cuddling against him. He didn't stir. She fell asleep for a while and when she woke it was late afternoon. Joe slept on, not even snoring, not noticing when she leaned over and kissed his scratchy cheek. She lay back and pondered what she should do. She should call Montana, call the hospital. They were probably worried sick, wondering what had happened to her and her patient. She wondered if she could tell them how they had been attacked by the woman, Heather, whom she had thought was her new friend. A woman who, from the little she had gleaned from Joe, was apparently a killer sent to track him down. It was not something she could imagine herself explaining, as unbelievable as her once-embraced notion of Joe as the new man, the angel from heaven.

Lord, she thought, how on earth did I get here? But here she was. She sat up and paced about, restless and anxious. Finally, she went to the bedside telephone and looked through the hotel folder until she learned how to make an outside call. She was waiting for the hospital to answer when Joe's hand reached around her and clamped down on the telephone rest, cutting off the call.

"What are you doing?" he asked, his eyes blinking, but wild. "What the hell are you doing?"

"Joe! You're awake. I . . . I'll order something from room service."

"Who were you calling?" he demanded. He looked angry.

"Nobody," Cateyo said. "I was calling the hospital. I just didn't want them to worry."

"Calling the hospital?" Joe said. He glanced around. It was not late, but the short winter day was already declining. He sat up. Cateyo replaced the phone on its stand.

Joe thought for a moment, running his hands through his thick black hair, rubbing his bearded face. "All right," he said, finally. "Go ahead, call them. Tell them you've run away. Say it any way you like. But don't tell them where we are. And don't call from here. You have to go out. Don't use the lobby pay phone. Go down the street. Call that nurse, your boss."

"I know," Cateyo said. "But I'm worried about the house."

"What house?"

"My house. It's winter up there. If the heat goes off, the pipes could freeze."

"Figure it out," Joe said. "Just don't tell them where you are. Say you're in Spokane, if you have to. You're at the . . . " Suddenly he remembered something. "Tell them you're in Idaho, at the Coeur d'Alene Resort Hotel. When you come back we'll get something to eat." He lay back and closed his eyes. "Go ahead. Call them. I'm just going to rest a little bit more."

By the time she had dressed, Joe seemed asleep again. She found a pay phone a block from the hotel, in a drugstore. It was dark out now, the downtown Christmas decorations glittering on the Salt Lake streets. She thought of getting Joe a present, some little thing, a surprise. Perhaps because of the sex, the failure of it, or just because it was on a shelf near the pay phone, she found herself looking at condoms and lubricant. On an impulse, she bought a plastic container of "personal lubricant." Perhaps that was all that was needed.

"I'm in Coeur d'Alene," Cateyo told her supervisor, Head Nurse Janice Work. It was the most direct and deliberate lie she had ever told, but she went boldly on with it. "We're getting married."

"Oh gosh," Nurse Work exclaimed. "Honey, are you sure? Do you really love him?"

"Janice, I have never known anything more securely," Cateyo said. "He's . . . well, he's . . . " She hesitated. She had been on the verge of saying, "He's my god." But that was wrong. "He's my lover," she said, a statement no more true than the other. Then she paused, and added, "Am I stupid? Am I crazy? I love him, Janice."

"Of course you're crazy." Janice laughed. "You're crazy as a loon. But you're in love." She thought about her own life, her husband who worked on the power company lines. He was out in the cold at that very moment, repairing downed lines from the storm. "Be in love. Do it. But Cateyo, are you sure you're all right? You weren't hurt in the fire?"

"What fire? What are you talking about? Of course I'm all right."

"There was a fire at the cabin, at Mr. Humann's cabin. Didn't you know? Several people were killed. We had the only survivor in here, just for a few minutes, and then they flew him to Salt Lake, to the burn center. The police are looking for you and Mr. Humann. They were afraid you might have been trapped in the fire. That detective from Detroit is back, asking about you and Mr. Humann."

Cateyo was stunned. All thoughts of sex and marriage and romance fled from her mind. "I didn't know," she said. "We didn't know a thing about it. We just left the cabin, it was all right. There wasn't any fire." She couldn't say anything about Heather, it was too complicated and, anyway, she didn't understand it herself. "Listen, Janice. I'll have to call back. But I'm okay, really I am." She hung up before Janice could reply.

Clutching Joe's present, the bottle of lubricant, she hurried along the cold, windy street, her eyes blurring with wind tears that made the Christmas lights blaze. But when she arrived in the room Joe was not there.

Joe didn't feel whole, but he felt a lot better. He thought about the debacle of the bed. He hadn't had sex in . . . well, he wasn't sure how long. He ought to have been randy as a goat, but what had happened? Still, she had certainly brought him off before, with her hand, and he'd had plenty of erections. Was it just that Cateyo was a virgin? Was that it? He didn't believe it. And now the image of Helen crept into his mind.

Helen! Somehow, he had forgotten Helen. He had never had any problems in bed with Helen. He thought about her slim, hairless body. Something weird there. Plenty weird, really. Where was Helen now, he wondered?

For that matter, where was Cateyo? He got up. The afternoon light had failed. She was gone. He didn't remember waking and talking to her, barely a half hour before. He dressed in the darkened room and went out.

He slipped out of the hotel and walked around the town for a while, enjoying the cold air and exercising his legs. It was amazing how weak he felt, but gradually his legs began to work better. There was something wrong with his right leg, but he couldn't figure out what it was. It didn't hurt, it just didn't do what he wanted it to do. But as he pushed along, it worked better, in a new way, than he could have hoped.

The area around the hotel was open, bare. This made little sense to Joe, but he didn't try to figure it out. Some kind of urban renewal, he decided. He walked along. It was dark. One could no longer see the cliffs and crags to the east of the city, but the street-lights and the house lights seemed to reflect off the Front. He understood then where he was. It was Salt Lake City. The mountains up there would be full of snow and skiers at Snowbird and Alta sitting in the taverns, sipping their après ski drinks and eating dinner. Down here, on the valley floor, there were just the most pleasant and comfortable people on the planet. Some of them were Mormons, but just as many were not. They were middle-class white people, white-bread folks, the median television audience—thinking about Christmas, running out to buy presents. Joe was not a Christmas-type guy. He disliked the lights, the decorations. They seemed false.

Joe walked away from this, as he thought, and soon entered a street filled with bars. "Filled" didn't seem quite the right word. There were bars, but there didn't seem to be anybody on the street. He was hungry, but he realized that he didn't have any money. He thought a drink would be a nice thing. A hot toddy, perhaps. He needed money, though.

He hadn't gone very far when two huge young men, much taller and bulkier than Joe by far, with large and dusky blunt faces approached. They looked odd, some kind of massive Hawaiian or Samoan giants, or maybe a mythical race of giants. They angled out, walking slowly, one of them cutting him off from the street so that he imperceptibly found himself herded toward the alley next to a bar. Joe stopped at the mouth of the alley.

The two men stopped, one of them on either side, a few feet away. Their huge faces were bland. "Dude," one of them said, "walk over here." He gestured at the alley. The one nearest him moved even closer and Joe felt something hard.

Joe went, at first. But a step or two into the alley, he turned and looked down at the gun. Without thinking he snatched the gun from the young man's hand. The thief's jaw dropped open. He stared down at the gun in Joe's hand. He started to reach for the gun, to take it back, but Joe smashed his hand with the barrel. The thief yelled and grabbed his hand in agony. The other man drew a gun, but Joe just shook his head.

"Give me," Joe said. The other man handed Joe the gun. Joe waved the two into the darkness of the alley. The thief grimaced and joined his partner against the wall. He was wringing his hand, trying to shake off the pain.

"I didn't mean nothin', man," the other thief said. "Hey, keep the fuckin' gun."

"You didn't mean nothin'?" Joe laughed, a little giddy with excitement; his eyes shone. "Well, thanks for the gun, anyway. Now empty your pockets."

"Oh, man," the second thief said. "I ain't got no money. We was lookin' for money when you. . . . All right, all right," he acquiesced as Joe raised the pistol. It was a .38. A Smith & Wesson. The thief hauled out a wad of bills and handed them to Joe.

Joe took the bills and shoved them into his pocket without examining them. "What's your name?" he asked the man quietly.

"My name? Whatchoo wanna know my name for? It's DC."

"DC? DC-10? What are you, a jumbo jet? What kind of name is DC? Well, let me guess," Joe said. "It's Dirty Cuntface, something like that, but nobody wants to be called that, so you go by DC. Right?"

DC glowered.

"What are you guys? Indians? Hawaiians? You"—he gestured at the one in pain—"squawk."

"We ain't no fuckin' Indians," DC said, while Joe took another wad of bills from the injured thief. "You dumb fuck, you in deep shit. We're Tongans. You fuckin' with a Tongan posse. You dead already."

"*I'm* in trouble?" Joe shook his head, laughing, almost giggling. "What the hell are Tongans? I never heard of Tongans. Are they big around here?"

"Tongans run this place," DC said. "You dead."

"So who's the head Tonk?" Joe asked. "Who's the Tonk, if I told him you assholes tried to rob me but instead I robbed you, would be most likely to kick your jumbo butts?"

The two kids just stared at him, mouths hanging open.

"Okay. I'm not giving these guns back to you, because you'd probably shoot yourselves," Joe said, "but there must be somebody around here who would want to know if somebody was busting into the business. I'm busting in. Can you figure this out?"

DC couldn't figure it out. He launched himself at Joe, thumbs poised to take out the eyes. Joe whacked him across the side of his head with the pistol and stumbled aside, none too lithely. DC flopped to the dirty concrete of the alley, his immense carcass almost shaking the ground. He lay there, moaning and weeping. The other Tongan took the opportunity to bolt. Joe let him go. Then he kicked DC in the butt. DC curled into a ball. Joe felt inordinately angry with the hapless robber. He wanted to shoot him, he was so enraged at the ineptness, the stupidity, the futility . . . but then he abruptly cooled and felt calm.

Joe leaned against the brick wall of the building. It was cold and rough under his hand. He breathed heavily, staring down at the abject DC. "Well, who is it?" he asked. "Who the hell runs things around here?" He prodded the kid with his foot.

The kid flinched, but then, in a muffled voice, he said, "Cap'n . . . Cap'n Lite."

Joe stepped back. "What is this?" He gestured at the brick wall. "A bar?" When the kid said yes, Joe told him, "Go see Cap'n Lite. Tell him . . . ah." He racked his brain for something suitably

stupid. "Tell him Bongo Billy is waiting for him in the bar. Go on."
He kicked the boy in the ass. "Get going."

DC scrambled up and jogged ponderously down the alley. Joe
went out onto the street, then walked into the bar. There was some
kind of music playing. A jukebox, he thought, peering into the
gloom. There were people sitting at tables, men and women. They
were black people and a few giants—Tongans? Some turned to look
at him, but not with much interest. The music was very loud. Everybody seemed remarkably spaced out. There wasn't a bartender, or a
barmaid. Perhaps it wasn't a real bar. He hadn't noticed a sign. It
was more like a store, or a meeting room, perhaps. There was a glass-
fronted counter or display case along one wall, but there was nothing on the counter or on display in the case, except for a few empty
candy bar cartons—the Oh Henry! bars were gone. People sat about
at tables, on folding chairs. They had bottles, some of them in paper
sacks. Joe stood at the counter until a woman, a thick, sturdy woman
with an islander's face, got up and came to the counter.

"I want something to drink," Joe said.

"What?" she said. "I got Mad Dog."

"Okay, give me that." He peeled off a ten-dollar bill from one
of the rolls he'd taken from DC. She handed him the fortified wine,
a pint of it in a paper bag.

Joe sat down at an empty table. He opened the wine and
drank. It burned all the way down, but it made him feel warm and
good. His eyes glittered. People turned to look at him, but then they
looked away. They looked back to the end of the room, to a low
platform on which there was a piano. It was being played by a very
strange black man. There was a fancy well-lit jukebox, as well, but
the music was coming from the bizarre piano player, whose fantastic fingers filled the room with sound.

Joe took a jolt of the wine and leaned forward. It was just a
single man on the little stage, playing an upright piano that wasn't

in great shape, but putting out an incredible amount of sound. The piano player was strikingly thin, wearing a spangled jumpsuit. He had one of those topiary haircuts, a kind of spirally flame-shaped hairdo that ran straight up into the sky, resembling certain kinds of decorative light bulbs. He was like a spider monkey, or it may have been a tree frog. His fingers were long and spatulate. He wasn't seated—the piano stool had toppled over—but he was dancing and leaping while he played, his ornate cowboy boots flashing brass toes.

Suddenly he slammed out three clanking descending chords and screamed, "Well, I see you standin' out there in the cold and the rai-yain. . . . Come on in my house! YES! Come on in my house! You done gittin' soakin' wet. . . . Come on in my house!" And suddenly he zipped into: "I been dying! Yes! Yes, I been dying and I got the blues! I say YES! I can't never be alo-owo-oo-wo-oo-wooooone." The scream went soaring off into space, a shocking scream of despair. This wasn't a person singing the blues. This was someone afflicted with awful, terminal blues.

The night frog turned to Joe, his yellow eyes gleaming over his shoulder. The piano chords slammed and the blues arpeggios whirled. His lips were huge and peeled back in a painful grimace. His chin was extended by a long and narrow stiff beard. "Am I right!" he screamed. "Oh God, let it be over." Then he humped up, his beard wagging, his eyes flashing, every part of his body arcing, and his fingers flew at the keyboard while he screamed: "Yoo, del, oh-oh-oh-oh-ver!" The voice oscillated. "Let it be!" He hit a peak. "Yodellay he over!" Then, as everybody else shouted with him, "Whoo, hoo, hoo, over. Judas priest, I got over," he finished with a descending murmur, the blues chords rattling down in his left hand as disconsolately as the final breath of a dying man.

This was immediately succeeded by the most incredible stream of piano chords that Joe had ever heard, accompanying a running right hand that crackled up the keyboard, the fingers flying, dinging like a fusillade of bullets. Art Tatum came to mind. A splintering, cascading, and thundering piano SLAM!

And on the other side of this crescendo . . . the spider monkey walking the beat away. Oh, my, the good walking bass.

Joe stared at this freak, spellbound. He had never seen anyone like him. Obviously some kind of maniac, a warped and misshapen monster, but oh, how he could play. He had righted the stool and now he was sitting, just comping, riding along with his hands walking the keyboard quietly, coming down, his body slumped, his head down, trying to relax.

Joe went up to the stand, stumbling past the people, the wine buzzing in his head. He looked down at the player. He knew this man! He *knew* him. But he didn't know from where. The player peeped up at him, over his spangled shoulder, his wide froglike mouth smirking.

"Is it you?" Joe said.

"Man," the player rasped back, "is it *you!*"

And then the Tongans arrived. Somebody said something, or it may have been that the night frog looked over Joe's shoulder. Whatever, Joe turned and saw them coming, saw the guns.

Joe drew his pistols from either pocket and shot the first one in the face and strolled easily toward the others, shooting with both hands, shooting right and left. The other people screamed and tumbled, running and hiding and crawling under the tables. There were four with guns. They all went down in the blaze from Joe's hands. He walked straight on out of the bar, the music and the thunder of the guns still ringing in his head, and turned back toward the glow of the downtown lights.

Fifteen minutes later, chilled, he rode up in the elevator. Cateyo was standing in the room when he entered. "Oh, oh Joe, where have you been?" she cried. "I couldn't find you. I was so worried. The desk said they didn't see you leave. I . . . "

Joe undressed without a reply and got into bed. She stared at him. He looked so weird, so crazy. She was afraid to say anything about the fire, about what Janice had told her. He beckoned and she undressed and crawled in with him. "I'm tired," Joe said. "You get on top."

"I got some stuff, Joe," she said. "It'll help. It'll make it easier."

He nodded, smiling as she worked the lubricant over his steadily hardening cock. When he seemed ready, she straddled him and lowered her wet cunt to his slippery cock. She gasped as she slid down the pole, into his arms.

2

A Good Time

The precinct wag had clipped a few lines out of a magazine, taped them to a piece of paper, and taped that to the door of Mulheisen's so-called office, in the Ninth Precinct. It said: "Of this I am certain, that we are not here for a good time." Under this the anonymous jokester had written in awkward pencil, "L. Witgenstien, a.k.a. Mullhiesen."

Mulheisen had crossed out the names with his precise Tombo razor-point pen and corrected the philosopher's name: "L. Wittgenstein." He had also added the line: "Well, not *all* the time, anyway," and signed it "F. Mulheisen."

Detective Lieutenant Jimmy Marshall stared at this signature. He was alone in the tiny office, the door open, the note gleaming. He had never seen that "F." before. He was sure of it. What could it mean?

At this very moment Mulheisen was lying between the legs of a ditch rider, in a cramped trailer house in Montana that was rocking not only from his considerable, impassioned exertions but also from the wind buffeting the building. This ditch rider was named Sally McIntyre. She was lean and rugged, an outdoor person for sure, but there was ample softness about her.

It was a very cold day with a bleak, dirty sun that struggled through the ragged clouds blowing off the mountains. A fluctuating blanket of airborne snow swirled across the valley floor and hissed about the aluminum box. The house was warm, though, too warm. It was heated by a black iron woodstove that kept the temperature well above seventy degrees. The exertions of the lovers had them both in a lather. Neither of them were used to this, not that they were inexperienced. It was just that for a forty-year-old man who had been sexually inactive of late, and a single woman in her midthirties who was raising a couple of children by herself . . . well, they just weren't used to sex. They were certainly wallowing in it now, though. Indeed, Mulheisen was dimly thinking—to the extent that he could think at all in this moment of sexual oblivion—that he couldn't recall it ever being quite this good.

As for the ditch rider, she wasn't thinking, in the usual sense. She was intensely conscious. She could feel this man deep inside her, his arms along her sides, his thighs against hers, his warm breath on her face, his lips on her forehead . . . and then began a stunning sequence of orgasm, wave after wave of it sweeping up her body, her belly quaking and her legs trembling weakly. She moaned softly and prayed that it would continue. It felt like a tactile version of the northern lights, sheets of energy and ecstasy rippling and crackling across her body.

"Don't stop," she whispered hoarsely. But Mulheisen had no notion of stopping. He had still not reached his own orgasm.

And that's when she heard the sound. She didn't place it at first, even though she registered it with alarm. Then it popped into her consciousness: it was the distant sound of the school bus grinding up the long, low rise. On that school bus would be her two children, Jason and Jennifer. From the sound of it, she knew the bus would arrive in approximately one minute. It would pull up past her driveway to turn around on the road that went to the two ranches that lay above her little five acres. The driver was an old crank who wore a filthy, battered cowboy hat. He wouldn't let the children off until he had turned around and was aiming back down the hill. Five kids got off here, three of them belonging to a ranch almost a mile further up. Even in this bitter wind they would have to struggle on up the hill, one of them only seven years old. Sally's two kids would run whooping to the house. All of this would take about two minutes at the most, unless the driver detained them all for another minute of scolding for not staying seated, for writing dirty words on the frosted windows, for fighting and tossing Christmas candy at each other and at him.

Sally wanted Mulheisen to finish and be damn quick about it. She reached down and grabbed his buttocks and began to slam her groin upward while rhythmically contracting every muscle in her vagina. "Oh, come on, come *on*," she demanded.

Mulheisen, oblivious to the approaching bus, was surprised but thrilled. He responded willingly, furiously. In a remarkably short time, seconds it seemed to him, he could feel the cream rising to the top. It was an excruciating and thrilling progress, but an inexorable one: before he knew it the moment arrived, almost simultaneously with the school bus, which he heard for the first time. He groaned loudly and at the same instant was stunned when Sally McIntyre's strong arms flung him aside. He crashed to the floor next to her bed, his cock still spurting and looked up in shock as she leapt about the tiny bedroom, literally dripping his semen down her thighs, frantically tugging on jeans and a sweatshirt without bothering with panties or bra.

She shrieked at him, "For Christ's sake, get the hell up and get some clothes on! The kids are home!"

Then she was gone, slamming the door behind her. Mulheisen stumbled to his feet and hastily dressed. He heard her go outside. A moment later he cautiously peeked out the door. Through a large window in the front of the narrow trailer he could see Sally, her great frizzy mass of red hair billowing in the wind, her tin coat flapping unbuttoned, as she ran up the path in Sorel boots (no socks, he was sure) and greeted her children with hugs. By the time the three of them returned to the house, Mulheisen was calmly seated at the kitchen table, his pale thinning hair only slightly disheveled, his necktie in his pocket. He smiled weakly at the children and said, "Hello."

The boy, already as tall as his mother, had her red hair and a lot of freckles. His face was ruddy from the cold. He held out his hand suspiciously and looked around the trailer—wondering who else was there? Checking for telltale signs of lust? The girl was also red haired, with beautiful pale skin that looked even paler with the bright red spots on her cheeks. She was very pretty, about eleven years old.

"You're a cop?" the boy said skeptically. He wore a down ski jacket and jeans. "You don't look like a cop."

"I'm not from here," Mulheisen said. He was disconcerted by this bold kid, who seemed to know more than he should. How much did this kid suspect about him and his mother? "I was just asking your mother a few questions," he said lamely, "about the people who were involved in that fire the other night."

"Ma found a dead man up there last fall," the little girl, Jennifer, proclaimed.

"Yes, well, she's been very helpful." Mulheisen stood up. "Now I guess I better be going." He stuck out his hand and Sally took it. Hers was cold and dry, very strong. She smiled at him and pressed his hand.

"Don't run off," Sally said. "Kids, take off your coats and sit down. We'll have some soup, then we'll go for the tree." This distracted them. She ladled hot stew with large chunks of potatoes, turnips, carrots, onions, parsnips, and beef out of a crockpot and sawed off thick slices of home-baked bread for them. Mulheisen stood about. When the kids were eating, Sally walked Mulheisen out to the car he had borrowed from the Butte–Silver Bow sheriff.

The wind was bitter and it was getting dark already. She did not hug him, although she longed to, but she stood very close, letting him shelter her from the stinging snow that swirled around them. "You don't have to go," she said. "Why don't you come along and get the Christmas tree? It's just a couple miles up to the woods." She gestured up toward the green trees that blanketed the low mountain a few miles away, the peak obscured by low clouds and blowing snow. "I'll cook us a good dinner and we'll decorate the tree and later, when the kids get to bed . . . " She didn't finish.

Mulheisen was truly tempted. But then he felt a measure of fear. He didn't know anything about kids. It didn't sound like his kind of party. He was more used to women he'd met in a bar, or at work; women who lived in apartments, wore sexy, non-indestructible clothes and careful makeup, had no children, weren't scrambling for an existence on a bleak Montana hillside. Women who didn't heave him out of bed like a bale of hay when the rural school bus approached. This woman was outside his experience. She had powerful needs. She needed a lot. Could he give it to her?

Sally sensed this. She suppressed her anger and her pride; she wouldn't beg any man to stay. But there was something about this man, something very different from the ones she had known, including the father of Jason and Jennifer. "The beef stew is real good," she said, "but I could make chicken 'n' dumplings, if you'd rather. I've got some fresh side pork."

Mulheisen had a fleeting vision of the bedroom, the tumbled bedclothes, the heat and passion of this woman. The bedroom was so small and the walls so thin. It was only a trailer house, but it was neat and clean, except for the plethora of books wedged into every cranny and stacked on all available horizontal space, including the floor in odd places. And the pictures taped to the walls: pictures of animals from magazines, the blue planet from space, postcards of van Gogh, Winslow Homer, Mary Cassatt, alongside crayon drawings by the kids—a cow looking out the window of a pickup truck. He glanced at the trailer and saw the heads of the children, bent over their steaming bowls. He remembered the suspicious look of the boy.

"No," he said, "I've got to get back." Her face fell and he felt bad. He leaned forward, taking her by the upper arms and kissing her cold lips briefly. "But I'll call."

"Promise?"

He promised.

Johnny Antoni, the county prosecutor, was still in his office. He was an old friend of Mulheisen's, although they had only recently become reacquainted after many years. They had spent months together in an air force technical school in Illinois, more than twenty years earlier. They were exactly the same age, practically the same birthday, having arrived in Texas a few days after each had turned eighteen. Antoni was taller and more handsome and looked five years or more younger. He was a prosperous man and a successful politician who would soon be running for state attorney general. He had silvery iron hair that was stylishly cut, wore pin-stripe suits tailored in a Western style, with elegant cowboy boots made of exotic leathers. He was athletic and tanned, a hunter and fly fisher, married to a pretty woman and the father of two strapping athletic teenagers, as well as a late addition who was only three.

Also in Antoni's office was Jacky Lee, a hulking sheriff's deputy who seemed to be an Indian, though evidently not a Montana Indian: his large face resembled one of those stone Toltec head sculptures one saw in *National Geographic* magazines, discovered in the jungles of the Yucatán.

They were discussing the case that had brought them all together here in Butte, seventeen hundred miles from Detroit. It cen-

tered on Helen Sedlacek. Now Antoni was explaining to Mulheisen
why he was going to release Helen from the county jail.

"Okay," said Antoni briskly, "this guy, Mario Soper, had slugs
in him from two different guns. We've got the guns—the ditch rider
found one and Jacky the other, in the hot springs where the body
was. The trouble is these guns have too many fingerprints, including Soper's, the ditch rider's, Jacky's, plus a couple on the .38 from
Humann, but no definitive ones from Helen Sedlacek. I'm surprised
you didn't get your mitts on them, Mul. You see my point. The .38
is registered to Joseph Humann—he purchased it last year in a Butte
gun shop. The other, a .32, is reported stolen in New Jersey—probably belonged to Soper. We have no eyewitness, no other evidence
at all. Also, the slugs recovered from Mr. Humann, who Jacky found
out on the highway, near death, are from the .32. Therefore,
Humann and Soper had an encounter. Soper is dead, Humann
is not, though he probably should have been. We don't have an
accurate time of death for Soper, but it looks like he died at roughly
the same time that Humann's body was found on the highway—
probably the same day, anyway. So, did Humann kill Soper and toss
him into an irrigation ditch on his own property and then get shot
himself, forty-some miles away, with a gun bearing Soper's prints,
and then get left by the side of the interstate? That'd be a hell of a
trick, but it could be done."

"Maybe Soper shot Joe," Mulheisen suggested, "out on the
highway, then went on to Joe's house looking for Helen and she
got the drop on him."

Antoni rolled his eyes, but he conceded, "Sure, sure, why not?
Obviously, other unknown persons are involved. Your scenario is
as good as anyone's, Mul, but we don't have the slightest evidence
that Helen Sedlacek shot anybody."

Antoni paused and swiveled his chair behind the big desk.
He pulled a typewriter platform out of the desk and put his elegant

Western boots up on it, leaning back in the upholstered leather chair and puffing on a cigar. "So where in all this is Ms. Sedlacek? Mul? Jacky?"

"How about the gun I recovered from Helen?" Mulheisen asked. "The Dan Wesson—a .357, I believe."

"That gun was also the legitimate possession of Joseph Humann, who purchased it earlier this year in Missoula. It'd been fired recently, but not at Soper. Or, at least, neither Soper nor Humann had any bullets from it in them. And now Humann has disappeared."

The deputy spoke up. "Miss Yoder's supervisor at the hospital, Janice Work, received a call from her this afternoon. Nurse Work is confident it was from Miss Yoder. She said she was calling to say she was all right, that she and Humann were in Coeur d'Alene, that they were going to get married. We checked it out with the Coeur d'Alene police: there was no one of those names or descriptions at the hotel where she said she was staying and nobody has applied for a marriage license at the town hall. For the time being we're still treating it as a kidnap. The FBI has been notified."

"I don't see how we can call it kidnapping," Antoni said, irritably. "Who kidnapped who? Whom. As far as I know, Humann was in no shape to kidnap anyone. A man is kidnapped by his nurse? Or did he just run off with his nurse? But, what the hell . . . we don't have them and if this nurse or Humann surfaces we can forget that line. But let's get back to Helen. Mul?"

"Our forensic people in Detroit have found traces of blood and human tissue on the sawed-off shotgun I discovered in Joseph Humann's cabin. They've matched it with blood and tissue from Carmine Busoni. Also on the gun are Helen Sedlacek's fingerprints, as well as those of Joseph Humann. We think Humann is a known mob associate who goes by the name of Joe Service. This is pretty heavy evidence, Johnny. The trouble is, the Wayne County prosecutor is not willing to seek an indictment against Helen Sedlacek based on this evidence. But we would like to extradite her on another charge, or rather a different process: protective custody."

Antoni lowered his feet with a muffled thump onto the well-carpeted floor. "How's that, Mul?"

"Mario Soper was a professional hit man sent out here to avenge the killing of Carmine Busoni," Mulheisen explained patiently. "His targets would be Joseph Humann, a.k.a. Joe Service, and Helen Sedlacek. He almost got Joe, but he didn't succeed with Helen. I think, and Jacky agrees"—he nodded at the deputy—"that Helen got him. Now, I accept that you don't have enough to hold Helen for this; it's just supposition. But there is a precedent for extraditing a person and holding them as a material witness, for his or her protection."

"You have talked to Helen," Antoni said. "Did she agree to this protective custody?"

"No," Mulheisen said. "In fact, she wouldn't talk at all. She didn't have a lawyer, not yet, anyway. But I think she's scared. She knows the mob is after her. It's possible she may consent, but even if she doesn't, there is some precedent for holding a material witness against their will."

Antoni shook his head, a sour expression on his face. "Maybe in Detroit, Mul, but I've never seen it in Montana. I don't know, maybe you could get a governor's warrant, but I doubt it. It's a mutual backscratcher deal with these governors, only I think your governor is a Democrat and ours is a fuckin' Republican. But get your governor to ask, if you want. And I have to tell you, Mul, that Ms. Sedlacek has obtained the services of Daphne Z. Stonborough. You won't like Ms. Stonborough, Mul. Well, you'll like her at first, to look at, but you won't like dealing with her. She'll put up a killer argument against extradition on such unusual grounds. She'll point out that the shotgun you confiscated doesn't belong to Ms. Sedlacek, that Sedlacek resided in a place where the gun was stored and in the natural course of her residence probably had occasion to innocently handle the weapon, which accounts for the fingerprints . . . that there are no eyewitnesses that link Ms. Sedlacek to the murder of Carmine Busoni . . . that she has no previous criminal record or indication that she is a violent person . . . and, of course, you found the gun months after the murder, not at the scene of Busoni's death but seventeen hundred miles away, and so on and so forth."

Antoni frowned at Mulheisen. "I imagine that would be just Daphne's openers, Mul, speaking as a lawyer myself. Montana judges are familiar with Daphne. They have had cases overturned where she was counsel. She's about as good a lawyer as we've got, out here. I wouldn't count on seeing Helen Sedlacek in Detroit soon. I don't think you have a chance in hell. I'm dropping all charges and releasing her."

Mulheisen sat back and considered this statement. "What about the assault charge?" he asked. "She struck me with the .357, she tried to flee—"

"Mul, the lady was naked, bathing in a hot springs on property where she was a resident. You're not a Montana law officer . . . hell, if she'd *shot* you just about any Montana jury would let her walk. You disturbed a lady in her bath."

Mulheisen was a little puzzled by his friend Antoni's cool attitude. When the case had begun, months before, Johnny had been enthusiastic. Now he seemed indifferent, perhaps even hostile. Antoni looked pained and said, "Do you really want to do this, Mul? If it got to court you'd have to come back out here to testify . . . Daphne would say you weren't qualified to make an arrest . . . all that sort of crap. Frankly, I'm happy to see these Detroit hoods out of here."

After an uncomfortable moment, Mulheisen said quietly, "Johnny, you've had a citizen in good standing nearly murdered, now

he's disappeared . . . you have a dead hit man on the citizen's property . . . you have five men killed in an explosion and fire at the
man's home . . . and you're going to shrug it off?"

"Tell me how I can hold Helen Sedlacek, Mul." He shook
his head. "You talked to her, didn't you? What did she say?"

"She didn't say anything."

"And now she has Daphne Z. Stonborough," Antoni said.
"Talk to Daphne Z. See where it gets you."

Mulheisen didn't know how to respond. Later, he discussed
it with the deputy, Jacky Lee. Jacky snorted, "What'd you expect
from a politician, Mul? I know he's an old buddy of yours, but he
also wants to be attorney general. That's how you get to be governor. I s'pose it's the same in Michigan, isn't it?"

Mulheisen agreed that it was one of the ways, all right, but
still. . . . When he'd first come to Montana, months earlier, Antoni
had actually tried to hire him to take a job with something called
the Northern Tier Organized Crime Task Force; they were worried
about the mob moving in on gambling on the Indian reservations.
Antoni had promised him the top job, anything he wanted.

"But you turned him down," Jacky pointed out. "I s'pose that
didn't sit too well. He was hoping to make a splash with that
program. Now he'll have to find someone else. The way it looks to
me, all this mob stuff—hired killers, Colombians flying in, Detroit
detectives poking around—probably it doesn't look so good to
Antoni. The Northern Tier thing may still fly, but I 'spect he's happy
to see the last of Helen Sedlacek and Joe Service."

The following day Mulheisen was sitting on an air-
plane, headed back to Detroit, via Salt Lake City. He was trying to
think about his investigation, but images of Sally McIntyre kept
intruding. Every time he pictured the mountaintop hideway to
which he had tracked Helen and her accomplice lover, Joe Service,
he thought of the hot springs nearby. In that hot springs he had first

44

looked upon the naked flesh of Sally McIntyre. Later, he had also looked upon the naked flesh of Helen there. It was a great hot springs, but it was Sally's form that he kept seeing. He made a great effort to push those images to the back of his mind. No pale breasts with blue veins faintly visible, no pale belly, no smooth but power-ful thighs, no strangely rough lips, no arms, no tender throat out-stretched to receive kisses, no. . . . No. No.

He succeeded finally, by switching his thoughts to the redoubtable Daphne Z. Stonborough, attorney at law. He had met her only a couple of hours earlier. A remarkable woman, he thought. Attractive, but even more impressive on a nonphysical plane. Her handsome face was strong but amiable—indeed, when she smiled, as she did readily, Mulheisen had felt a kind of relief, a reprieve, from the powerful intelligence that seemed to radiate from that smooth brow and shining dark eyes. She looked Russian, possibly Jewish. A Stonborough she might be, but the Anglo-Saxon heri-tage didn't give her those almond eyes or smooth olive skin. She was tall, very trim, in her late thirties. When it came down to busi-ness, she was as solid as a brick outhouse. There was no way that her client was going back to Detroit to be interrogated for a crime for which the Wayne County prosecutor had as yet been unable to obtain an indictment. Period. If Mulheisen wanted to question Ms. Sedlacek here, that was fine, but Ms. Stonborough would be present.

The questioning didn't get anywhere. Helen was calm and looking fine, confident, even. She was a small, dark woman with a mane of black hair that had a silver streak running through. She was smartly dressed, having been released from the Butte–Silver Bow jail that morning, the assault charges dropped. The interview took place in Daphne Stonborough's office, a wood-paneled affair with a view of the Continental Divide, the craggy mountains to the east of Butte. It was an old building, uptown, and from here you could see the great white figure of Our Lady of the Rockies, perched on the Divide.

Helen was friendly, calling Mulheisen "Mul" and responding pleasantly with only a few conferences with Ms. Stonborough.
They had clearly gone over what she would say. She admitted knowing a man named Joe Service, although she had no idea what he
did for a living other than manage his own estate. She knew that
he went by the name of Joseph Humann. They were not married.
They had met in Detroit when he had come to her house to visit
one of her late father's associates. She had no idea where Mr. Service was now. For the past three months she had been traveling,
although she knew that Mr. Service was in the hospital. They had
agreed to separate a few days before Mr. Service's hospitalization.
When she heard about his misfortune she had consulted the hospital and learned that he apparently had no insurance, so she had
contributed some money toward his care. She understood he was
now released, or had at least left the hospital. No, she had not seen
him since September, when he'd left on a road trip. No, she had no
idea where he'd been headed at that time. Once again, she had no
idea where he might be now. As for her plans, she was unsure.

Mulheisen wasn't discouraged by any of this. All in
all, it had been a successful investigation. If it hadn't solved any
crime, at least he'd learned a lot. Some things, he knew with a kind
of fatalistic certainty, would never be satisfactorily explained. But
he felt confident that the main questions were well on their way to
being answered. For one thing, he now knew the identity, more or
less, of a man who had plagued his investigations for some time:
Joe Service, a man with an ambiguous relationship to the Detroit
mob. Apparently, he was not himself a mobster—not a "made
man"—but his ties to the mob ran deep. That would be where to
look for him, Mulheisen suspected.

Just knowing who you were looking for was a step forward,
Mulheisen felt. He was reminded of an old partner of his, a mentor

actually, a rough, crude, unconventional crazy man of a detective, now deceased, named Grootka. "The world is round," Grootka would say, by which he meant that criminals kept on being criminals and if you didn't nail them on this rap, they'd offer you another opportunity sooner rather than later. In this case, Mulheisen felt that the trail was definitely warming up.

In fact, having arrived in Salt Lake City and standing on the moving conveyor that bore him to another concourse, where he would wait for his connecting flight, Mulheisen felt that the trail was very warm. Just a few weeks earlier he had spotted Helen Sedlacek on this same people-mover, passing in the opposite direction. He had not apprehended her at the time, but it had eventually led to a successful tracking of her movements. He had felt at the time that she hadn't been in Salt Lake City coincidentally, that there was a good chance that she had been staying somewhere in the area. Just a hunch, a vague notion. He had the same notion, now, not only about Helen, but about Joe Service.

When Joe Service had been dangling between life and death at St. James Hospital in Butte a few months ago, money for his medical expenses had been sent via Federal Express from Salt Lake City. It came in the form of cashier's checks from an anonymous donor for just less than three thousand dollars each (the maximum amount purchasable under current law without filing a telltale IRS form), purchased at several Salt Lake City banks. Subsequent checks had come from other cities around the West, but again, from time to time, from Salt Lake City. The pattern had suggested to Mulheisen at the time that Helen Sedlacek was using the Mormon capital as a base. He now made a little leap of logic: if Helen had been sending money for Joe Service's care, as she had admitted this morning in Daphne Stonborough's office, she must have access to a good deal of cash, inasmuch as she chose to purchase only those amounts under three grand. Otherwise, like any honest citizen, she would have sent a personal check. Of course, the reason could be that she hadn't wished to write a check, to remain anonymous, but Mulheisen felt the first reason was the more likely. It strongly indicated access to a lot of cash. Further, it was known that a large amount of drug cash was missing from a scam that had been run on the mob by Helen Sedlacek's late mobster father, Big Sid. It seemed reasonable, therefore, to believe that Helen had some or all of that money, and that it could well be in Salt Lake City, and that Joe Service knew it.

A lot of assumptions, but there was a behavior pattern here that had become familiar to police all over America. The cocaine business had generated a frankly mind-boggling amount of money in the U.S. for at least the past fifteen years. This money—always cash—had to be washed, made clean, if it was going to be used as real wealth is used, in investments that would themselves earn money. And the money had to get back to Colombia, somehow. One of the ways this was done was by "smurfing." Teams of men and women were sent out by the drug operators to process cash into legitimate monetary instruments that could be mailed and deposited in, say, Panama banks. The process was precisely like the one that Helen had used to send money to the Butte hospital. It was illegal to "smurf," but it was difficult, if not impossible, to prove that the cash the smurfer used was not legitimate. However, the cash could be impounded until the smurf could provide a legitimate source. This, of course, the true smurf never did. In fact, the smurf simply went on his or her way, rarely to be seen again. The amount of money was presumably written off by the drug bosses. Why bother with a few thousands when you were dealing in tens and hundreds of millions, even billions?

But Mulheisen didn't think Helen was a smurf, not in the usual sense, at least. If she was smurfing, it was on her own behalf, not some drug lord's. Her money had come out of the drug scam her father had run. He sat down in one of those busy little snack shops that flourish in large, regional air-traffic hubs like Salt Lake City and drank a cup of coffee while he gazed at the blue skies of Utah and contemplated the assumptions he had just formulated on the people-mover. He had a three-hour layover here. He had noticed before that the airport was not too distant from the city. Conceivably, he could go into town and look around. But for what? A pile of money? Mulheisen hadn't *that* much confidence in hunches. But he thought he'd take a little jaunt into town. In the meantime, looking at the striking mountains that glistened in the winter sunlight, he couldn't help wondering what Sally McIntyre was doing at that moment.

Jimmy Marshall stopped Leonard Stanos in the hallway that led from the precinct lobby back to the detectives' offices and interrogation rooms. Stanos was a hulking, raw-looking man, now a full-fledged member of the Big 4, the "cruiser bruisers." Marshall and Stanos had been squad car partners, once, in their youth. They were about as different as two men could be, but Stanos had once saved Marshall's life and this act had cemented a life bond: Marshall was certainly the only person of African descent for whom Stanos had any regard at all; that is, Stanos actually thought of Marshall as a person, and an important person, even (if he were capable of searching his inner being, his soul) a person he *liked*. Why the saver rather than the saved should be more changed and moved by the act is a ponderable curiosity. Jimmy Marshall wasn't unmoved—he tended to forgive Stanos for any number of ignorant racist utterances and acts—but Stanos was clearly more affected.

Marshall showed Leonard the note on Mulheisen's door. He pointed to the "F." in Mulheisen's signature. "What do you think of that?" he asked. "What does 'F.' mean?"

Stanos stared at the note, his thick brow ridged in pretend thought and his mouth hanging open, as always. "Fuckin' Mulheisen," he said quickly, glibly. But then, aware that Jimmy didn't take kindly to adverse comments on his mentor, he said, "That ain't a eff. That's a Catholic seven."

"A Catholic seven? What the hell's a Catholic seven?"

"You know," Stanos said, gesturing with a huge hand in a kind of rotary fashion, a gesture of linguistic or intellectual incapacity, "a seven like a Catholic'd make. It has a little cross on it, like a 'tee,' or a 'eff.'"

"Ah." Marshall understood that Stanos was referring to what he thought of as a European 7. He had never connected it to a religion however, and he asked Stanos about that.

"Sister Mary Hilda, at St. John Berchman's, al's made us cross our sevens," Stanos said.

Marshall nodded. "But." He pointed at the signature. "Seven Mulheisen? What does that mean?"

Stanos pondered the signature for a long moment, then he said, "That ain't 'Mulheisen,' that's 'McIlhenny.' Yanh. McIlhenny was a famous football player. I heard my dad talk about him. Hugh McIlhenny. I think he played for the Rams or the 49ers, back in the fifties. His number was prob'ly seven." And he walked away, leaving Marshall to stare at his back.

At this moment, Mulheisen was riding in a taxi into Salt Lake City, considering what he knew about "Joe Service." He visualized the name with quotation marks because he wasn't in any way confident that it was the man's real name. It didn't sound any more real than Joseph Humann, the name he had used to buy land and establish himself as a legitimate citizen in western Montana. Fingerprints, taken while he was in the Butte hospital, had not turned up any previous identity, nor even any previous history as Joseph Humann. The name Joe Service was one Mulheisen and his Detroit colleagues, especially the Rackets and Conspiracy bureau, had heard in connection with the mob. It was said that he was an outside man, a resource man. Someone who was called in to investigate problems within the mob. A mob detective. But he was not known to be a hit man.

Mulheisen could recall a half dozen cases in which it seemed that his own work had been hampered by the efforts of this "Joe Service" character. He imagined that, like any corporate body, the mob had inevitable internal problems with theft and embezzlement—no doubt much more than General Motors or the First Bank of Detroit experienced. The familial and hierarchical arrangements inside such a body as the mob must be horrendous to deal with. In order to avoid outright bloodshed, street war, such as had characterized the clashes of mobs in the twenties and thirties, the services of a man like Joe Service must have seemed very valuable. But he must have come from somewhere. It wasn't a job description that one could advertise in the classified section of the *Free Press*. How did he get to be "Joe Service"?

Mulheisen thought he could start here, in Salt Lake City. Maybe here he could pick up a trail that would lead back, little by little, to the real "Joe Service."

3

Catch Your Death
of Cold

Sally McIntyre was bucking bales on the Garland Ranch, feeding cattle. It was a bitter cold day in Montana, but she was grinning into the stinging wind. It howled around the pickup, swirling snow and hurling chaff into her face. She wore a hood and liner made of some modern stuff that was very warm under her brown duck tin coat, with an oversized checked wool cap jammed on her head with the flaps down, but she could feel the brutality of the wind tearing at the edges, trying to strip away her protection. She was used to it. She didn't let it get to her.

She jumped up onto the tailgate and hauled the heavy bales out, clipped the baler twine, and let them tumble to the frozen, shit-stained snow, there to fall apart for the cows that crowded about. She ducked back into the cab of the truck and drove another twenty feet to dump another bale or two, making a long trail of broken bales for the cattle to feed on. She was laughing about the spectacle of Mulheisen tumbling out of her bed, sprawling naked as she scrambled after her clothes.

When she had broken the last bale she drove back to the gate, opened it, and drove through. She refastened the gate and climbed back into the blessed heat of the cab, out of the wind that threatened to flay her alive. Her face was nearly numb. She sat gratefully, drinking hot coffee from the steel vacuum bottle and munching a thick meat-loaf sandwich smeared with ketchup. She was still thinking about yesterday afternoon, the incredibly warm and delicious ecstasy of bedding a real man, a decent man, in the hothouse atmosphere of her little trailer house. After the brutality of her marriage she'd been to bed with a couple of men, including the Butte–Silver Bow sheriff's deputy, Jacky Lee, plus an amiable cowboy named Gary. They were both satisfying lovers, she had to concede (although they'd had the usual male tendency to try to control the action), but she'd never really supposed they were men she could live with. She hoped to hell that something would come of this, but she was realistic.

Mulheisen was a city man. He lived in Detroit, nearly two thousand miles away. A rough woman, as she saw herself, with two young kids—how could she interest a man like that? He hadn't said anything about her hard hands, her blackened thumbnail where she'd smacked it with fencing pliers, her raw skin. When would she ever see him again? And how could anything really come of it? A single man his age—she figured he was about forty or so—and her with two kids; a poor woman with a high school education. She wasn't pretty, or at least she didn't think of herself that way, though she knew damn well that when she had a chance to show her body it was still sexy enough to interest a cowboy in the Tinstar Saloon. But she didn't have any nice clothes, nor anywhere to wear them, even if she found the time to go out. How could she hope to hold the attention of a man like Mulheisen? Especially if she heaved him out of bed at the moment of truth.

She laughed, refusing to be depressed. She still had work to do. She drove back to the hay barn for another load. Later, having fed the last of the cattle, she paused on the access road above Grace Garland's ranch house. She hadn't seen Grace in a couple of days, although Grace's pickup truck was parked outside the white frame house, so she must be home. But now she noticed that the snow had drifted across the driveway and, in fact, had made a little bowl around the parked vehicle. Obviously, the truck hadn't moved recently. But there was a recently broken path, only partially drifted over, between the house and the barn and chicken coop, and smoke was streaming out of the chimney. Sally sat in her pickup, wondering if she should drive down to the house and see if Grace was doing all right. It would be a neighborly thing to do. It was coming on to Christmas and Grace was all alone.

Grace was a widow in her sixties, very hardy (not to say tough as an old saddle) and certainly capable of taking care of herself. Her daughter Calla, a biologist over in Bozeman, would surely be coming to visit for Christmas. Sally knew Calla from school days. Calla was unmarried, as far as Sally knew. About the son, Cal Jr., Sally knew very little. He was at least five years older than the daughter. She'd heard he was an accountant in Seattle, also unmarried. The story was that he was gay, which had led to a falling out with his father.

Sally decided not to go down. She'd have to get out of the warm pickup and open the gate. She was cold and tired and didn't feel like opening another gate. She was due to collect her wages at the end of the week. She'd see Grace then. Smoke was fairly whistling out of the chimney. Grace was surely all right. Sally decided to call her when she got home. She drove away.

Grace watched her go, from the living room window, looking through the dusty white muslin curtains. She needed to wash these curtains, she thought. Since Cal had died she had neglected that sort of thing. She would do it after Christmas, after New Year's. She would take down all the curtains and wash them and then set up her old wooden curtain stretchers with their pin-lined frames in the dining room and the upstairs hallway. The house would look very bleak and naked for a day, a look that she had always hated as a child, the very image of January, but one that was inevitable after Christmas and New Year's, anyway, what with the tree and the other decorations coming down. Not that she had a tree or decorations this year. She just hadn't found time, and anyway, there were no kids here to enjoy them. She had already sent a present, a sweater, to Cal Jr. (a name she pronounced as a single word), and she expected Calla to come by for her present (a sweater) on Christmas Day.

It was funny, she thought, how nothing ever worked out the way you thought it would. You figured you worked hard when you were young to kind of make things easier for when you were old, but it didn't seem to work out. When you were old your husband died—well, you had to expect that, more or less—and your kids moved away and one of them tells you in a single sentence on the long-distance line that he's gay and he's got AIDS. It was a stunning blow. The first statement would have been a blow all by itself. She was glad that Cal hadn't been alive to hear the second.

You got old and found that you hadn't made things easier. Your daughter, a fine young woman, a professor at State, a research scientist, never got married and brought grandkids around. In fact, she hardly ever called. Once a month, if you were lucky. And if your old friends hadn't died, they moved away to Arizona. So despite all the hardship of early days, building up the ranch, you had to look back on them as the golden days. But you weren't even aware of it at the time, so you hadn't really enjoyed it the way you should have.

But she wasn't bitter. You just never knew how things were going to turn out. In a good year with lots of rain you might get hit by wheat blight, or beef prices might drop out of sight. Then in a drought year, when you thought you were going to lose it all, beef prices would skyrocket and it would turn out that the XOX was the only outfit in the valley that had any cattle to sell. And here she was, thinking that she'd be alone for Christmas, and along comes a young woman in need.

"Well, she's gone on," Grace said to the woman tucked up on the couch. "I kinda thought she'd stop in, but she's got plenty to do, I expect."

"Who?" said the woman hoarsely, alarmed. "Who's out there?"

"Just Sally, the ditch rider. She's feeding cattle for me, up on the butte meadow. Looked like she was thinking of stopping by, but she went on. Honey, how you doing? Did you drink that tea? Let me get you some more."

"No, no, I'm all right," the woman said. "I think I'll sleep. I'm feeling a lot better, though."

"Well, you just go ahead and sleep, honey. It'll do you a world of good. After a while I'll look at that . . . " Grace hesitated, unsure whether to call the woman's affliction a wound or a sore, or what. "That gash. Change the dressing. It looks clean, no infection, and seems to be healing. You lost aplenty of blood, though. Sure you don't want me to take you on into Butte, to the hospital? Them doctors ain't like to do you no better, but I expect them nurses could tell you whether it's all right or not."

"I'm fine, really," the woman said. "You've been so kind. Anyway, I'm tough." She forced a smile. She was a handsome woman (that was the right word, Grace thought) and obviously strong. She looked worlds better than when she'd come stumbling up to the back door, three days earlier. Fallen and hurt herself, gashed herself with a ski pole, cross-country skiing, she'd said. Grace didn't know a thing about skiing. An accident like that could happen, she thought. She supposed one could strap skis onto those winter boots. No skis, though. The gal had left them out in the snow, she'd said.

"Well, you look so much better," Grace said. "I'm surprised you didn't catch your death of cold."

The woman had come along about dark, the day after poor Mr. Humann's cabin had burned down. Grace was not ordinarily a garrulous woman, but now that her husband was gone, why she didn't often get to set and talk much, so she was happy the woman was up and alert, finally, her first day out of the downstairs bedroom, which had been Calla's room. Grace had been telling the woman about her neighbor's fire. It had been a lucky thing for Mr. Humann that he hadn't been to home, Grace had told her, otherwise he might've got burned up. She couldn't hardly think of nothing worse than a house fire in the middle of winter.

And now that Grace thought about it, here was another of those things that just hadn't worked out. When she sold Mr. Humann the springs property, after Cal died, it had seemed like a good thing all around. Mr. Humann seemed like a darn nice feller, for a flatlander. He wanted his privacy, but she'd still be able to graze cattle up on his meadow and he'd deferred the water rights on Tinstar Creek, so it wasn't even as if she'd lost land or water. Humann was often gone for days, even weeks at a time, but he'd stop in, now and then, and Grace had begun to think that she'd acquired a genuine neighbor. But then Humann had come back with a girlfriend and that was just about the beginning of everything going wrong.

Just this morning Grace had seen on the news that Mr. Humann's girlfriend had been arrested for something, but Grace couldn't make out what it was all about.

"Not that I ever cared much for the woman," Grace told her guest, "though I shouldn't tell stories on the poor thing."

The girlfriend, Helen (Grace hadn't even known her last name until she saw it on the news), was a little, dark woman. "At first I thought she might be Mr. Humann's sister, they looked so much alike," Grace said, "both of them small and athletic, but I soon enough saw that Helen wasn't Mr. Humann's sister, not by a long shot. Not that they were married—I could see that. People don't seem to get married, these days. She wasn't friendly, like Mr. Humann, didn't seem interested in the country. She asked me once if I didn't get awful lonely, living by myself way out here. 'Way out here?' Why the country is filling up, mostly with Californicators. It's nothing to what it used to be. At night to look out on the valley you can see lights in just about any direction, and not too darn far off."

Grace said she couldn't see why a friendly feller like Joseph, or Joe, as he asked to be called, "would drag a cat like that out of the city and set her up in a cabin in the mountains. Anyone could see she wasn't cut out for this country, and now look what's happened. But it's none of my business. You can't hardly believe the stuff they put out on the TV these days. Now look at me! Here I am settin' here a-talking and I was going to make tea. You just lie back and get your rest and I'll have it out here in a jiffy."

From the kitchen window Grace could see a thin plume of smoke still swirling from over the ridge, from what used to be Joseph Humann's cabin. She filled the blue enameled kettle and set it on the electric range to boil. What an awful thing to get burned out in the dead of winter, she thought. Used to be you'd ride over and offer a hand, but there'd been aplenty of fire engines and sheriffs up there, and of course Mr. Humann wasn't there, anyway. He was in the hospital. Shot by a hitchhiker.

Mr. Humann was such a nice feller, Grace thought, but then there was all that shooting going on. The man was a shootin' fool. When he was home he was shooting every day, sometimes for hours. An awful lot of ammo, and ammo wasn't cheap. But Mr. Humann had plenty of money, that's for sure. She reckoned losing his cabin wouldn't be as hard on him as it would be on most others, although it was always hard to lose your stuff—photographs and suchlike. Hard to have sympathy for the rich, though, even in moments of tragedy.

Gun crazy, she thought. And then he gets shot in the head. Picked up a hitchhiker. It was too bad, but he was asking for it, she supposed. Used to be, out in this country you didn't dare *not* pick up a person out on the road, leastaways in the winter. But nowadays, the best thing to do was call the sheriff. Don't stop. And now this fire. Sometimes bad luck just came in bunches. The deputy, Jacky Lee, had stopped by to tell her all about it, the morning after the fire. Some burglars had broken into Mr. Humann's cabin and set it on fire. What next? The country was getting like L.A. Well, you live long enough you see ever' darn thing, she thought. She'd lived long enough, that was sure. She'd seen blizzards that went on for weeks with temperatures of forty below at night and never got over twenty below in the day; she'd seen cattle struck by lightning; earthquakes that dammed up the Madison River and flooded hundreds of people out; wind bursts that knocked down forty acres of trees in a second; whole summers of forest fires filling the valley with smoke so thick you couldn't see the mountains . . . why a burnt-out cabin or a handful of shootings wasn't nothing, come to look at it.

Humann's house, or what was left of it—ashes, Grace reckoned—lay only a mile or so away, over the ridge. The night of the fire she had not heard a thing, not even the boom when the propane tank blew up. They'd had fire engines up there, cops, even helicopters, people coming and going all night, and she hadn't heard a darn thing. Well, she'd always slept sound. She worked hard was why. A body works hard, a body sleeps hard. If that Indin deputy, Jacky Lee, hadn't come by when he saw her out in the barnyard, she'd have had no idea about it. It hadn't made much sense to her. The burglars had started a fire that had blown up the darn propane tank, killing all but one of them. Well, it was too bad about Mr. Humann's house, but at least he wasn't caught in it. It was just too darn much for Grace to figure out: who could keep track of these new people, the way they lived?

Then when everything had pretty much quietened down, the next day along about dusk the woman had appeared, though it wasn't clear exactly where she did come from, but she was on the back porch, knocking real slow but hard, and she was in awful shape, bleeding stopped but it'd been considerable, and near froze to death.

Grace poured the boiling water into the teapot, onto a spoonful of Darjeeling. Calla had given her this tea. It was real English tea, from Jackson's of Piccadilly. She didn't ordinarily drink tea. She was a coffee drinker. But when you were sick tea was the thing. And soup. She had made a very earthy chicken soup that she'd fed to the young woman: a whole hen (one of the old nonlayers) in the big stockpot, along with root vegetables—a whole onion, an entire head of garlic, a couple of carrots, a small turnip, a parsnip, a couple stalks of celery with the leaves on, a potato. And when it had cooked enough she strained it and set the broth out in the snow until the fat set up. She skimmed most of the fat and reheated the broth and practically funneled it down the woman's throat. It would have made a dead man grin. And there was no doubt about it, the woman was better.

She sat up when Grace brought her more soup and tea, this time with a little toast. The woman was looking worlds better, much more alert. She asked about the ditch rider again and Grace told her. Then she asked if anybody had been about, asking about her, but nobody had.

"Who's your folks, dear?" Grace asked. This was the first chance they'd really had to talk.

"No folks," the woman said. She drank more soup and lay back on the couch. "I'm just an orphan, I guess."

"Well, even a orphan's got a name, I expect," Grace said. She sat in the rocker a few feet away, next to the big black iron wood-stove that pumped out mind-swamping heat. In the house Grace wore long underwear under gray sweatpants and a gray sweatshirt that had "Montana State University Bobcats" printed on it, a gift from Calla, who was on the faculty there, although she spent most of her time in Yellowstone Park. On her feet were thick wool socks pulled up over the legs of the sweatpants so she could easily slip them into the shit-encrusted Sorel boots that sat by the kitchen door when she went out to do chores or fetch in more firewood. In the house she either went in stocking feet or sometimes, when she remembered, she would wear sheepskin-lined moccasins. She was not a big woman, but very angular, a square-built woman. She gave the impression of a cow, without looking in any specific way like a cow. She did have a long face, but her eyes weren't big and brown like a cow's, nor was she bosomy, but she had that angularity of the hips, a kind of awkward, bandy-legged hitch to her walk. She had stiff gray hair that still had a hint of its original red color, cut rather short.

"Heather," the convalescent woman said. "Heather Bloom."

"Why, what a lovely name, Heather. Now, must be someone bound to be worried about you. No one? Oh, that's too bad," Grace said. And she introduced herself, stepping across to shake hands. "You wouldn't know it," she said with a laugh, touching her gray hair, "but most ever'body calls me Red. But I prefer Grace."

To Heather's question in turn Grace replied that Yes, she was alone, pretty much, though she expected her daughter, Calla, to come by any day now. "But where'd you leave your car? Out on the highway?"

Heather said no, she'd left it in town, in Tinstar, which was just a few miles down the highway, and she'd set off to do a little cross-country skiing, but she'd run into trouble, which she had already explained. She wasn't expected anywhere, there wasn't anybody fretting about her. She'd worked for a while in Butte, but she was just setting out to go south, look for work down in Arizona, maybe. She was a kind of troubleshooter, she said, for computer systems. She never had any trouble finding jobs. She'd work for a while somewhere, then move on. It was good work, she liked it. She liked moving around. She was sorry to be so much bother. She'd be out of here just as soon as she could. She had money, she could pay for her keep.

"Why honey, you ain't fit to go to the skunks' ball," Grace told her. "You're welcome to lay around here all you want. Glad for the company, really. You just make yourself to home. If you ain't expected nowhere, you might as well lay up for Christmas, anyway."

So it was pretty much settled. Except that later, Heather confided that she did want to kind of avoid someone, a man from Butte. He might be looking for her and she'd just as soon he didn't find her. "I've had enough of these jerks," Heather said. "I always seem to find the wrong ones. He seemed all right, but then he started drinking and he seemed to think it was all right to take a poke at me when I wasn't willing to, you know, accommodate him."

"Honey, there is no reason for anyone to even know you're here. Don't you worry about a thing."

Grace shook her head. She'd heard this story often enough. Her late husband, Cal, had not been that sort of man. Didn't drink, didn't swear, just chewed snoose a bit. Cal hadn't been no Clark Gable . . . Grace's mind flickered back to a hand they'd hired, a moment in the barn. . . . But plenty of the gals in Tinstar had run into just the same luck as Heather. Sally McIntyre, for one. It was a damn shame that some of these men didn't use more of their energy doing a little useful work. She herself wasn't no saint, but she did like to read the Bible a bit. Nothing preachy. She liked the Old Testament stories best. Would Heather like to hear the story of Ruth? Heather said that would be fine.

Grace took down the old, well-worn Bible and began to read. But it was so warm, so cozy in the house with the fire and the wind howling safely outside, that before long the two women were fast asleep, one of them snoring in the rocking chair with her mouth wide open and dreaming about a hayloft, the sneezy sweet smell of hay, the shafts of sunlight piercing down, the soft mocking drone of the doves, a young man with an indistinct face but muscular arms.

It was dark but not late when they were awakened by the telephone. Heather sat up abruptly, then clutched at her shoulder, at the wound, with a little cry. Grace hurried to her, but Heather said she was all right and managed a smile. Grace went to the phone, which hung on the wall by the entry to the kitchen. She looked back at Heather, who watched her with alert, frightened eyes. It was Sally.

"Oh, no, I'm fine," Grace said. She put her hand over the speaker and whispered across the room that it was okay, it was just Sally. "I've got a visitor is why," she said into the phone. "A friend." Grace stared at Heather's worried face and grimaced in mock shame at fibbing, shaking her head with a little smile. "No, well, it's a lady friend, a cousin, or a niece . . . I guess she's rightly a second cousin, or third." Grace winked at Heather. "Come to visit for Christmas. Yes, it's nice to have someone for the holidays. Well, you stop on by and meet her. She's been feeling a little poorly, but she's settin' up now and as broody as a hen, so I guess she'll be all right. Why I'll have her out doin' chores before you know it, if this weather ever lets up. Well, Merry Christmas to you too, and to the kids. I'll have your check for you, anytime. No, we don't need a thing, we're just cozy as a coupla badgers in a den. Unh-hunh, well you take care of them kids and I'll see you maybe tomorrow."

Grace hung up. "Well, I didn't know but what you didn't want your whole life story spread all over the county. Sally's a fine gal, but she's out and about and I always thought it's just as well that nobody hears what they don't need to hear. Well, it was Cal, my late husband, who always said that, but it's true."

"Thank you," Heather said and she smiled a very warm smile that went right to Grace's heart. Then she lay back and closed her eyes.

"Well, I'll go out and see to them hens and such," Grace said, pulling on the brown duck overalls and the tin coat, then stuffing her feet into the felt-lined Sorels. "There's been a ferret about. I'll put a stop to him! And when I come in I'll get to making supper and afterward, why maybe you'd enjoy me to read you one of Dickens's Christmas stories. Would you like that?"

Heather said she'd like that and when the old woman went out she got up off the sofa, shocked at how weak she was. But it was necessary to take a look around. The first thing of interest that she found was a .30–.30 Winchester carbine, loaded, leaning against the wall near the door. Guns could be useful, Heather felt, but she had never really liked them: there was a tendency to rely too much on them and if they failed, as any mechanical device might fail, you were screwed. She preferred simpler methods—a stick, a stone. The gun could come in handy for Grace, however. She emptied the magazine and put the bullets in the pocket of the robe that Grace had provided her. She looked about the kitchen and then the rest of the downstairs, being careful not to stray too far from the couch, in case Grace should come back in and catch her.

The house was an old farmhouse, now somewhat modernized and better insulated than it had originally been. But it had the odor of old houses, not that the odor was familiar to Heather. It was a combination of years of wood smoke and years of the outdoors and the barnyard inevitably carried into the house by people who essentially lived outdoors. An odor of outdoor clothing and boots, of simple cooking. Not a scent of polish except for the wax on the dining room table and the old upright piano that was covered with a cloth and surmounted with a few family photos, including one of a rugged-looking man in a cowboy hat plus two of the kids. There was a faint tang of strong soap or piney-scented detergents. A homey odor, comfortable and warm.

Heather returned to the couch and snuggled up. She felt secure. She thought she could probably hang out here for another day or two, until she felt better, and then she would have to get moving. Grace had a pickup truck parked near the back porch. Heather figured she could use that, but it would mean having to take care of Grace. She felt no animosity toward Grace, quite the opposite: she couldn't recall when she'd felt so, well, at home. She hadn't lied about being an orphan, or not much. She had a vague notion of her mother but none of a father, and the succession of aunties and foster parents were not memories she cared to invoke. But she would have to do something about Grace when the time came. She drifted into sleep.

4

Deal Me In

Young lovers on awakening do what they did before falling asleep, but when Joe and Cateyo awoke he was suffering what she diagnosed as "bed spins." This is not a medical term, but a colloquial phrase more appropriate to the experience of a teenager when he or she first goes to bed drunk. In Joe Service's case it obviously had something to do with the brain injuries from which he had still not recovered. There was an alcoholic component, of course, having to do with drinking Mad Dog the night before, as well as some dreadful dreams he'd had about Tongans and a tree frog with an Egyptian or Assyrian beard who played fantastic blues on the piano—he could vividly see those long, spatulate fingers and that wide, wide, maniacal grin. In the dream the creature had also had black, leathery wings, which he didn't remember from the scene in the bar, or whatever it was. But it was difficult to sort the dream from the vision.

Sorting dreams from reality had been a problem for Joe since his brain injury, so when Cateyo went into the shower, he struggled up and searched his clothes: there were no pistols in his coat, but there were wads of money, about four hundred dollars. He wasn't sure what this meant; possibly he had disposed of the guns on the way back to the hotel, but he didn't recall doing so. He tried to imagine throwing them into the river as he walked across a bridge, but he had no memory of walking across a bridge. For that matter, he had the impression that Salt Lake City was one of those rare cities that is neither a harbor city, nor an island city, nor even a river city. Possibly an oasis city, he thought, except that here the water was brackish and salt and the city avoided its shores.

He was curious, in fact, about how he knew this, how he knew these things. How did he know anything? He was, by now, fairly confident about his own identity, although in the early days after he had awakened from the bullet-induced coma, in the hospital in Butte, that had been a very serious problem. Even now, the path that led back from the present to his remembered past was a narrow one, perilously faint, liable to disappear at any moment into the undifferentiated grasses of the plain. Or, he thought, perhaps like the wake of a canoe on a lake: you could look back and see it, and it told you where you had been, but it was clearly dissipating into the other currents and eddies of the water that lay all about you. . . . He shuddered, not wanting to think any more about it. Except that it seemed important.

Thus far, he had managed to retrace his steps—recover his memory—by simply trusting that he could. That is, he would, in effect, take a deep breath and boldly step toward where the path might be presumed to be. How he had hit on this tactic he hardly knew, but it seemed to work, most of the time. And a memory once recovered was strengthened, or the path to it was strengthened, but he wasn't completely confident of the technique. Perhaps there were different kinds of memories, short-term and long-term, habitual things as opposed to contemplative things. He didn't know. He wasn't a neurologist or even a person with an interest in medicine. But he had a good mind and he trusted it. Somehow, though, he knew that one couldn't do that *all the way back*. The farther back one went, the more difficult it would be to find the path, or the wake.

When Cateyo got out of the shower, toweling off that rosy young flesh, Joe put all thought of riverless cities, grassy paths, and dissipating wakes out of his fragile mind, gratefully yielding brain time to more urgent interests. He advised her to get into bed and wait until he had showered. This advice was eagerly taken and eagerly they replayed the sexual events of the night, this time with even more deeply satisfying results.

Afterward, Cateyo told him what she had been unable to convey the night before, concerning the cabin fire and the police search for them. To her surprise Joe didn't seem very concerned. He said something about how it would all work out and they went down to breakfast and the newspapers.

Looking into the restaurant, Joe was suddenly struck with the thought that he had been here before. This was not a good place to eat. The good place to eat was somewhere about five or six blocks away. . . . The railroad station? He remembered the Rio Grande Cafe. But it was too far. Then it hit him: the Market Street Grill and Oyster Bar. He was fairly certain that it was a "private club," which in Mormonland meant a place that served booze. They found it easily. Membership was five dollars for two weeks. They were soon bunkered in a comfortable banquette and eating a Hangtown Fry, made with very fresh oysters flown in that morning from Seattle.

There was nothing in the Salt Lake paper about the incident in Montana at Joe's cabin. They had picked up the Butte paper on the way and it carried the story on the front page, but it wasn't the lead. It had been three days, and even in Butte that is long enough for a story to lose interest. Apparently, the arson investigators had found nothing to suggest that it was anything other than an accident, perhaps precipitated by the damage the invading gangsters had done to the house: it seemed clear that they had been ripping out walls and perhaps disturbing electrical wiring and the propane-feed tubing. It was the explosion of the propane tank itself that had done the major damage, literally leveling the structure, and if propane explosions are not common they are at least not unheard-of in rural areas.

A reporter had asked, naturally, what the intruders might have been looking for, but no one had an opinion on that, although Deputy Jacques Lee had observed, pointedly, that the intruders were known gangsters and three of them were thought to be Colombians.

Joe was interested to learn that only one man, a Victor Echeverria, had survived. He was now in Salt Lake City, as it happened, in serious condition at the burn treatment center, where he'd been flown within hours of the explosion. It was not known if he would survive. The name meant nothing to Joe. It was more interesting to Joe to read that Helen Sedlacek, whom the press described as "the missing Joseph Humann's companion," was in the Butte jail and was expected to be charged with assault on a police officer and resisting arrest. He'd had no idea she was in town: he hadn't seen or heard from her since before he was shot.

What was bothersome, if laughable, was that the police were still treating the disappearance of himself and Nurse Cathleen Yoder as a possible kidnapping: who was the kidnapper and who the kidnapped, since Joe was also described as an invalid? Cateyo's call to Nurse Work had not made the papers.

Cateyo was worried more about Joe than the misunderstanding about her disappearance. He seemed anxious and withdrawn. He ransacked the newspapers, especially the *Salt Lake Tribune*. She had no way of knowing that he was looking for some reference to a shootout in a local bar. When he did find an article referring to a minor disturbance at a southside "social club," in which no one was reported injured despite several gunshots being fired, he seemed perplexed, but then he shrugged and seemed to lighten up.

Joe couldn't figure it out. Had everything that had happened to him last night been a dream? Had he simply imagined it? He didn't believe it, but he wasn't sure. For one thing, he had a pocketful of money, so presumably the attempted mugging, at least, had been for real. But no guns. Well, there would be ways to find out, and he knew the ways. But first things first.

"You have to go home," he told Cateyo. She argued and protested, but there was no good alternative. She had to show her unharmed self. And Joe could not. She would be questioned, and he had no confidence in her ability to withstand a police interrogation, but what did she know after all? The police would have to believe her when she told them that Joe was fine, that he was "traveling." If she could stick to that simple line. To that end, the less she knew about Joe and his program, the better. He was sure that the Detroit detective, Mulheisen, would be looking for him now. It was something that he had long feared but had always successfully avoided. Over the years he had been involved in a number of investigations for the Detroit mob, mainly for Carmine, the late and unlamented mob boss. Time and again, Detective Sergeant Mulheisen had come close to encountering Joe in his flittings and fleeings, but Joe was fairly confident that, until now, Mulheisen had never "made" him. Heretofore, Joe Service not only had no criminal record but not even an official existence, much less an identity. To be known was a new and serious danger to Joe's freedom. And he was concerned about how Cateyo would interact with Mulheisen, but perhaps she wouldn't have to: it would be a Butte–Silver Bow case, although Mulheisen was bound to stick his nose in, Joe thought, and maybe the FBI, as well. But Joe had no regard for the FBI.

She refused to go, even though Joe assured her that all she need do is return to Butte, talk to her superiors and the police, prepare her house for her absence and meet him . . . well, *somewhere*. She wanted to know much more about Joe, about his life, about the life they would have together. She couldn't possibly go back now . . . unless he enlightened her.

They went for a long walk. They found a large park, built around what Joe thought at first was a zoo, not very far from downtown. It wasn't a zoo; it was an elaborate aviary, populated now with ducks and geese in its outdoor ponds.

"Who is this Helen?" Cateyo wanted to know, as they strolled in the wintry sunlight. "I know she must be the one who was paying your medical bills, but is she . . . I mean . . . I guess you're not married?" She stalked along, not looking at him, her blond head buried in the collar of her ski jacket.

"No, I'm not married," Joe said. He was strangely confident of this. He wasn't finding it easy to keep up with her. They paced along a poorly cleared walk, gritty with dirty ice. The sun filtered coldly through the bare branches of cottonwoods, and a breeze blew off the mountains. Geese coughed and slid around on the iced ponds. In the caged areas there were odd-looking ducks.

Cateyo pleaded, "What is she to you . . . now?"

Joe appreciated the "now." "We were lovers," he said casually, "but it wasn't working out. I mean, even before *this*." He gestured at his head. "It was a mistake." He stopped on the lumpy path. Cateyo stopped and looked back at him.

Joe stared at the ground. It was true, he thought. It hadn't been working out and it had been a very grievous mistake. He realized for the first time since he'd been shot that it was Helen who had betrayed him. He wondered how it had happened. He was inclined to believe that it was something unintentional on her part. And then he knew what it must have been: she had contacted her mother, back in Detroit. A phone call, a postcard, a letter . . . something like that. He had vehemently warned her not to; it was worth nothing less than their lives. She had killed Carmine and he had helped her do it; the mob would never forget. Oh, the Fat Man, or

Humphrey (as he seemed to be calling himself these days), might want to cut Joe some slack, but it simply wasn't possible to forgive and forget the killing of a mob satrap. Humphrey was a patient man; he would have waited and, finally, when Helen made contact with her aged mother, Humphrey would have learned of it and would have acted. And that was what had happened.

"Joe? What is it?" Cateyo said, coming back to stand by him, taking his arm.

He looked at her. "Nothing. I made a mistake. It was my mistake. I should have known better." Joe uttered a brief dry laugh.

They walked on. Finally she stopped and turned to him. "Joe, don't you understand? I have to know more. Don't you care? Don't you want me . . . to stay . . . to be with you?"

"Of course I do, babe." It was true. He needed her. He wasn't well and she could help him. Also, he had feelings for her. He understood that she wanted him to be in love with her and he was willing to be in love with her, whatever that meant. He had been in love with Helen, perhaps. He certainly had been fascinated with her, almost obsessed. He thought it probably had been love. But he wasn't sure how he felt about Helen now. Betrayed. Alarmed. He wanted very much to see her and talk to her, but it didn't have much to do with desire or love, at this point. As for Cateyo . . . well, he thought she would be nothing if not loyal and faithful. He thought he could love her. He understood her need to know more about him and he wanted her to know more, but how much, and of what nature?

"Joe, are you a criminal?" she asked suddenly.

What an extraordinary question! Who on earth goes around saying such things? But there it was. That was what she wanted to know. Were they doing something wrong? Was Joe a bad guy? "How can you ask such a thing?" he replied, with a show of indignation.

"Joe," she pleaded, "you were found on the highway, shot. The paper says the guy who shot you was a professional killer, and his body was found on your property. You were living with a woman who the cops think killed a gangster in Detroit." Cateyo recounted these things as calmly as she could, but finally she turned to him with tears in her eyes, near despair at his maddening nonchalance. "That detective from Detroit, he told me that you were not what I thought, that you were a criminal, that your friends were drug dealers and killers.

"Joe, I never really believed in professional killers," she said. "I thought they were something that was made up for movies. It's hard to believe in things like the Mafia, gangsters, when you live in Montana. Oh, I suppose there are such things . . . "

"In the Butte paper this morning," Joe retorted, "there was an item about a seventy-five-year-old farmer up on the Hi-Line who gave two punks from Great Falls two thousand dollars to kill his forty-nine-year-old second wife. He thought she was ripping him off and having an affair with the hired man. The punks were supposed to make it look like the hired man did it, but the hired man spotted them sneaking around the property and called the sheriff."

"Well, they must not have been professional killers," Cateyo said, derisively.

"No doubt," Joe said, drily, "but what about the woman in the Salt Lake paper? From Spokane? She hired a guy from Seattle to kill her estranged husband? He was almost beaten to death—for five hundred dollars!"

"Okay, there *are* hired killers. My point is, Joe, that I didn't know about such things and now I find out that you're involved. I mean, you're the victim, but you were also living with a woman who was involved. Six gangsters were in your cabin. That woman Heather—you said she was a killer. Why was she hanging around me? What am I supposed to think? If I'm going to be with you I need to know why you . . . well, why you know such people."

It was at that moment that Joe saw the Tongans.

Joe took her arm almost casually and turned her aside onto another path that disappeared behind some aviaries. "I'm not a

gangster," he said, laughing. He felt inspired, suddenly. "I'm just a
guy who has—or had—a lot of money. Crooks are always interested
in money, regardless of the source. It's a fact of life; all rich people
understand this. Regardless of how they came by their wealth,
they're constantly besieged and harassed by thieves and hustlers and
con men." He uttered these words as he hurried her along a path
around other aviaries. Some disconsolate mallards poked along
muddy little pseudocreeks. They quacked softly, or rather grunted,
oppressed by the cold.

"Are you rich, Joe? I thought you were broke."

"I've *got* money, I just don't *have* it, on hand. It's not readily
available. I earned my money and I want to put it to good use, but
the law doesn't seem to understand what I'm doing. They want to
talk to me, and . . . " He glanced over his shoulder as he turned Cateyo
down another path, catching a glimpse of a hulking body and a large
head, stopped at a junction of paths, craning around—he didn't think
they'd seen him, but where were the others? "I'd like to talk to the
cops and I plan to, but right now they would interfere with my plans
and it would mean hardship for many innocent people."

What on earth he was talking about he didn't know. But he
babbled on as he swiftly but without panic guided Cateyo onto
another path, around another building, casually eyeballing the area.
There were some Tongans over there, big heads looming near the
park entry, a young couple, hand in hand. Maybe these Tongans
weren't after him? Maybe they were just incidental Tongans, young
lovers in the park. Joe Service wasn't prepared to believe this; it
wasn't the season for young lovers in parks.

"What innocent people?" Cateyo wanted to know.

"Poor folks who are dying," Joe said. "I have access, or had
access, to a lot of funds that I've gathered over a period of time, to
aid people with terminal illnesses. But, thanks to Helen, I've temporarily lost contact with my funds. This," he said, gesturing at his

head again, hunched down in the collar of his coat, "has upset my plans. I've got to get back to my work."

Cateyo was astounded. It was the first she'd heard of Joe's altruistic purposes. In fact, it was the first time he'd ever spoken of his work, his plans. She was eager to know more, but he was hustling her now, moving with surprising speed along the rim of a little rise that blocked any view of them from the other side of the park, toward where her car was parked. He opened the door of the driver's side and pushed her in behind the wheel.

"Go," he said. "Trust me, please. Go back to the hotel and pack your stuff. Don't bother to check out—I'll take care of it. Meet me at the Market Street Grill in about an hour. Go." He slammed the door and walked rapidly on, disappearing over the ridge of the little rise. She was tempted to get out and follow him, but his urgency had infected her. She started the car and drove out of the lot, passing two large, dark men, who were plodding heavily along in what for them may have been a jogging gait.

Joe cut directly across the park and now he could see two more pairs of Tongans headed his way. He grinned. The sun had disappeared and the air was cold, but he felt good. His head was light and almost empty. He glanced back and, for the first time, noticed that both the Tongans he could see were carrying hand-held phones of some kind. One of them was talking on the phone. That was ominous, but he wasn't too alarmed. For one thing, he was practically out of the park. Once into the streets he felt that he would be like Brer Rabbit in his briar patch.

He made it to a one-way street and was slipping across the slowly moving spotty traffic when a car pulled past him and a door opened. A large hand reached out and hauled him in. It was done very smoothly, very simply, and he was almost admiring of the maneuver, except that he found himself jammed between two very large men with large heads in the back seat of the car. It struck him that he'd been herded out of the park like a rabbit and that he'd practically dived into this back seat as into a falsely welcoming burrow. Not the briar patch—more like Wonderland.

A much smaller man in the passenger seat up front turned and said, "Hello. You must be Bongo Billy." The man extended a hand over the back of the seat. It was a thin, papery hand. "I'm Cap'n Lite," he said. His voice was weak and whispery.

He had a small head, bony, with bright blue eyes and a sharp nose. He had small brownish teeth. Joe shook the hand briefly and let it drop back onto the top of the seat. The man wore a green felt hat, sort of Tyrolean looking, but it seemed large for his head. Joe had the impression that the man was ill. He didn't seem to have much hair. Perhaps he was undergoing chemotherapy.

"Hi," Joe said. He swiveled his head to look at the two men on either side of him. They were massive, filling up the otherwise wide back seat of the big car. Another similar sort was behind the wheel. The car turned and started smoothly up a long boulevard toward the mountains.

"I heard you were looking for me," Cap'n Lite said. "But then it seems like you changed your mind."

Joe shrugged. "I didn't like the look of those guys in the park. I've never really gotten along with giants. Well, that's not exactly true . . . I don't mind the odd giant, it's when they come in clumps, if you know what I mean."

The man laughed. It was a wheezy laugh and ended in a little cough. "Sorry," Cap'n Lite said, then: "I know what you mean. But what can I do for you?"

Joe looked at him carefully. He was trying to think, but then he shook his head irritably, as if dislodging a fly that was bothering him. It didn't do to think, he reminded himself. Just wing it. That was his only chance. "Aagh," he gasped as a huge hand thudded none too gently into his right rib cage. "Well, yeah," he wheezed, "I need a little help. I lost something and I thought the, uh . . . " He hesitated, then recalled the phrase of last night: "The head Tonk might be the guy who could help me find what I lost." The man on the left lifted his arm slightly and powered a dull thumping fist into Joe's left rib cage, just over Joe's heart. Joe thought this might be dangerous. He wished he could think of some way to get them to stop. They could kill him accidentally.

Now it was Cap'n Lite's turn to study Joe. "You lost some money," he said at last, barely breathing the words.

Joe smiled weakly. "That's it! Amazing! Well, we're headed in the right direction, anyway."

"We are?" Cap'n Lite said. "Pull over, Tutu," he said to the driver. They parked on the street. They were facing uphill, not a steep incline, but definitely a hill. There were a lot of largish, modern houses around. Not really fancy, but the homes of the modestly well-off. "How much did you lose?"

"I'm not sure," Joe said. "I'd have to count it when I find it. But a sizable amount. Say, a couple hundred thousand?"

"Don't ask me," Cap'n Lite said. "I didn't take it."

"I know who took it," Joe said, "I just don't know how much she got away with. Could be . . . oh, three hundred thousand. If you could help me find it there would be a generous reward."

Cap'n Lite pondered this. "The blond, you mean?" he said finally, nodding down the hill.

Joe shook his head. "No, this one was dark. Small. She had a silver streak in her hair."

The blue eyes were paler than Joe's. They weren't in any way expressive. Just pale blue eyes. The man had little or no expression, except for an occasional small smile alternated with a grimace of pain. "You hurt some of our people," he said, with a faint tone of reproach.

"I did? I wasn't sure. It was dar— ooogh!" A fist the size of a baby's head slammed into his ribs. It didn't seem to have broken anything. Joe was grateful for the down lining in his ski jacket. He slumped passively between the two men, both of whom gazed straight ahead. He looked up at the little head on the seat back.

Cap'n Lite rested his bony chin on the seat and when he spoke his head moved up and down, a childish gesture. "What's your regular name? No Bongo Billys now. Hunh?"

"They call me Joe. Little Joe, from Kokomo." He smiled at the man hopefully, then added: "Joe Service, at your service." When he finally got the man to crack a smile, Joe tipped his head left and right at the two pillars of flesh on either side and said, with a very sincere expression: "Can we talk, Cap'n?"

Cap'n Lite was still bouncing his head off his jaw as he replied, equally sincerely, "I've heard of Joe Service. I think. Okay, we can talk. These are my friends. You can talk in front of them."

"Obviously, you're free to relay to these gentlemen anything I tell you," Joe said, "but I'd rather you decided, after you've heard me out. And I'd prefer to just talk to one man than blat it all over town."

Cap'n Lite considered this for a moment, then he lifted his chin from the seat back and addressed the three Tongans as one: "You heard him, my friends. Could you leave us alone for a few minutes?" He was quite polite about it, genuinely asking their forbearance, rather than making a conventional request for them to beat it. They shrugged and got out of the car, causing it to rock violently in their leaving. The driver took with him a telephone. They gathered by the trunk, hands in pockets and staring around at the white-bread neighborhood, two of them talking in low tones to each other in their rumbling language, while the driver spoke into the phone.

"Who are these guys?" Joe asked. "Where the hell did you pick them up? I mean, they're nice and hefty, a regular wall around you, but . . . "

"They picked me up," Cap'n Lite said. "They're Tongans. The Mormons run a big mission effort in the islands. The Tongans come here to see Jerusalem, or Rome, or Mecca, whatever. They're good people, most of them, but . . . " He shrugged philosophically. "You don't know about Tongans? They got a reputation out there." He gestured with his head, presumably at the distant Pacific Ocean. "What's the phrase? 'Tonga-heart.' I think it means not very caring, maybe. The thing is, they don't give a shit about us, about the U.S., maybe not even about the angel Moroni. Tonga is all they care about." He sighed. He seemed tired. But he went on: "They hang out here for a while, just to make a pile, or what they figure will be a pile back in Tonga, then they go home and as far as they're concerned we can all blow ourselves to kingdom come with A-bombs, or whatever. They picked me 'cause they figure I know the ropes and I can help them take care of business. Street business. Also, they're some kinda comedians—the idea of a little boss tickles them. But there's some other boss, a Big Boss. I don't know who he is. They weren't amused by what you did to their pals, though."

"It's their own fault," Joe said. "I didn't pick on them. I was just walking down the street, minding my own business. The others, they shot first."

The little man looked at Joe sadly, as if to say, Get serious. He said, "Their business *was* you, but it don't matter. They'd like to take you for a drive up the canyons." He looked thoughtful, then said, "Joe Service is a name. You get around. You have connections. Mitch in New York, the Fat Man in Detroit. You were in Vancouver not too long ago, weren't you? Something about the Chinese? Something like that?"

Joe didn't answer, just looked at him. After a moment the man sighed and said, "I'll do what I can, Joe, but I don't know if they'll let you off with just a beating."

"*Just* a beating? That doesn't sound very nice," Joe said. "I don't know if I could handle a beating, right now," he added, with only a seasoning of irony. "Uh, just what *did* I do to their pals? I'm not kidding, it was kind of dark in the bar."

"Shootin' guns off in people's faces. You could have hurt somebody, Joe. Nobody dead, anyway," Cap'n Lite said. "That's one thing in your favor. These boys are literal minded—maybe it's the religion, I don't know—but an eye for an eye is pretty much the rate of exchange."

Joe winced. "Did any of them lose an eye?"

Cap'n Lite shook his head. "Tell me more about this lady who lost your money for you. Money is sometimes a satisfactory exchange medium, in part at least."

"She didn't lose it. She's got it, but she's not in town. I think the money's in town, though, if I could find out where she was holed up."

"Tell me about it," Cap'n Lite said. He rested his chin on his arm and listened while Joe told him as much and no more than he figured was needful. "Is that it?" he said, when Joe stopped talking. "Maybe three big ones? And this is Big Sid's daughter?" He shook his head. "Chip off the block."

"If you help me find it, ten percent is yours," Joe said. "That'd be—"

"I know how much that'd be," Cap'n Lite said. "It's shit. I'm thinkin' more like fifty-fifty."

A sense of release flooded through Joe. The man wanted to deal. Joe liked people who would deal. "Twenty-five," he countered.

Cap'n Lite stared at him dreamily. The man seemed quite tired. The driver came over to the front door and rapped. He pointed at the phone and nodded. "Okay, okay," Cap'n Lite said, nodding. The driver walked back to join the other men. Cap'n Lite turned to Joe. "Thirty percent," he said.

"You got it," Joe said. He held out his hand. Cap'n Lite shook it limply.

"Okay, Mr. Joe Kokomo. I'm gonna get out now and I'll talk to the boys. When a bus comes down the hill, you get out and walk across the street to where that lady is waiting and you get on the bus. I hope the boys don't stop you. You call me every six hours." He gave Joe a phone number. "Maybe we can work this out. For old times' sake, being as you know the Fat Man."

"I'd appreciate anything you can do," Joe said. "Us wee folk have to stick together. It's a big world out there."

The little man grimaced and got out. He really was little, smaller and much slighter than Joe; the top of his hat didn't quite reach to the Tongans' armpits. He took the two back-seat heavies by their hands and walked them down the sidewalk about twenty feet, like Sabu leading elephants, his jaw jacking away. The driver followed, holding out the telephone.

A bus came into view. Joe opened the back door quietly and got out. The men turned to look at him, but Joe avoided eye contact. He set off across the wide street, hoping not to hear their elephantine trumpets bugle or the ponderous thumping of their feet. There was a pretty nice view of the city from here, the capitol over there, a university over here, the Great Salt Lake a distant haze. Joe didn't linger to enjoy it. He made it to the bus stop safely and got on. As the bus pulled away he could see the Tongans pointedly turning their backs on him while Cap'n Lite spoke into the phone.

Minutes later he got off the bus downtown. He went immediately to a phone booth and called the hotel, in case Cateyo had not left yet. There was no answer in the room. While he stood listening to the rings, he looked out of the telephone booth absently at the Zion National Bank. He felt a strange twinge of memory, but that was immediately vanquished when he saw Detective Sergeant Mulheisen of the Detroit police exit from the glass doors.

5

Cold Trail

Mulheisen was a man who felt comfortable with himself. He believed himself to be a man who took things easy, who didn't get too excited. It was true that he gave that appearance, generally, but it was also true that when exercised he was apt to depart from ordinary routes and tracks. He wasn't wedded to the comfortable. For instance, when he'd gotten off the Butte flight at Salt Lake City, he hadn't meant to do anything more than catch the Detroit flight. But now that he'd picked up a whiff of a trail, he didn't hesitate to risk missing his flight connection to spend a little time in the Mormon capital, even though it might cause some disruption, some trouble, mostly for himself.

At this point he wasn't sure what he was up to, but when he'd shown Helen's picture to various bank personnel and it had been readily identified as the picture of the woman who had purchased money orders for slightly less than three thousand dollars, he felt a tremor of the chase. He wanted to take a longer look. He had long suspected that her presence in Salt Lake City was more than casual. He wondered if she'd made a base for herself here. He didn't bother to go to the local police. It was hardly worth bothering with, at this early stage. Later, he would of course coordinate his investigation with them, but right now it was too tentative.

He was encouraged by his conversation with one woman, an officer at a downtown bank, who had initially interviewed Helen when she sought to purchase a cashier's check with a large amount of cash. She had recognized the photo—Helen was a striking woman, easily remembered—but she had no name to go with the face. "She came in here," the woman said, "carrying a small suitcase which was evidently full of cash. She didn't know about the three-thousand-dollar limit. She wanted to buy a fifty-thousand-dollar cashier's check—with cash! She said she was in a business where she had to handle a lot of cash. I explained the IRS reporting requirements to her. You know, it used to be that you could buy a cashier's check for less than ten thousand dollars without identifying yourself, but now we have to keep a log for anything three thousand and over. She purchased a check for less from the teller and naturally I was suspicious. I watched her walk right across the street and into another bank. I was sure she was trying to avoid IRS reporting requirements. She didn't look like a smurf, but they aren't supposed to, are they? So I called the FBI. They took the information and said they would pass it on to the proper agency, but they didn't seem particularly interested and I never heard anything more about it. I guess now I should have called the IRS, but I just didn't think about it. Did I do right?"

The woman looked concerned. Mulheisen had identified himself as a policeman, but she had hardly glanced at his identification—that homely, honest face was nearly always accepted at, well, face value. If he'd said he was a plumber, she probably would have pointed to the sink. He supposed she thought he might be a federal agent of some kind. "Oh, no problem," he assured her. "We're on the case, but since you did report your suspicions. . . . The fact is, she didn't do anything illegal as far as you were concerned, but I think you were right to be suspicious. Did she give any name? I know she didn't have to file a report, but did she give a name to you?"

The woman was sure she hadn't. "But I saw her in the bank again, a few days later, and then again some weeks later. She was no longer lugging that suitcase, but she was toting a very large hand-bag. I asked the teller when she left and found out she had purchased another cashier's check."

None of this had taken very long. Mulheisen walked around to a few of the hotels downtown and showed the picture. It wasn't recognized until he got to the Little America, a huge pile just south of the main business district. It seemed she had spent a couple of days there about the time of Joe Service's shooting, in September, some three months earlier. It looked like the hotel for her, suitably large, anonymous, but with some class. But he had another feeling: she wouldn't be happy in a hotel if she had a lot of cash to take care of. And this was another thing that was tentative, but convincing to Mulheisen: he suspected that she had quite a lot of money, in cash.

Nearly a year earlier, it had been widely rumored on the streets of Detroit that her father had skimmed—shoveled, really—somewhere between twenty and forty million dollars off drug deal-ings, which was why Carmine had ordered him dead. This money had never been recovered, according to street talk reported to Rack-ets and Conspiracy in the Detroit Police Department, but Mulheisen himself had found the man who had engineered the skimming for Big Sid Sedlacek: a small-time chiseler and wannabe hit man named Eugene Lande.

Mulheisen remembered the scene vividly; how could he for-get it? Lande was holding a .45 automatic and it was pointed at Mulheisen. Lande had said, almost offhandedly, that the take had been too much to disperse into the elaborate computer-banking scheme that he had set up. The money just kept rolling in, a scene reminiscent of the Sorcerer's Apprentice, where once the foolish apprentice got the juice flowing he didn't find it so easy to get it to stop. But Lande had managed to lay off all but about fifteen million dollars, he thought. Mulheisen had asked where that money was now. Lande had nodded toward the rear of the building in which they stood.

"You have fifteen million dollars here? In cash?" Mulheisen had asked. Lande wasn't certain how much was there.

"Fifteen mil is an awful lotta cash," Lande had told him, "even if it's all in fifties and hunnerds, which it was, 'cause you can't be screwin' aroun' with twennies and that little crap. Lessee." He'd done a quick calculation in his head. "If it's all hunnerds, that'd be a hunnerd fifty thousand bills, or somethin' like that. Now, if they was all new bills—you know, in little tight bun'les like the mint issues—you could prolly cram that much cash inna half dozen cardboard boxes, say like they put whiskey bottles in. But what I had was a couple dozen boxes, 'cause the money was used. . . . It's thicker." He went on to say that he had dumped some of the money—a fantastic tale of leaving it on the doorsteps of orphanages and missions for the homeless—but he still had a lot left. He thought he had perhaps got rid of another five or six million, he wasn't sure.

At the time Mulheisen had been skeptical of this tale (he hadn't heard anything about orphanages finding boxes of free money on their doorsteps). Besides, he was distracted, what with the wavering .45 in Lande's hand. Well, Lande had been drunk, and quite crazed. Ultimately, he had put the .45 into his own mouth and ended it. Afterward, Mulheisen had found a dozen or so boxes in the back, stuffed with old newspapers. At the time little attention was paid to this factor, but Mulheisen had reasoned that no one fills a cardboard box with newspaper, unless perhaps he wishes someone else (Lande, presumably) to think that the boxes were still full of what they were supposed to be full of—money. So perhaps there was something to Lande's story. Perhaps someone had elfed off with a few million. But it was all so speculative, so insubstantial that it hadn't seemed worth pursuing, not with the press of other events.

But Mulheisen hadn't forgotten. He had speculated that Joe Service might have taken the money and that it probably amounted to something in the neighborhood of ten million, or so. Too much money to be carrying around, if Helen had, in turn, taken it from Joe's place. And surely she would have taken the money. When the mob hit man Mario Soper had shown up at Joe's place, she must reasonably have believed that Joe was dead and the mob hot on her trail. She would flee and she would certainly take with her a portable fortune. And if she had it with her, well, it was portable but not comfortably portable; it wasn't something you would want to leave in the car while you went shopping or caught a movie. And if you checked into a hotel it wasn't something you could just have the bellboy bring up to the room: "Uh, boy! Do you have a dolly, a cart? I have several boxes here. Be careful! They're full of money!"

The desk man at the Little America hotel remembered Helen very well and he thrilled Mulheisen by checking their records to discover that she had used the name Helena Kaparich. This was Helen's mother's maiden name, a name by which Mulheisen had tracked her movements earlier. He kicked himself for not having remembered that. A phone call to the power company was in order.

The woman in the credit accounts department at Utah Power and Light was very cooperative, once she had received Mulheisen's PIN number—an identification number that verified that he was a police officer. Helena Kaparich had opened an account for electrical power at a single dwelling on Main Street in September. Her account was up to date. She was not the home owner, but the property was managed by a real estate firm in downtown Salt Lake City.

By now he had very little time if he still wanted to make his plane connection to Detroit, but Mulheisen didn't hesitate. The realtor was located in the Zion National Bank building, just a few blocks from the hotel. There the woman running the office recognized the photograph as that of a "Mrs. Helena Kaparich," who had leased the house on Main Street.

He walked out of the large, new building in which the realtor's office was located and stood on the corner. Salt Lake is one of those few cities with sensibly laid-out streets: 300 South, 700 East, and so on. From where he stood he figured the address was perhaps a mile or more south of the business district, on one of the few named streets, Main Street. Too far to walk, if he wanted to make his flight, but possibly a cab could take him by there quickly and still get him to the airport on time.

He never saw Joe Service standing across the street. He took the cab and within a few minutes they had pulled up in front of the house that Mrs. Helena Kaparich had leased, with an option to buy. The cab stood outside the stucco bungalow and Mulheisen got out and walked up to the house. He rang the bell, but he knew before ringing it that no one was home. He glanced about the neighborhood. He loved it. It was a house a Detroit girl could like. The house was small and discreet and had a style that had been prevalent in the Midwest for nearly a century. A house like this one could be found on the same streets of Detroit where Helen had grown up. He knew the floor plan just by looking at it: front living room, a bedroom on the side, a dining room, a kitchen in the rear, the bathroom off a little hall between the front room and the kitchen, and upstairs there would be two bedrooms with a bathroom between them. He would bet on it. And he was right.

There would be a basement, probably. A laundry room, a furnace, perhaps a room converted into a den or family room. . . . The money would be there, he guessed. But what to do now? Go to the Salt Lake City police? Get them to watch the place? Try to get a search warrant? He wasn't sure. He doubted that the local police, although inclined to be helpful, would be able to spare any men for a close watch. They might be able to keep a rolling surveillance, advising patrols to eyeball the place in passing. A warrant, though . . . he doubted it. Unless he could come up with something else.

"What time is it?" he asked the cab driver. Mulheisen could never seem to keep a timepiece—even fine watches went dead on his wrist. He had a half hour till flight time. "Airport," he told the driver.

Joe Service had been unable to find a cab in time, but he was energized. He set off down Main Street, walking as fast as he could. He was able to keep the cab in sight for some ways, but eventually it was lost to his view, though not having turned off, evidently. He stopped, finally, and turned back. He felt exhilarated. Who knew what Mulheisen was up to? But he felt that he knew his man. Mulheisen was on to something. Mulheisen wouldn't just be driving around the town looking at the sights. But now he'd lost him. Still, he knew where Mulheisen had been and he knew the number of the cab. He could find out what Mulheisen had been up to by backtracking.

He walked to the Market Street Grill and Oyster Bar, where he was supposed to meet Cateyo. She wasn't around. He ordered a bowl of clam chowder and it tasted tremendous. None of the waiters and waitresses could remember seeing Cateyo, but they had just changed shifts and it had been at least two hours since she could have first come in. Where would she have gone? He walked out into the cold afternoon—it was only four o'clock, but it was already getting dark—and headed over to Main, just looking around, wondering what had happened to Cateyo. He felt tired, exhausted, in fact. He wasn't used to all this walking. He soon found himself simply standing on the street, getting cold, pondering, when he noticed the huge Zion National Bank building, from which he'd seen Mulheisen exit. There was something about this bank. It nagged at him. He'd had the same feeling when he'd first seen it, but then he'd ignored it when Mulheisen came out. What could it be?

It was a sensation with which he was becoming familiar. It had something to do with his perforated memory. There was something about the bank that had to do with him and as he had learned, it didn't do to push his memory. It would come to him if he just let it. He walked across the street and entered the bank. It was even more familiar now. He had been here before. But what had he done? Well, what did people do at a bank? They deposited money, they withdrew money, they applied for loans, they bought cashier's checks. . . . He recalled that Helen had sent a cashier's check from this bank, according to Cateyo, to pay for his medical bills. That must be it. That was probably why Mulheisen had come here. He was on the trail of Helen. But there was something unsatisfactory about this explanation and then he realized that he had missed a turning somewhere. He was not on the same track as the one which had brought him in here. Mulheisen's pursuit of Helen was not why this bank had seemed familiar to him. And then it simply appeared in his mind: he had an account here. In fact, the rental car from Avarris was billing this account. He smiled delightedly. One minute he didn't remember and the next minute the hole was filled in as if it had never existed. No bells, no whistles, no bright lights . . . just another piece of the memory back.

In his travels about the West he had often stashed money in accounts, for emergency purposes. But under what name? Well, Avarris was billing Joseph Humann. He went to a cashier and said, "Hi. I'm just in town for the night and I realized that I need some cash, but I forgot my account number. Is there any way I can do this?"

The woman behind the counter was young and pretty. She looked at the handsome, if somewhat drawn young man standing before her and smiled. "Sure," she said. "What's the name?"

"Joseph Humann."

The woman took the spelling and typed it into a computer terminal. "Mr. Joseph Humann? Tinstar, Montana?"

Joe nodded.

"Do you have any identification?"

Joe did. He pulled out his wallet and handed over his legitimate Joseph Humann driver's license from the state of Montana. It had his picture on it and everything. She squinted at it and said, "You didn't have the beard when this was taken."

Joe shrugged and smiled. "Yeah, I know. What do you think? Should I shave it? I never really had a beard before."

"No, it looks . . . interesting. It makes you look older, more distinguished."

Joe laughed. "Now I'm definitely going to shave it."

She laughed too and said, "You want to make a withdrawal?"

"How much is the total?" Joe asked.

She wrote down a number from the screen and passed the piece of paper across to him. $10,672.34. Joe frowned. "Isn't this an interest-drawing account?" he asked.

"It's a checking account, but it does draw interest. Not as much as a savings account, or a money market account. It's three percent, but all checking services are free, including checks and—"

"I guess I'll close this out," Joe said, "or, no . . . just let me have, mmm, nine thousand. You have five-hundreds? Good. Mostly five-hundreds then and the rest in hundreds and a few twenties."

A minute later he was on the street and hailed down the first City Cab he saw. "Hey," he said sticking his head in the door, "can you get hold of number forty-seven for me? I think I may have lost something in the back seat."

"Number forty-seven?" the driver said. "Hunh." He picked up his mike and asked the dispatcher for the whereabouts of number forty-seven. The dispatcher said forty-seven was on his way back from the airport with a passenger, going to the Red Lion Hotel. Joe hopped in the cab and said "Take me there." When he got out he laid a twenty on the startled driver and told him to keep the change. Five minutes later number forty-seven showed up in the semicircular drive of the Red Lion. The driver discharged a man and a woman and Joe approached him as soon as he was free.

"You just take a guy to the airport?" he asked. "Big guy, kind of long teeth. Friendly guy?"

The driver, a skinny kid with long lank hair and a scraggly little chin beard, eyed Joe warily. "What's a matter?" he said. "You a cop?"

"Do I look like a cop?" Joe said. "Did you take him to the airport?"

"So what?"

"So he called me from the airport," Joe said. "Come on." He got into the back of the cab. The driver got in.

"What's this?" the driver said, looking at the twenty that Joe had placed in his hand.

"My friend forgot to get the address of the place you took him. What was it, out on Main?"

"Yeah. Main. He never told me the address," the driver said. "He just told me to drive and then he told me to pull over and he got out and rung the bell, but nobody was home. Then we went to the airport."

"Right," Joe said. "Take me to the house and there's another twenty for you. I have to get the exact address."

The driver looked at him in the mirror, then shrugged and drove away. Five minutes later he pulled up at the house. Joe looked at the house from the car. "This is the right house?" Joe said.

"Sure. We stopped and he walked up there and rung the bell and then he come back and he said 'Take me to the airport.'"

"He didn't go in the house?" Joe said.

The driver looked at Joe in the mirror. "No. He didn't get no answer when he rung the bell. He didn't go in. Nobody came out of the house. Nobody came by. . . . You *are* a cop, ain 'choo?"

Joe handed the man the other twenty and sat back in the seat. "No. I'm not a cop. Take me to . . ." He thought for a second. "Zion Bank." He glanced back as they drove away and tried to imagine what Mulheisen had seen here. He had an odd feeling.

The cab let him out at the bank. This was where he had seen Mulheisen in town, and then Mulheisen had taken the cab down Main Street. Joe wondered what else was in this building, what Mulheisen might have found here. He looked at the listing of offices and saw that one of them was a realtor. Finally it penetrated Joe's mind. He almost didn't need to go to the realtor. But when he got there and asked if they had something for sale on South Main, oh, say, between Fifteenth and Twentieth, the woman showed him a couple of properties and mentioned that she had a place currently under lease, with an option to buy, but she had a feeling that the lady who had the lease would probably buy. Joe felt exultation.

"I wonder if the lady would consider a buyout of the lease," Joe said. "It's just about in the area I want. Do you think you could check?"

"We could try," the realtor said. She didn't say anything about Mulheisen's visit, but she was suspicious about this inquiry. She got out a file and laid it on her desk. Joe stood up and paced about, whistling softly while the lady tapped out a phone number. Joe wandered casually away to the window, hands in jeans pockets. When she put down the phone and said, "Sorry, she seems to be out," Joe sauntered back and perched on the edge of the desk, nothing threatening, just friendly and interested. He leaned over. "What were those other two properties?"

The realtor's suspicions vanished. She shoved the folder aside, but not before Joe had seen the name "Helena Kaparich" and the phone number. She scribbled down the two other addresses for him on her card. Joe said he'd go take a peek at them and he'd check back with her.

It was beautiful, he thought, walking away in the cold. It was dark now, the Christmas lights blinking on. Helena Kaparich! He loved it.

He hurried back to the Market Street Grill, eager for warmth, for Cateyo. But when he waved his membership card at the entry and walked in, there was still no Cateyo. He sat there, sipping a drink, until suddenly he was alarmed. Cateyo was not a foolish woman. She had been upset when he left her, but she wouldn't do anything silly like stand him up. He walked to the hotel, hoping that Cateyo might have given up on finding him and had returned to the room. But she wasn't there. He threw himself on the bed and thought.

Something was amiss. He examined the room. All of her gear was gone. She had followed his instructions, come back to the hotel and left. Presumably she was still down on the street. But she hadn't been to the cafe. That was clear.

He lay on the bed thinking about this until, quite exhausted, he fell asleep.

6

Some Like It Chilly

Humphrey DiEbola was a big man but it was clear that he was not as big as he once was. He had once weighed three hundred and fifteen pounds, which did not sit lightly on a five foot, eight inch frame. But now he was down to two hundred and fifty pounds, which had begun to seem like a manageable weight. He wasn't sure he wanted to weigh much less. Two twenty-five looked like the reasonable lower limit to Humphrey. Any less than that and he would begin to seem a small man; not an attractive prospect. He had no desire to be a small man.

He attributed his new svelteness to his diet—an overliberal use of chili peppers, in all their myriad forms—and a modest regimen of exercise: regular, if not very long or arduous walks along the lake shore by his Grosse Pointe home and about the spacious grounds. He was a man who had never exercised, had never worked physically. The basis for muscles just wasn't there. He could lose weight, but he couldn't really be lean.

It was the chili pepper that was most important. He believed that peppers actually consumed fat, burned it off somehow. Obviously, the hotter the pepper the greater the conflagration and the more fat was consumed. Thus, his favorite was the habanero, that incredibly volatile pod from the Cobán region of Guatemala, with its 200,000 to 300,000 Scoville Units of fieriness (the hottest jalapeño registered only 5,000). But he liked all kinds of peppers. He had graduated from merely buying bottles of prepared sauces (although he still harbored a fondness for Salsa Picante de la Viuda, a de Arbol pepper sauce from Jalisco, mainly because the photo of the dowdy "widow" on the label reminded him of his late mother) to buying dried peppers from various suppliers who advertised in *Chile Pepper* magazine, lately his favorite reading. Besides the nearly combustible habanero (what on earth did it have to do with Havana? he wondered), he was fond of the beautiful if relatively mild casca-bel, with its reddish-black shiny skin; the wonderfully hot little cobanero, also from Guatemala; the nippy little wild tepins and pequins, or the pico de parajo (bird's beak) peppers; the lovely long red de Arbol, burning at a respectable 15,000 to 30,000 S.U. Ah, there was no end to this study. He was in correspondence now with the poet Harrington, debating the merits of peppers and trading recipes for menudo and nam prik sauce (employing "prik ki nu," or "mouse droppings" chilies grown by expatriate Thais).

At the moment, a stormy winter afternoon with the wind howling off frozen Lake St. Clair and hammering the French doors of his living room, causing the fire in the fireplace to huff and roar, he had the first inkling that others were beginning to find him too small. Specifically, a visitor from New York, who was sampling Humphrey's good Scotch and pointedly remarking that Humphrey's Detroit crime fiefdom had declined. Not so, Humphrey mildly protested.

"All my indicators are up," Humphrey said. "Collections, real income . . . all up significantly."

"Good," the wise guy from the East said, "but you could expect that, once Carmine was gone. He was a drag on business. But it isn't up, I bet, from what it should be." The wise guy didn't have any figures, of course, or not any reliable figures, but he had a general perception of business. Any figure was bound to be less than "what it should be."

"The thing is, you have lost respect," the wise guy said. "Not only is Carmine still not revenged, but you lost three guys in that business out in Montana, which you know your business best but it looks like a total screwup, plus the Colombians lost a couple guys and even Vetch, our best contact, your best contact, looks like he'll croak. . . . I'm telling you, Fa—" The visitor almost made the mistake of calling Humphrey by his once universal nickname, Fat, but caught himself in time. "Er, Humphrey, it looks like you're weak. I'm not saying you *are* weak, but it *looks* like you're weak."

Humphrey almost shrugged, but he didn't. He wasn't weak. He knew the business was better than ever, much better, in fact. Better than the Eastern organizations could imagine. The Detroit organization was solid, now that he no longer had to contend with Carmine's foolish arrogance and unproductive gestures of old world mafiosimo. He contented himself with remarking that business was never up as much as one might hope. How could it be? But it was up plenty.

Privately, he knew damn well that this visit wasn't prompted by any notions of disinterested concern on the part of the Eastern mob. True, they had lost their man Mario Soper, the man they had sent to kill Joe Service, with Humphrey's grudging assent. But they were nosy and greedy. He supposed what they were most curious about was just how deeply the Detroit mob had been into the Colombian drug market and how much was involved. That was all Carmine's doing, against Humphrey's advice. A negligible part-timer named Eugene Lande had pulled off a scam with Big Sid Sedlacek. All the principals were now dead. The money had not been recovered. It wasn't even known how much was involved. The key figure here was Helen Sedlacek, of course. She was presently in

jail in Butte, Montana, but Humphrey expected her to be released
on bail, soon. He had every intention of discussing this problem with
Helen herself, but he didn't need the Eastern mob poking around
and he especially resented implications that he was weak, that he
wasn't as big as he used to be.

He decided to cut down on the habanero sauce and empha-
size some of the milder peppers, although he loved the flavor of
habanero above all others. He would draw the line at two hundred
and twenty-five pounds. It would make his tailor happy, anyway.

"Everything is in hand," he told the man from the East, and
he made a slight gesture of gripping and crushing that did give the
visitor pause. "I'll do the right thing about Carmine and your boy
Soper. I could give a shit about the Colombians, especially that
back-stabbing Vetch Echeverria, but they too will be avenged. You
know, revenge is a dish best served cold. I think Edgar Allan Poe
said that. It's supposed to be a Spanish saying, eh? Though what
the Spaniards know about cold dishes I can't imagine. Myself, I like
it hot."

"Everybody likes it hot," the man said.

"Not like I like it hot," Humphrey assured him. "Still, you
gotta face up to reality. If you don't get it hot you gotta settle for
cold. When hot goes cold it's too late for hot."

The wind whumped against the French doors and the fire
roared.

"So turn up the heat," the man said. "I hope you are including Joe Service on your platter of cold cuts. Mitch asked me to
mention Joe especially. You know, Carmine almost had Joe popped
just before he went down himself. Did you know that? He thought
he could handle Joe, but it looks like he thought wrong."

"Carmine, God rest him, never figured Joe right. He was forever screwing him over. I guess Joe finally got fed up. That don't make
it right—*if* Joe was behind Carmine's death. I don't have no proof."

"Proof! You want proof? What are we, the fuckin' D.A.? Rules of evidence don't apply here. We know what happened. The guy was in it with Big Sid's kid. She ran off with him, didn't she? She couldn't of done nothing like that on her own."

Humphrey shrugged. "Maybe we underestimate Helen. She's very capable. She took down your prick, Mario. And Joe was in the hospital at the time. That was *your* man's fuckup. Mario left him breathing. I didn't recommend Mario. That was you guys. So please, don't tell me what Helen can do. She's a handful. It looks like she also took down one of my own."

The man from the East was interested. "I never heard about that. Who was the guy?"

"A loser," Humphrey said, as offhandedly as he could manage. It had just slipped out, in his annoyance. He was not about to admit that his hitter had been a woman, someone the traitor Rossamani had recommended. In a way, he considered the Butte episode successful since it had flushed out some disloyal figures in his own operation, but that wasn't something he wanted to discuss with the Eastern boys, either. "No one you ever heard of," he said. "But let me tell you, I'm not totally convinced Joe had anything to do with Carmine's killing. Plus, you gotta consider that over the years Joe did good work for all the organizations, never screwed over anybody, even when Carmine was jacking him around. Did Joe ever screw over you guys? No, I didn't think so. A useful kinda guy, I'd say. But, if it turns out he was in it with Helen, I'll deal with it. You can count on it."

"Where is Joe, anyway?" the man asked.

"Who knows? He got out of the cabin before my people and Vetch got there. He's running, obviously. But we'll hear from him, don't worry. He's not a guy to lay low forever. In the meantime, I'll deal with little Miss Sid."

The Easterner didn't comment. Humphrey took that to mean that they weren't dropping their interest but that they were withholding judgment. The wind blew and the man held up his empty glass. "This is good shit," he said. Humphrey poured him another glass.

When the man had left, Humphrey sat for a long while, pondering. It was strange, he thought, that all the years when he was serving Carmine, making the dumb asshole's decisions for him and cleaning up after his messes, he had never given a thought to the need for someone like himself when, and if, he were ever to succeed Carmine. He had taken it for granted that he would be able to handle everything himself. But it couldn't be. The boss can't do everything. He had inherited Rossamani, one of Carmine's lesser lieutenants, and Rossie had turned out to be a snake. Rossie had foisted the killer Heather onto him. She had evidently perished in Montana, no doubt whacked by Helen. Rossie had collaborated with Vetch Echeverria. Rossie had been a traitor. Humphrey was glad he was gone. But who did he have to help him now? A boss had to have dependable lieutenants. Joe would have made a great one. A very capable man, Joe. Maybe too independent, but Humphrey had always gotten along with him. What he couldn't really figure, however, was why Joe had helped Helen whack Carmine.

Helen he felt he understood. He had known her since infancy. She used to call him Unca Umby, from his real name, Umberto. She had been a willful child, impossibly indulged by her adoring papa, Sid. When Sid was whacked—and it had to be done, Sid just had never learned to keep his fingers out of the pie—there was no way she was going to let it go. She hadn't been brought up that way. He could see why Joe would like her: they were pods from the same plant. But how could Joe fall so completely for her that he would help her whack Carmine? Joe wasn't that kind of fool. Or so Humphrey had thought. Loyalty was the highest virtue. Joe had always been loyal, if complaining.

Humphrey pondered now if there wasn't some way he could work around Joe's disloyalty. Let's be practical, he told himself. Is there ever a time when disloyalty can be okay, when it can be overlooked? Ever? He considered, for instance, if there could be a higher loyalty, say to the organization. How 'bout if you saw that the leader was betraying the group itself? Wouldn't a man have the responsibility, even the right, to act against the leader? He mistrusted this notion. It wasn't right for a follower to decide for himself when the leader had gone too far. Maybe a guy, if the boss was actually threatening his life, had a right to strike first. That could be, he thought. He had been shocked when he had first learned that Carmine had contemplated a contract on Joe. Carmine had said nothing to him about it, at the time. Oh, he recalled an occasion, or two, when Carmine had angrily exclaimed that if Joe didn't straighten up and do what Carmine wanted, then Joe could be whacked too. But that had been anger, a momentary thing, the kind of thing that anybody might say, not really meaning it. But to go so far as to suggest to the New York mob that Joe was expendable. . . . Humphrey had never heard that kind of thing, not until after Carmine's death. But maybe *Joe* had heard it. Maybe Joe had learned about it, somehow. Joe had a way of learning things like that. If he had heard it, he might have decided he had to cap Carmine first. Was that justified? Humphrey wasn't sure. He himself had sometimes thought that Carmine was running down the whole business and if it went too far *he* might have had to take steps. But he hadn't taken steps.

And then it occurred to him that maybe Joe had been loyal to *him*, to Humphrey himself. Maybe Joe had seen that Humphrey was the guy who should be running things. He had to admit that he liked this idea, but he also didn't like it. He didn't like the idea that an underling, a guy who was in a lot of ways not really part of the organization, not on the inside, anyway, would set himself up as a kingmaker.

Joe had a peculiar status: he was an independent investigator for the mob, he worked for everybody. But he was not an inside man, not a made man. That had been the whole point. Sometimes, when things went wrong in a large, loose affiliation like the national mob, a truly independent investigator was invaluable. You needed someone who had no particular loyalty to any particular member of that loose federation—that is, no deep, essential, familial loyalty. That was where Joe came in. It was a role that Carmine had imperfectly understood: he grasped the principle, but he was too old-fashioned, or wanted to be: the grand don, everybody's papa, *padrino*. He had treated Joe like his personal tool, and that wasn't right. Or was it? Maybe a truly independent figure like Joe was unique and maybe it was a role that couldn't be sustained over the long haul. In fact, now that he thought about it, before Joe Service there hadn't ever been an independent investigator. Now that he thought about it, Joe Service had come up with the idea himself.

Humphrey sighed. This wasn't getting him very far. He needed someone, he felt. The only confidant he had these days was his chef, Pepe, and they didn't always see eye to eye. Pepe was a Mexican, but not very interested in hot cuisines. He had trained as a French chef, in Paris. He saw all his expertise going sadly to waste in Humphrey's kitchen. He knew how to make menudo, how to cook posole, even, but it wasn't what he wanted to cook. It was peon food. Lately, however, he had begun to come around to Humphrey's point of view. He had decided to pursue this chili business, to see just how much heat his boss could take. So far, Humphrey could take anything he dished out and ask for seconds.

The cold wind huffed against the French doors. Humphrey looked out at the bitter lake. He caught a glimpse of one of his people, bundled up in a bulky down coat and a wool hat, standing near one of the fir trees, out of the wind. The guard was obviously making his rounds, talking on his portable phone. Humphrey shivered. It was cold out there. He wanted heat. He picked up a copy of *Chile Pepper* magazine and leafed through it. Suddenly, he leaped to his feet—much more nimble these days—and raced into the kitchen, shouting "Pepe! Pepe!"

It was a good thing that Pepe heard his still quite hefty boss pounding down the corridor that led to the kitchen, for he was at that moment in the act of penetrating the sumptuous Caroline, the maid. She was bending over the butcher block, her tiny skirt flipped up over her buttocks, her panties around her ankles, and Pepe's white duck pants were coiled about his own ankles.

"*Madre de dios!*" Pepe exclaimed, hiking his pants up and shoving the horrified maid into the pantry. Humphrey burst through the swinging door seconds later.

"Pepe! Listen to this!" He brandished the magazine, his face glowing with delight. "Some guys in England—scientists!—have proved that capsaicin actually consumes calories! They gave a bunch of volunteers the same amount of food each day, but some days they added chili powder. On the chili days the volunteers consumed twenty-five percent more calories, on the average! See! See!" He held the magazine open to the article. "It's like I always told you. I *knew* the chilies burned fat. But you laughed. You laughed!" Humphrey laughed.

Pepe adjusted the belt of his trousers surreptitiously under his apron while he looked at the article, which Humphrey had spread on the butcher block. "May temporarily accelerate the metabolic rate . . ." he read. He pursed his lips judgmentally, then smiled. He noted, "It does not say that it burns fat, boss, it says calories."

"Fat is calories," Humphrey retorted.

Pepe shrugged. "So? Perhaps."

"Perhaps? There ain't no perhaps about it." Humphrey sniffed then. "What's that? You cookin' something?" He sniffed again. "Fish?"

Pepe turned his back to him, standing by the maple cutting-board counter, rummaging in a paper sack. Suddenly he spun around and held up his hand with a small orange-colored thing in it. "Voilà!" he exclaimed.

"What?" Humphrey said. "What's that . . . a—it can't be."

"Is," Pepe said, grinning broadly. "I was gon' to surprise you. This is habanero. *Fresh* habanero."

"Where did you get it?" Humphrey asked, his voice low, almost whispering in awe.

"It comes from Belize, this habanero. It comes on *aeroplano*. A fran of mine has bring him to me." He turned triumphantly to the paper sack and dumped it on the counter. There were at least two dozen of the golden, glowing pods.

Humphrey hastened to them, picking one up in his hands. "They're beautiful," he breathed, slowly rotating the golden vegetable, his eyes devouring the smooth, shiny skin, the fascinating wrinkles.

"Careful, boss," Pepe said, gently removing it from his fingers. "Wash your hands. This pepper is so, so—*très* volatile. You handle this and then you rub your eyes . . . wow! Your eyes on fire!"

Humphrey ran the water and soaped his hands, asking, "What are you going to do with them? What do you have planned?"

"Many things. A habanero salsa, for your grilled salmon." He pointed to the fresh salmon, lying on the counter, cut into thick steaks. "This salsa also have roasted New Mexican chilies, almost no fat at all, some green peppercorns, a little dill . . . " He gestured theatrically, lifting his eyes to the ceiling. "Later, I use the habanero in some other dish . . . I don't know."

"Pepe, you are a genius." Humphrey stared at him gratefully. He felt like hugging the handsome young man. He felt almost, well, affection. "You know, Pepe, perhaps you *are* a genius. I wonder if we could talk? I mean about some other things? Not just food, though that too, of course."

"Of course," Pepe said. "But now I must begin to chop. I make the salsa."

"I'll watch. I can help."

Pepe held up his hands. "Boss. Boss. Por favor. You will talk. I will chop off my fingers. I will fuck up the salsa. Blood in the salsa!"

"All right, all right," Humphrey said. "I understand. But later, we will talk." He picked up the magazine from the block. "Vindicated," he declared, gazing down at the article. He sniffed, lifting the paper to his nose. "Must be the salmon," he muttered, walking out. Pepe was already washing and coring the peppers.

As soon as he was gone, Caroline issued from the pantry. "My god," she whispered, "what if he'd caught us?"

Pepe shrugged, wiping his hands on a towel. He flung it onto the counter and approached her. He swept her into his arms, although she fought a little, still fearful. He hiked up her dress and slid his hands under her panties. She quivered, still kissing him. But when the kiss was over, she said, "He'd kill us. He'd kill me, anyway."

"Diablo? He kill nobody. Here." He eased her panties off and gently pressed her to bend over the butcher block again. He fumbled with his trousers. When he was ready, stroking his penis to hasten its stiffening, he grasped her by the hips and eased himself into her moist warmth.

After a few moments, she gasped. "It's hot! Why is it so hot? My pussy's on fire!"

Pepe could feel it, too. At first, he'd thought it was just that her vagina was warm inside, but quickly he realized that it was more than that. Just the few seconds he had spent coring and chopping the habaneros, brushing the seeds away, they had released enough capsaicin on his hands . . . and when he'd touched his penis, then entered her . . . it was damned hot! My cock is a flaming sword, he thought. Fantastic!

A few minutes later, pulling up her panties and still rubbing her crotch, Caroline said, "But he does kill people, Pepe. You don't know."

"How do you know?" Pepe asked, skeptically. He was washing his hands with warm water and plenty of soap. His penis was still tingling. He decided to soap and wash that, too. It didn't help much, but the sensations were diminishing slightly.

"We're in the family, sort of," Caroline said. "Believe me, I know. I'm afraid of him. Papa said not to be afraid, that Mr. DiEbola wouldn't bother me, that he wasn't interested in that sort of thing. But he also said, 'If he does . . .'" She waggled her hand in a gesture that was presumably a replication of her father's gesture. It meant that she was on her own, as Pepe understood the gesture. "Papa told me, 'Be careful,'" Caroline said. "And lately, since Mr. DiEbola's lost so much weight, he's been looking at me funny. I think I'm going to quit."

"No, you don't quit," Pepe said. He embraced her, crushing her ample bosom to his flat chest. "Pepe will look after you. You don't worry. Now you go." He pushed her away with a spank on her butt. "Pepe has to make salsa for the devil."

After dinner, which Humphrey clearly relished, along with a bottle of Oregon pinot noir (Humphrey detested white wines, except occasionally on hot summer days), he congratulated Pepe on the salmon, particularly the stunning salsa. Then he beckoned him into the study. This was a very comfortable room, with soft leather chairs and couch, lined with books that Humphrey had actually read, although he often pretended that they were just for decor. He poured them both some MacCallan and when they were seated he said, "You know, I'm thinking I'm losing too much weight, Pepe. What do you think? It isn't good to lose too much, too fast. Maybe a few more pounds."

Pepe, comfortable in wool slacks and a cashmere pullover, made a face that suggested it was foolish to worry. He felt very comfortable here, sipping this excellent whiskey. He accepted a Cuban cigar. "You look good, boss. You feel good?"

"I feel great."

"So? What is the problem? The women they are chasing you, making your life too, too . . . ?" Pepe waved his hand, searching for the correct phrase.

"Fuck women," Humphrey said. "They're murder. They can drive you crazy. That little what's-her-name, Carla? Caroline? She's always leering at me." He mimicked a leer. Pepe had to laugh. "I might have to send her away."

"Oh, she is okay, boss. If you want, I tell her to watch herself."

"I'd appreciate that, Pepe. But women are a problem, especially one woman." He shook his head.

"What is it?" Pepe asked.

"There's a woman named Helen," Humphrey said. He went on to describe the situation in some depth, ending by leaning forward to pour them both more Scotch and fastening Pepe's eyes with his own. "I'm telling you this because I believe I can trust you, Pepe. You're a smart fellow, a man of the world. You know what kind of business I'm in. It's the real world, not the polite world that an ordinary businessman thinks he lives in. This is the world where I have to make life-and-death decisions for many people. I have to provide for them. I don't mind doing this, Pepe, but it isn't easy, you can imagine."

Pepe was suddenly chilled, despite the fire burning brightly in the nearby fireplace. He realized that a fateful step had been made. He had become the confidant of a dangerous man, an unimaginably powerful man. He wasn't sure that he wanted this, but it wasn't for him to decide. It had been thrust upon him. In effect, his employer had just confessed to murder—not in so many words, but there could be no doubt about what he had said. And his employer's manner was such that Pepe knew that the man was confident that he could (and would) deal with any betrayal of that confidence.

"What do you think I should do about her?" Humphrey asked.

Pepe was stunned. He was a cook. But, he thought, now more than a cook. All he could think to say was, "Oh boss, how do I know?"

Humphrey laughed. "I know, you're just the chef. A great chef, though. You've helped me a lot, Pepe. But, like I said, you're also smart, a man of the world. What do you do about a woman like this?"

Pepe thought for a long moment, then asked, "Boss, is this woman a threat to *you?*" He pointed a finger at Humphrey.

"To me? To me personally? No. No, she's not. But there are many sides to this. If I don't do something about her, maybe someone sees me as weak. Also, she has something I want: a lot of my, *our*, money. That money don't belong to Helen."

Pepe digested this in silence for a long minute or two, then said, "Maybe if she gives up the money, you find some way . . . you know. Maybe she can be useful to you."

"Yes," Humphrey said, enthusiastically, sitting forward, "that's what I've been thinking. I don't wanta whack her. I've known her all her life. She's a fucking pain in the ass, but she's also cute."

"Cute?"

"Well, I like her. I'd like to help her."

And you would like her money, Pepe thought. Aloud, he said, "But what about this Joe Service? He is her lover?"

"Joe. Yeah, well Joe is a problem too. It's about the same, though. He really oughta be whacked, but somehow it don't go down right. It don't feel quite right. It don't feel good. But the others," he continued waving his hand at the rest of the national mob, presumably, "they want him knocked. They think he's dangerous, a loose cannon, or something."

Pepe lifted both hands, palms up. "So, let them find him and do it."

Humphrey shook his head. "They can't. They tried it already, in Montana, and it almost worked, but in the end it was their own boy got knocked. Joe isn't just good, he's lucky."

"Nobody can find this man? Nobody can hit him?" Pepe frowned. "He must be Superman, hey?" But after a minute, he brightened and said, "Boss, if this Helen can find him, and if she . . . " He made an obscure, jerking motion with his right hand, a tightening of a rope perhaps, or a stabbing gesture? "Then maybe you can say to these others, 'I have got the money and she has got the man, so she can come . . . '" Now Pepe made a kind of gathering gesture with both hands and arms, as if gathering the lamb to the breast.

Humphrey beamed. "Pepe, you are a genius." But then he frowned and said, "But what if . . . what if Joe whacks *her?*"

"Is also good," Pepe responded.

DiEbola nodded. "Yes, except that I wouldn't have the money. Though, maybe . . . but we can deal with that later, if it turns out that way. You know, Pepe, I don't pay you enough."

Pepe shrugged, nonchalantly allowing the well-deserved praise to roll gracefully from his shoulders.

7

Girl in Hand

Joe was awakened by the telephone. He glanced at the clock radio on the bedside table. Only 9:16. He had fallen asleep. He must have been very tired. He picked up the phone.

"Mr. Humann? This is Margaret from billing?"

It was an irritating voice, invariably lifting in an interrogative manner at the end of each statement. "What do you want?" Joe said.

"We were wondering? Since Ms. Yoder left without signing the bill? If you were planning to take care of this with a credit card? Or would that be cash." The final question in the series was phrased as a descending scale that ended with a flat landing that was a bit disconcerting, even bordering on brutal. "Or would that be *cash*." Chink-ching-clink-clank—crash.

"Hunh?" Joe blinked. His mind wasn't working too well. Finally, the thrust of her question struck home. Obviously, someone had noticed that Cateyo had gone out with her bags, just as Joe had asked her to when he'd sent her away in the park. And the hotel bill was on her credit card. But she hadn't signed the bill. And Joe was still here. The hotel was not blind.

"Cash," he said, remembering gratefully that he now had some nine thousand dollars in his pockets.

"Oh very good." For once no lift at the end of the statement. But then, "Could you come down to the desk? Or we could send someone up?"

"Now? You want me to pay my bill now? It's . . . it's 9:21. I'll stop by the desk later, maybe tonight."

"Well, sir? With cash? Without a credit card? We require a deposit?"

"Cheesecrackersgotallmuddy," he muttered, a phrase from his childhood, a joke involving a priest who overhears the curses of a child who has dropped his cheese crackers into a puddle. "Okay, send someone up." He almost crashed the phone down but, instead, gently replaced it on its cradle. He got up and put on a robe in anticipation of the bellboy, or whoever. While he waited he thought about Cateyo. What on earth had happened to her? He had returned to the hotel after looking for her at the Market Street Grill, thinking she might have come back when he didn't appear, but there was no sign of her. Her bags were gone. And then he'd been so tired, he'd lain down to rest, and the next thing he knew that irritating woman had called.

So where was Cateyo? He decided she must simply have taken off for Montana. Apparently his urgings had finally penetrated her innocent brain. He sighed. He missed her. But, he told himself, it was all for the best. She had to go back anyway, to reassure everyone, to look after her house, to make sure of her job at the hospital. He just wished that he'd had more of a chance to discuss it with her. There were a few things she could have taken care of for him while she was up there—mainly, spying out the land. He would like to know, at least in a general way, what the authorities were thinking about him. Of course, when Cateyo was questioned by the cops she would, willy-nilly, pick up on what they were after. But there were some inquiries she could make, as well. Anyway, he was sure that once she got there he could contact her and he could give her some advice or suggestions.

It was the woman from billing, herself, who came to his door. She seemed pleasant enough; her voice didn't seem nearly as irritating face-to-face. Perhaps it was only on the telephone that she adopted that intonation. But she wanted a thousand dollars.

"You must be kidding," Joe said. "A thousand dollars? For this?" He gestured around the room, which actually was quite large and pleasant, if not furnished in exceptional splendor, with a dazzling view of the lights of the city through the partially closed drapes. The woman looked around herself, clearly unaccustomed to this top-floor luxury. "Well, I mean," Joe amended, "it's *nice*, sure, but it isn't three-hundred-dollars-a-night nice, and this is only Salt Lake City . . . it isn't San Francisco, or Paris. I've only been here a couple of nights. Not two *full* nights."

The woman, a young woman, perhaps no more than twenty-five, nice looking, intelligent looking, but seemingly without a sense of humor, listened patiently, interestedly. Joe had a feeling she was a Mormon. He equated pleasantness, humorlessness, blandness, and earnestness with the kind of low-temperature religiosity that characterized the Latter-Day Saints, at least in his experience. These people were very business oriented, to his mind, implacable really, but they weren't fervent Holy Rollers or Snake Chunkers. Still, they were not to be diverted from their purpose.

"How many nights were you planning to stay?" she asked.

"I don't know," Joe said. "At these rates, not many. What are the rates, anyway?"

"The room is one hundred fifty dollars a night," she said, "but without a credit card?" There was that lifted tone. "We require a deposit?" And now a back-to-earth, gliding crash landing: "Which will be returned at checkout." And then a further, muffled *flump*, perhaps the explosion of the wreckage: "Less additional charges." She stood there in her blue skirt and low heels, her hands clasped placidly over her crotch, sort of smiling at him, but not really.

"I'll give you five hundred," Joe said, "and I'm out of here in the morning."

She settled for that.

An hour or so later, having taken a soothing shower in the luxurious bath, where so recently he had soaped and caressed the lovely body of Cateyo, Joe was sound asleep when he was again awakened by the telephone. This time it was a sinister voice that whispered in his ear.

"Joe, Joe, from Kokomo," the voice whispered, "I thought you were gonna call."

"Cap'n Lite?" Joe guessed.

"You got it. You're making my job hard, Joe. How come you didn't call?"

"I guess I forgot," Joe said, honestly. "I came back here and I fell asleep. Well, so now I'm calling. What did you find out about Helen? Anything?"

"Joe, you don't understand," Cap'n Lite insisted. "You were supposed to call, every six hours. The boys got pissed."

"Every six hours? You mean right through the night? I'm gonna wake up at four in the morning so I can make my call?" He glanced at the clock; it was only 11:15. "So I'm talking to you. What have you got?"

"What I got is a little blond lady. I've also got some information about your previous girlfriend. You're kinda careless with your girlfriends. But what I need is you, Joe."

"Now why would you have Cateyo?" Joe asked coldly. "That isn't very nice. She isn't part of this deal. I hope she's all right." He spoke matter-of-factly, but with an edge of menace.

"She's all right so far," Cap'n Lite said, "but a couple of the boys are quite attracted to her, although she ain't really their style. She's kind of small and these are very large boys, Joe, as you recall. I don't think they'd really hurt her, but in the passion of the moment, who knows? By the time you got her back she might need to be rebushed. So we need to talk to you, in person. I got things to tell you; you got things to tell me."

"Well, I'm happy to talk, Cap'n, I'm always ready to talk. Let's talk."

"In person, Joe."

"You know, Cap'n, that doesn't really strike me as a great idea. I mean, you've already got Cateyo, which means you've got my attention, but how does having *me* help the situation? My ribs are still sore from our last conversation."

"Joe, I got people who have more than sore ribs. And the point is, we got Blondie. We gotta talk, Joe. Face-to-face."

"You know, I'm hearing something here," Joe said. "I'm hearing something that doesn't have anything to do with Cateyo. I'm hearing . . . " He pretended to listen for a couple of seconds, then whispered, "The sound of money."

"Me too," Cap'n Lite said. "I been hearing it louder and louder since I let you outta the car, up on Sunnyside. It wasn't just a hundred thousand decibels, either. It was more like a couple million decibels. It really caught my ear."

"I'm glad, Cap'n, because it's got my attention, too. Did you get any sense of the direction that sound was coming from?"

"I did, Joe, but I can't really point it out at the moment. Face-to-face I could give you some suggestions. Say, aren't you worried about this little lady? She's just sitting over there on the bed—she's still got all her clothes on, for now—but she looks kind of worried. You wanta talk to her?"

"Nah," Joe said. "What can she say that would help?"

"He don't want to talk to you, honey." Cap'n Lite spoke, ostensibly to Cateyo.

"Joe!" came an answering yelp, from some distance. It was Cateyo's voice, all right.

"All right, I heard her," Joe said, "but it doesn't change anything. I hear Cateyo; you hear money. Who talks loudest? It's always money, right Cap'n? Mmm-hmm. But it doesn't change anything, except that you think you've got a little more leverage. I concede that the money is probably—that's *probably*, mind you, 'cause I really have no way of knowing—more in the million range. Maybe it's two million. So instead of a hundred big ones, you get three hundred big ones, or six hundred big ones. What's the big deal?"

"We didn't really talk enough about the deal, Joe. I trusted you, I let you out of the car, and then you don't call and in the meantime I find out that you low-graded the take by at least a hundred percent. Thirty percent of a hundred grand is exactly thirty thousand dollars. A good day's work, but that's it. I figure, no matter how much the take really is, if I leave it in your hands, it'll turn out to mean thirty gees for me, us. So I covered my bet with a little insurance, in case the take is a little higher. And since you didn't live up to the rules, I gotta increase the percentage. Fifty-fifty, Joe. And don't argue," he added, cutting off Joe's protest, "'cause I'm thinking we can maybe find this shit by ourselves, and you know what that means."

"What does that mean?" Joe asked, calmly, although he was fairly certain of the answer.

The answer was as expected. "It means a hundred percent, which means we don't need you and we don't need Blondie, which means you won't be around, neither of you." This chilling statement was followed by a good measure of silence, before Cap'n Lite spoke again: "You there? So, get dressed, go for a walk, and someone will pick you up."

"Forget it," Joe said.

"Then forget Blondie," Cap'n Lite retorted.

"Well . . . I hate to disappoint you, Cap'n, but I just can't see putting myself in your hands. I don't see how it helps *me* and if you think about it, it doesn't help you either. You said you found out something about Helen. What did you learn?"

"Why am I gonna tell you this, if you won't cooperate?" Cap'n Lite complained. "Here, your girlfriend wants to talk to you." He spoke to Cateyo: "Talk to this chump. He don't seem to care what happens to you. He needs to come here."

Cateyo's voice said, "Joe? Joe?" She sounded very worried, very frightened. "Joe, can you come here? Please?"

"I can't do that, honey. It wouldn't help. They—"

"Joe! They're pulling my clo— He's pulling my jeans off! Joe! Please, please, help me!"

"Honey, what can I do?" Joe sounded very calm. Cateyo wailed, her voice fading as the phone was obviously taken from her and she was removed to another part of the room.

"Joe from Kokomo," Cap'n Lite said, "how come you're not worried about your girlfriend? Jesus, you are a tough guy. I don't think Tutu and Polly will really hurt her, I mean not permanently, but she ain't gonna like you for letting them have her."

"Can't be helped, Cap'n," Joe said. "Pussy's not like sliced bread, a guy takes a piece and there's that much less in the loaf. But don't be hard on her. I thought we had a deal: you help me, I compensate you. Instead, you want to fuck with me. Well, that's a bad choice of words, but let's quit all this screwing around. And Cap'n, please don't tell me how it was my own fault for not allowing myself to get mugged. I didn't come looking for you folks, did I? Now you snatch an innocent woman who knows nothing, who isn't any part of my business. How does this help? No, no, you listen to me." Joe resisted Cap'n Lite's efforts to interrupt. "You want to make some money? Okay, there probably is more than I mentioned, but I'm leveling with you—I don't have any way of knowing how much money it is. It could be nothing—you heard me, nothing. Zero. Nada. But, it could be a couple million. I don't know. First I gotta find out what Helen was doing here. If you can help me with that then, okay, I'll go fifty-fifty with you. But don't give me any more of this crap about how I hurt your people. I don't give a damn about a bunch of Tongans. Okay?"

"Joe, Blondie ain't no loaf of bread. What's the matter with you? These guys got dicks on them like ponies, man. That what you want for a sweet little blond lady like her?"

"You're breaking my heart," Joe said. "But all right, all right, I'm not going to come to you, but I guess we could meet in some neutral place. You can hang onto Cateyo and we'll talk. In a public place. Say, the Market Street Grill, you know it? Leave the girl alone, you come to see me. Okay? If you've got something worthwhile about Helen, then we can work together. If not, not."

As soon as he'd hung up, Joe threw what little he had in the way of clothes and toilet articles into an athletic-equipment bag that Cateyo had purchased earlier that day. Then he went down to the desk and settled the bill. There were no further charges. "I've decided to split," he explained sourly. They were solicitous at the desk. The bellman took off for the car. Joe followed him into the elevator that went to the underground parking garage and rode down with him. Joe gave him a fresh fifty and told him to drive the Cadillac down the street and park it. "Just leave the keys in it and go on back to the hotel. I'll be in the back seat." The bellman looked at him with misgiving and Joe handed him another fifty. Joe got into the back seat and lay down until they had driven away and parked on the street. When the man had gone, Joe slipped over the seat and behind the wheel.

The streets of Salt Lake City were practically empty. Joe started the car and drove around for a few blocks, checking his mirror for a tail. When he was convinced that no one was trailing him he circled back to the hotel. He parked in a lot near the Market Street Grill and waited. Within ten minutes he had spotted the setup. A couple of heavies were plodding down the street, then back. One walked from the west and one from the east, on opposite sides of the street. They were Tongans, he thought, but a little smaller than some he'd seen. Plenty big, though. They had phones in their coat pockets and they occasionally stopped, ostensibly to light a cigarette, but obviously to make telephone contact, stepping into the darkened doorways of stores. Cap'n Lite's Cadillac pulled up in front of the grill and he got out with one of his huge pals. The car drove off as the two men went into the club. Joe waited. He figured they would give it at least ten minutes, maybe fifteen. The two outside men had gone past the club and down the street, almost certainly to cross over and return, like sentries on patrol. In the meantime, Cap'n Lite's Cadillac would no doubt orbit the area, maintaining contact.

It was a very good arrangement, Joe thought. They had the numbers, communications, and certainly arms. He had nothing but himself. He sighed. He watched until he saw the Cadillac pass a block away, headed east toward Main Street. He hopped out of his car and moved as quickly as he could toward the man who was walking west. He caught up to him as they passed an abandoned furniture store. It wasn't difficult at all. He kicked the back of the man's knee, snatched the phone out of his hand as the man sagged to the cold concrete, then kicked him in the balls and the side of the head. He had the man's Glock out of his pocket a second later and stepped back into the doorway, racking the slide on the automatic. The gun was huge and blocky, a 9mm. Joe didn't care for it, but he squatted in the darkness, showing the gun to the frightened eyes of the man while he held the phone to his ear.

His victim's other half was babbling something in a language that Joe could not understand. He looked down at the phone, pressed buttons until the instrument emitted a weird squawk, then switched it off. He laid it on the concrete and brought the butt of the gun down on it hard enough to shatter the plastic.

"Don't make me kill you, chief," he said to the downed Tongan. "Come on, let's go for a hike." The Tongan got laboriously to his feet and with Joe's urging moved, limping and groaning, over to the lot where Joe had left his rented Cadillac. "You drive, chief," Joe said. He got into the back seat, directly behind the Tongan. He jammed the Glock into the base of the man's skull and said, "Drive."

The man started the car. "Where we goin', man?" he said.

"You tell me, chief. Where the girl is."

They drove south, right past the house on Main Street that Helen had rented, on for several blocks, and then turned west. The Tongan pulled the Cadillac up in front of a small apartment building, three stories, brick, belonging to a different era. The Tongan said, "This is where she is."

"Let's go get her," Joe said.

They got out and Joe followed him through a small lobby and up the stairs to the second floor. There were only four apartments on each floor, a front and a back apartment on each side of the central staircase. The Tongan knocked on the west front door and when a voice on the other side said something in, presumably, Tongan and got a grunted response, the door was opened and Joe and his hostage pushed inside. The single guard left with Cateyo was a big one, but docile. He handed over his weapon, another Glock, and backed into the living room with his hands held at half-mast. Both of the men looked calm and unconcerned. They didn't seem angry or even nervous. Cateyo was sitting on the couch, staring wide-eyed.

"You all right, babe?" Joe asked.

She came to him quickly. "I'm okay," she said.

"They hurt you?"

"No. I'm fine," she said. "I thought you didn't care what happened to me."

"What was all that about tearing your jeans off?"

"It's okay, Joe. They didn't hurt me."

He looked at her closely. She seemed all right. She was nervous, though. She was eager to get out of there. Joe felt relaxed. In fact, he felt better than he had in several days. He had the two Glocks, one in each hand; he had the Tongans at bay. It seemed reminiscent of the night at the bar, the night that had turned out to be some kind of blend of dream and reality. He looked around the room. Was *this* real? Was this a dream? He didn't think so. He didn't think that his mind, capable as it might be of conjuring up surreal froggy blues pianists, shadowy rooms full of zombies sipping Mad Dog, guns blazing . . . that mind couldn't imagine this faded wallpaper with its dead roses on ocher background, the mouse-colored velveteen drapes, the electric wall sconces with shaded twenty-five-watt bulbs, the sagging nappy couch, the Formica-topped kitchen table and white metal cabinets.

"Okay," he said, "if everything's hunky-dory, let's go. You got all your stuff?"

She held up her purse. It had been lying on the kitchen table. "My bags are in the car," she said.

"Where's the car?" When she shrugged, Joe asked the Tongan he'd abducted, "Where's her car?" The man nodded toward the back of the building, but when Joe asked for the keys he just shrugged and mumbled something that Joe didn't understand exactly, but took to mean that he didn't have the keys and didn't know where they were.

"Joe, come on," Cateyo said, impatiently. She tugged at his arm.

"Hang on, honey. I'm trying to get your car. You don't want to go off and leave your car, do you?" Joe pointed the right-hand Glock at the guard. "How about you? Where's her car keys?" When this oaf shrugged Joe sighed and stuffed the left-hand Glock into his belt, then took aim at the man's knee. BAM! The noise of the gun was loud but well contained in this overstuffed room. The sofa behind the two standing men was knocked a few inches back against the wall and gave off a puff of dust. Joe frowned and looked at the end of the barrel. The guard looked down between his legs, wide-eyed now. He looked up with a sickly smile, glad that the bullet hadn't hit him but now convinced that Joe would really shoot.

"Cap'n got 'em," he said.

"Cap'n got the keys?" Joe said. The man nodded his big head rapidly. "Well darn," Joe said. "Okay, come on, honey. You guys sit down. Wait for the Cap'n. Don't come out."

He and Cateyo left the apartment building and Joe put her in the front seat of the Cadillac. He stood on the street, looking about in the cold Utah air. It was a run-down street, bordering on an industrial zone, but even so it had what he was beginning to think of as a kind of Mormon cleanliness. It wasn't spick-and-span, but a street like this in Detroit, or Oakland, would have a hell of a lot more debris, more graffiti, more vandalism.

"Jo-oe," Cateyo whined, "come *onnn!*"

"Okay, okay, keep your pants on." Joe got in the car and drove around to the alley behind the building. There was a small parking lot and Cateyo's Ford was parked in it. Joe got out and tried the driver's door. It was unlocked. Not only that, the keys were in the ignition.

"Can you believe this?" Joe said. "Middle of the city, they leave the keys in the ignition! What are they thinking about? Well, code of the West, I guess. Come on, babe."

But Cateyo didn't want to get out of the Cadillac. "Joe, I'm afraid. Can't we just go? I can come back for the car some other time."

Now it was Joe's turn to be impatient. "Oh for crying out loud, Catey . . . get your butt in here. We haven't got all night. Those bastards will be back here in a minute or two."

Grumbling, she got in her car and at his request followed him while he drove over to the freeway. They took the northbound interstate, toward Montana. There was a large truck plaza north of town, the Flying J, open all night. They stopped there. It was after two A.M.

By now, as Joe had anticipated, Cateyo was furious. She'd had time to recover from her fear and it had been amply replaced by indignation. She felt abused. Well, she had been abused, but not by him and he had rescued her from the abusers. But her gratitude had dissipated. They sat down to a large breakfast of ham and eggs with buttery toast, hash brown potatoes drenched in gravy. Joe listened patiently to her voluble complaints—how he had kept her in the dark, how he had abandoned her, how he ignored her needs—while she packed in the carbohydrates and fats. When her blood sugar was up they both felt better, calmer, and even a little groggy. They drove their cars to the nearest motel. They were both in the mood for love and it was very successful, very pleasant. Afterward they lay together comfortably and Cateyo told him again all about her fears of her abductors, that he had abandoned her and didn't love her. Joe explained that he'd had to do it that way.

"If I hadn't, Cap'n Lite wouldn't have fallen for my trap. He'll be pissed now, though. That's another reason why you've got to get out of town." He explained what she should do in Montana, how she should listen to the kinds of questions the cops asked her, how she shouldn't be afraid of their threats. "They'll think of some charges that they're going to throw at you, but don't believe it. They have nothing on you. You're just a nurse who ran off with a patient. If the hospital comes down on you, well, I'm sorry. Find a good lawyer, someone who'll stand by you and won't let you answer questions you shouldn't. Hang tight. I'm close to my money now, so we shouldn't have any problems."

Suddenly she sat up. "Joe, I just remembered! I had a great idea while I was waiting for you. Do you want to hear it?"

"What?" Joe asked. He smiled in the darkness.

"You could open an AIDS house," she said.

"An AIDS house? Why would I want to open an AIDS house? What *is* an AIDS house?"

She rushed on to tell him. The idea had just come to her in a flash, she said. She'd known a woman in Butte who had worked in Tacoma at a place where they took in indigent AIDS patients, people who were dying. They had gotten some grants together and they provided a decent, simple, dignified atmosphere for a few patients, a place for people to go and die.

Joe sighed. It sounded discouraging and unpleasant. The very idea of AIDS . . . it wasn't something that he liked to think about. He didn't say so, however. He just said, "Well, it sounds noble, a decent thing to do, honey, but what does it have to do with me? I mean, why would I put money into that? Doesn't the government take care of people like that?"

"No, they don't, Joe," Cateyo said. "People think they do, but mostly these people are just warehoused, they're just shuffled aside. Insurance companies cut off their benefits, society doesn't want to deal with it, and they're so poor, they have nothing. You said you wanted to help people. These people need help. Nobody needs help more."

And suddenly Joe saw it. Cateyo wouldn't see it his way, he realized, because she didn't know what his real purpose was. But she had unwittingly hit upon what looked like an ideal answer to his needs. What Joe needed were dead people. He needed dead people who were intestate, or seemingly intestate. But these people were even better, they were living dead people, people who could make a will. They could be destitute, ostensibly, but it would be found, after their death, that they had actually been in possession of at least modest estates. These estates would have been left to Joe, or his various legal personifications. They would in no case amount to more than $600,000, because that much could be inherited tax free. Oh, once in a while the estate might amount to, say $650,000—Joe didn't mind paying taxes on fifty grand. And once inherited it would be legitimate money, money that could be invested.

Joe sat up and embraced Cateyo. She felt warm in his arms. "It's an idea," he said, delightedly. They lay back in their embrace, which led to further lovemaking. A half hour later, he said to the tousled blond head resting on his arm, "Tell me, hon, these houses . . . are they like foundations? I mean, could a guy set up a foundation, expressly for this purpose, something maybe *you* could run?" She didn't answer. She was asleep. But the answers were there. He could almost see them. He wondered how much it would cost, on the average, to provide a comfortable last few months, weeks, days, for an AIDS patient.

Yeah, he thought, the poor people would come to the home—he'd have to think of a good name: the Last Resort?—to die, and they'd sign away their nonexistent worldly goods and then, Lo!, after the funeral $550,000 in cash would be found, stuffed in a mattress, buried in the back yard, stuck in a safe-deposit box . . . hell, in a duffel bag in a bus-terminal locker. He thought it could work. And best of all, he would be doing good. Doing well by doing good, he thought. The Last Resort. He liked it. He couldn't wait to start serving his fellow man, his less fortunate brothers and sisters.

But first he had to have his money.

He slipped out of bed without waking Cateyo. It was still well before dawn. He sat down and wrote out a brief instruction sheet for Cateyo on the motel stationery. Essentially, it bade her to drive home, see to her affairs, go back to work if she wanted, tell the cops anything except that he was in Salt Lake City, find out what she could about AIDS houses, and stand by the phone until he called. He dropped a couple of five-hundred-dollar bills on the note and then he was out the door and gone.

Within a half hour he parked the Cadillac in the alley behind the house that Helen had rented, on Main Street. There was a garage—locked, of course—and a high wooden fence with a locked gate. Joe stood on the fender of the Cadillac to get a foot on the top of the fence, then he hopped over. In the small back yard an old, unkempt fruit tree of some kind took up one corner. Dawn was efflorescing on the tops of the mountains to the west, he noticed, the light spilling over the formidable Wasatch Range to the east. It was a cold, still morning in the city but with a sagey whiff of the range in the air, nonetheless. He approached the back door and gave the handle a tentative tug, then leaned closer to peer through the dirty pane of a storm door. Within was a small, glassed porch that was being used for at least temporary storage. Several cardboard boxes, empty, were stacked in the usual treelike way, half-tucked into one another. He recognized the boxes. They had once held Jack Daniel's whiskey and Smirnoff vodka. They had also held a few million dollars.

Joe was happy to see these boxes. He opened out a blade of a small pocketknife and a few seconds later was inside the back porch. The lock on the house door, he noticed, was new. In fact, there were two new locks. He was gazing at them thoughtfully, arms crossed, his right forefinger stroking his lip, when he heard the hinges of the storm door creak ever so slightly and a voice said, "Good morning."

Joe turned around slowly and carefully. The man was about fifty, he thought. Slim, average height. He had clear blue eyes. A nice-looking fellow, wearing khaki pants and an old air force flight jacket that had a name patch on the breast that read, "Col. Vernon Tucker, USAF." He wasn't wearing a hat, but his hair was the thick, steel-wool type, and Joe had a notion that it kept his head warm enough. He was holding a gun in his right hand, Joe noticed.

"Now let me guess," Joe said, not uncrossing his arms but shifting his forefinger to his chin, "that's a Colt Mark IV, Government Model .45 automatic. Right?"

"Series '70," the man said, nodding. He gazed confidently at Joe. "I was wondering which of you would be back first," he said.

"Which of which?" Joe said.

"C'mon." The man nodded toward the yard. "We can talk about it where it's warm. I've got some coffee brewing."

"Sounds good," Joe said. "Lead on, partner."

8

Home Bodies

By the time he got to Detroit, Mulheisen had decided what to do. He explained it to Lieutenant Jimmy Marshall, now his superior but formerly his protégé, as they drove into the city from the airport. He was uncertain about how to conduct himself with Lieutenant Marshall, but he knew that it would all work out. In any formal situation Jimmy must lead, or be seen to lead, and Mulheisen would be the veteran who stood in the background and offered advice and support. In any informal situation it wouldn't matter. They had never stood on much ceremony with each other, not for years, anyway. But the way Mulheisen couched his plans now was more in the way of "Here's the way it looks to me, Jim—what do you think?" And Jimmy listened attentively, serious as always, with his dark-rimmed glasses and his widow's peak, unconsciously brushing his fine thick mustache from time to time. And then he agreed, naturally.

They would contact the Salt Lake City police, not formally, but through some detectives that they both knew, and get a casual monitor put on the house on Main Street. This was probably the best they could get, a drive-by obvservation once or twice a shift. They would send out a bulletin on Joseph Humann, a.k.a. Joe Service, including prints and as good an artist's rendering as Mulheisen could evoke, with a request that Mr. Humann be detained for questioning, if possible. They would have to be careful here, since there was no hope of obtaining an arrest warrant, but just about anyone can be held a few hours for questioning in the matter of a serious crime; even processing a traffic ticket can take hours, when necessary. In this case the serious crime was arson. If they got lucky, some Salt Lake cop might spot Joe Service, and within a few hours Mulheisen could be there.

"For what?" Jimmy asked. "You mean to question him?"

"Hunh? No, no," Mulheisen said vaguely, although that had been the idea, but now he realized that questioning Joe Service wasn't likely to be very productive. He had visited the man in St. James Hospital, in Butte, when he was recovering from gunshot wounds to the head. He'd been awake, seemingly alert, but not talking, not responding. Nonetheless, Mulheisen had felt that Service heard what he was saying, that he understood. Service, he believed, was a remarkably devious, cunning man with a formidable mind. Questioning him, even if you could do it without a lawyer present, was pointless. "I was thinking more of a tail," Mulheisen said, "try to get a line on where he's going, who he sees."

"And you would be the tail?" Marshall said. "Somebody he knows by sight, somebody who doesn't know the turf?"

"We're not going to get a Salt Lake sleuth," Mulheisen pointed out, "and anyway, I've been there. Also, though you might not know it, I'm a pretty good tail." This last statement was true. Jimmy Marshall didn't know it, but he believed it. The fact was, he revered Mulheisen and believed him eminently masterful in the trade. He shrugged a careless agreement.

Mulheisen went on: they could go over the forensic data on the killing of Carmine and any other cases where they suspected that Joe Service might have had a hand. They could also review all the material they had on Helen Sedlacek. In fact, Helen was a key element here. Mulheisen believed that once released from jail in Butte, she would go to one of two places: Salt Lake City, where he was confident he had found her base, or Detroit. He was relying on Sheriff's Deputy Jacky Lee to discover and inform him of the destination. He explained to Jimmy his theory about the missing drug-scam money.

At this point they were nearly back in the city from the Detroit Metropolitan airport and Lieutenant Marshall broke into Mulheisen's reprise of ideas he had conjured during his flight, with, "You know, Mul, we've got a hell of a lot of murders unsolved in the Ninth, especially since you've been gone."

"I've only been gone a few days, Jim. Anyway, these *are* Detroit murders, Ninth Precinct murders."

"Old murders, Mul. We can't be fooling around with murders once they get to a certain age. We'd never keep up. You know, and I know, if a murder isn't cracked in the first few days it probably won't be cracked—or at least, the odds go down quickly."

This was the new lieutenant talking, Mulheisen saw, but he also saw that it was patiently, politely, and prudently said. He sighed. "Yeah, you're right, Jim." He rode quietly for a few minutes, gazing at but not really seeing the old familiar mess and jumble of Detroit. It was not a very attractive city, but he didn't think of it that way. It was his city, the city he knew, the very basis of his notion of what a city was. He probably wouldn't say he loved it, if asked, but there was no doubt that he did care for the battered town and was even proud of it in parts. He admired its hard-nosed spirit, its cranky, half-cynical self-derision and humor. And anyway, it was what he was used to. He had come to resent the knowing look on Montanan's faces when he said he was from Detroit. What were they so proud of? The land? It was pretty, sure, but they hadn't made it so—quite the reverse, from what he'd seen. But Detroit was the product of three centuries of endeavor by people of many cultures and races. You might not like its current condition, but you couldn't ignore the history behind it.

By the time they reached the John C. Lodge Freeway interchange, he said, gently, "Still, when you have fresh evidence . . . when it appears that a little effort might break an old case open . . . I think you've got to go for it, Jim."

Marshall glanced over at him and smiled, all the while driving quickly and masterfully changing lanes (a good Detroit driver, in a city of good fast drivers—drivers in Montana were awful) and said, "Sure, Mul. I don't mean we can ignore it. It's just that we have to keep things in perspective. And this is a mob case."

That was important, they both agreed with a glance. It was one thing when a citizen flipped and murdered, another when it was the work of an organization that was dedicated to crime, determined to thwart and subvert law and order. Mob cases were properly the business of Rackets and Conspiracy, as well as Homicide, but any precinct detective knew that they were more significant than casual murder, as it were. Marshall made a further concession when he asked when Helen Sedlacek would be released.

"Probably tomorrow," Mulheisen said. Then, his concession: "How many murders?"

Marshall shrugged. "I'm not sure. Five?"

"Five's not bad," Mulheisen said. "Any interesting ones?"

"That's five this week," Marshall said. "Mostly gang stuff—a kid noticed another kid wearing the wrong colors, so he shot him, that kind of crap—plus a lady tried to rob a supermarket and three different folks shot her. She had a fake gun, it turned out, but they didn't. Actually, that's not rated a murder, at this point, but Ayeh heard that one of the people who shot her was screwin' her old man." Ayeh, otherwise known as Ahab, was a still young and dashing detective on the Ninth.

This seemed interesting indeed to Mulheisen. The possibilities instantly bloomed in his policeman's mind. Had the dead woman been set up? Was it the husband? The mistress? What about the other two people, were they part of it? Was there a way one could find out? He cocked a pale eyebrow at Marshall, who didn't return the glance, but as if reading Mul's mind, said, "Ayeh and Maki are checking out all of the shooters."

"And the fake gun," Mulheisen said.

"That too. So, Mul . . . any more naked cowgirls?" Marshall changed the topic. The reference was to an earlier visit to Montana, from which Mulheisen had returned to report that he'd seen a naked teenager in her father's sauna as well as a naked ditch rider in Joseph Humann's hot springs. He was happy to report that this time he had, in fact, seen Helen Sedlacek naked, in that same hot springs.

"Really?" Jimmy said. "What does she look like?"

"She looks like a boy," Mulheisen said. This sprightly topic engrossed the two men until they reached the precinct, although Mulheisen's thoughts kept straying to Sally McIntyre, the ditch rider. He felt he had to call her soon.

It was nearly eight o'clock and Detroit was glittering with Christmas lights. It was cold and damp, quite unlike the brisk, dry cold of the West. A thin, sharp snow was seeping down out of a brownish mist, almost rain or sleet, but not quite. Just walking from the parking lot Mulheisen could feel it soaking into his bones, despite his warm and dry clothing. But at least the temperature was low enough to prevent icing. He looked through the latest reports briefly, with Jimmy, including the one on the woman who had fatally presented a false weapon in a public place in Detroit. It was intriguing and he caught himself on the verge of instructing Jimmy on how to proceed, but he kept his own counsel.

Soon enough he said good night to everyone and fled for home, but not before he had to endure a number of handshakes and hellos from colleagues who invariably addressed him as "Fuckin' Mulheisen." He was surprised and annoyed the first few times, until Jimmy Marshall pointed out that the notice on his office door had been further amended, either by the wit who had posted it initially or by some subsequent jokester. It now read:

Of this I am certain, that we are not here
for a good time.
~~L. Witgenstien, a.k.a. Mulhiesen~~
L. Wittgenstein
Well, not a__ll__ the time, anyway.
(F.) Mulheisen

Fuckin! — Fang, you mean!

Jimmy had looked at him expectantly, hoping that Mulheisen would enlighten him as to the true meaning of that "F." But Mul only laughed and added in his Tombo razor point the letter "A," following "Fuckin'." "Fang," of course, was the old street moniker that had long been attached to Mulheisen, apparently in reference to his rather long teeth, though also perhaps in recognition of his tenacious bite. It was an epithet that Mulheisen had never acknowledged.

Driving his solid old Checker through the holiday traffic out of Detroit toward his home in St. Clair Flats, Mulheisen mused for the first leg on the fact that to his colleagues, the joke aside, it appeared that he was still considered the boss of the detectives, although everyone seemed equally to concede that Jimmy Marshall was the nominal boss. But the comments made and questions asked, after those about the naked ladies of Montana, were the expected ones about their own cases, seeking his advice and guidance. He saw that it was incumbent on him to make clear that Lieutenant Marshall was the boss. This was fine with him. He knew, however, that he would continue to be the éminence grise, as it were.

Long before he approached the still somewhat rural lane off which stood the house in which he had been born, his mind had turned to Sally McIntyre again. He had to talk to her, he had to know what she was thinking. That is, he needed to know if she was thinking about him. He was alarmed by this feeling. He couldn't recall ever feeling this way before. And when he considered the situation as rationally as he could, he had to figuratively shake his head. A woman in her thirties? Living in an underinsulated trailer house on the side of a sage-dotted range hill with two young kids? What was he thinking about? Well, he knew what he was thinking about: red hair and soft breasts, a hard, lean belly and welcoming thighs. But also sweet lips and an easy laugh, the kind of mind that is serious and thoughtful but also eager to find the humor in every situation.

He found the humor here, himself. He also found himself hoping simultaneously that his mother would be home and that she would not be there to interfere with his call. It was already ten o'clock, which would make it . . . ah, only eight o'clock in Montana. That was not too late to call.

The house was dark and not very warm. His mother never kept the thermostat very high, but clearly she had turned it down even more. It was set at fifty-five degrees. The note on the refrigerator door, pinned with a magnet that carried an Audubon Society emblem, was dated a couple of days earlier. It read:

Dear Mul,
Sorry to miss you for Xmas. Your present is on the dining room table. I decided not to put up a tree. It seemed so pointless. I'll be back after New Year's. I asked Mrs. Munger to look in and water the

plants, poor things. I hope they survive. I'm afraid there is nothing to eat, although there is plenty in the freezer.

—Ma

P.S. I'm in the Galapagos. If it is absolutely necessary to reach me (heaven forbid!), please call Mrs. Munger, who has all the important numbers and dates and locations (too many to write down!).

There was also a Christmas card, depicting many colorful birds on and around a snow-laden fir tree; it was inscribed, "Merry Christmas, son" and signed "Ma." Mulheisen sighed, realizing that he had not gotten her a Christmas present. He hadn't even thought of it. What could one buy an eighty-year-old woman who seemed to be getting younger? Something in Spandex? New binoculars? Certainly not jewelry. Gore-Tex hiking boots?

He put the water on to boil and ground Mocha Java beans for coffee. He looked in the freezer. There was a plastic-wrapped meat loaf, which he gratefully popped into the microwave. He turned up the heat and put on a CD of Steven Isserlis playing Boccherini cello pieces. He wandered through the house, sipping coffee and touching things, sitting in different chairs, listening to the winding cello. The wind had picked up and the near sleet had changed into a definite snow that blew about the house. He suddenly felt that he was home. He had been looking at the city and even the house with the eyes of a stranger, although he had not been gone long. He was surprised. Evidently, he had very readily slipped into a Montanan, or at least a Western, outlook. He attributed it to a kind of affinity for the Western landscape. The wind buffeting the house recalled a similar wind shaking Sally's mobile home. A second thought: he had slipped into Sally. Maybe that had disoriented him.

She answered on the first ring and he had an image of her sitting next to the phone at the Formica kitchen table. She sounded great, clearly happy to hear from him. She spoke rather quietly, guardedly; Mulheisen supposed the kids had just gone to bed and were not, perhaps, quite securely asleep.

"I wasn't sure you'd call," she said. "After that . . . mmm, after the way I, ah, evicted you. I'm sorry about that."

"Oh no," Mul assured her. "What could you do? The bus was coming."

"So were you." She laughed quietly. "Sorry, Mul. Maybe, next time . . . "

Nothing she could have said would have pleased him more. "Yeah, next time," he readily agreed. "So . . . how are the kids? No harm done?"

"I don't think so, although Jennifer asked me if you were my boyfriend."

"What did you tell her?"

"Oh, I just kind of put her off. I told her it was all I could do to look after her and Jason, much less a boyfriend. I think she likes you. But Jason . . . well, Jason seems a little troubled. But that's natural," she hastened to add. "I've gone out with a few guys, very few, since I ran their father off, but none of them ever came here. I mean, they came here, to pick me up, but they didn't stay . . . I mean."

Mulheisen said he understood. He knew that she'd had some kind of affair with Jacky Lee, the Butte deputy sheriff, though evidently that was long ended. It had contributed some uneasiness between him and Jacky, which he hadn't picked up on at first, but now it seemed resolved. He liked Jacky. He was a good cop and a smart detective. Mulheisen admired his reconstruction of the situation at Humann's, plausibly demonstrating how the Mafia killer Mario Soper must have been shot and killed at the hot springs.

When he asked her if they'd gotten a tree, she told him all about it, about the tramping through the high country above the house, chopping down a small fir, setting it up—"It takes up half the living room!"—and decorating it. Mulheisen wished privately that he could have gotten the kids, and her, some presents, but it seemed rather early days for that kind of intimacy. He told her about his mother being away and she said that it was awful to spend Christmas alone.

"Well, you're alone," he pointed out, "except for the kids, I mean."

There was a brief silence and then she said, "Well, not really. Their old man is back."

Mulheisen felt cold. "Oh?" was all he could say. Then, "Is he there . . . now?"

"He's passed out," she said. Her voice took on an unbecoming tone of almost whispered pleading. "What could I do, Mul? He's their father. He showed up about six, not in too bad a shape, with a bunch of presents. The kids were thrilled. Nothing was wrapped, of course, so they've already been playing with the dolls and the video games. So much for Christmas surprise. He also brought a bottle of Jim Beam."

She didn't sound very happy now, clearly angry, but also depressed. Mulheisen's heart sank. "Jesus," he said, and, "Damn. I'm sorry, hon . . . I . . . ," but he didn't know what to say. He was surprised that he'd said "hon."

"It's all right," she said, her voice brightening. She had obviously caught the endearment, too. "It's fine, I—"

A distant man's voice said, gruffly, "Who's that? Who you talkin' to?"

"Nobody," she said. Then, to Mulheisen, she whispered, "I'll talk to you later. Bye." And she hung up.

Mulheisen sat stupidly, holding the dead phone. He was swept by jumbled emotions, anger and fear and a kind of grief. He was alarmed enough to think for a moment that he had to leave, he had to get back out there and help her. He had visions of a drunken lout, probably naked, swaying angrily over Sally. She had told him little or nothing about her ex-husband except to say that she had one, but her manner and expressions when referring to him had led him to believe that it was not a pleasant subject. He had a feeling that it had been a sordid relationship. He imagined drunkenness and abuse. Still, what could he do? She was seventeen hundred miles away. Then he considered that she was a strong, competent woman. She may have been abused, once, but she had gotten rid of the man. Perhaps she was now strong enough to keep him at bay. If that was what she wanted. Maybe she wanted him back. He didn't know. Had they been to bed—not when he'd called, obviously, but earlier? He guessed not, if the kids had sat up late playing and then the man had passed out.

In desperation, he called the Butte–Silver Bow sheriff's department. Jacky Lee was off duty and the dispatcher wouldn't give Mulheisen his home phone number, but she said she'd pass along his message. He paced about, unable to eat his warmed-up meat loaf, sipping a snifter of brandy, until Jacky called, collect.

"What's up?" Jacky said.

Mulheisen explained. He tried to phrase it as delicately as possible, but Jacky brushed that aside. He understood the situation. He himself had met Sally by responding to her calls for help when her husband had beaten her—not once, but at least three times. Later, they had gotten intimately involved (now it was Jacky's turn to be diffident). He was very concerned.

"This guy is bad news, Mul," Jacky said. "He's spent some time in Deer Lodge for assault and we've had our eye on him in the past for some robbery investigations. He was out of state, I heard. We don't have anything current on him, but there's a standing order out that he's not supposed to go near Sally. But you know how these things are. We can't just rush out there, even with the standing order, if she doesn't complain."

"Well hell, Jacky, if there's a standing order . . . "

Jacky was sympathetic, and shortly he came up with an idea. He would get Carrie Conlin, a sheriff's deputy who lived in Tinstar, to call Sally. Carrie and Sally weren't good friends, he said, but they got along and Carrie was a woman, which might help in a situation like this. If Carrie felt that Sally was in trouble, or needed help, she could respond to the scene. This sounded like a plan and Mulheisen asked that Carrie, or Jacky, let him know what developed. He would be home, waiting.

"Could be a long wait," Jacky said. "It's snowing and blowing. Carrie might be out in it, probably is."

"Again?" Mulheisen said. "You just had a blizzard, a week ago."

"This is Montana," Jacky said, "high country. We like the snow. We need the snow pack to get through the summer. We've been having some dry winters, Mul."

"Well, I'm not going anywhere. It's snowing here, too. Have Carrie call me. Or if you can't get hold of her, call me."

It was very snug up at Grace Garland's ranch, the XOX. Grace was reading a Christmas story aloud to her convalescing visitor. It was a Charles Dickens story, but not the familiar one about Scrooge and Tiny Tim. This one was about a cricket on the hearth. Heather was enchanted. It had been a very long time since anyone had read to her. She felt like a child, a Christmas child, coddled and comforted and loved. The snow swirled about the farmhouse but the iron woodstove hummed, filling the house with a delicious heat. She lay on the big sofa, wrapped in a down comforter, wearing one of Grace's flannel nightgowns and listening to that homey voice read about the kettle on the hob and people with names like Peerybingle. By her side was a stand with a tray bearing tea and the remains of toasted home-baked bread and home-canned serviceberry jam. She couldn't remember when she had felt like this and perhaps she never had, but had only heard about such things. But she wasn't going to think about that now.

Heather was feeling much better. Her bullet wound was healing—the bullet had struck her just to the right of her right breast, cracking a rib and deflecting through the muscle tissue of her inner right arm—and she had recovered from the shock. Lying on the sofa listening to sweet Grace, listening to the lovely twistings and turnings of Dickens's nineteenth-century prose, she was able to detach at least a part of her mind to other things. In the sentimental nature of the holiday and the story and the prose, this detachment took the form of misty regret. Two things she regretted: never actually having *had* the delicious Cate Yoder, whose luscious golden body had tormented her for weeks, and not having succeeded in killing Joe Service. These thoughts entertained her while Grace's reedy voice rode over the humming of the stove.

Some deals just never work out, Heather thought. The contract on Joe Service had looked like a cinch job—a man lying helpless in a hospital—until she'd fallen for Cateyo. That had distracted her, caused her to prolong the business. But she'd bungled it. She'd never failed before, but then it wasn't over yet, was it? She was alive. She was feeling much, much stronger. It could still be done. All she'd have to do is contact DiEbola and get on with it. DiEbola might be a problem, though.

She must have frowned because Grace looked up from her book and said, "What is it, dear? Are you all right? Do you need some more tea?" Despite Heather's protests, the old woman got up and carried the teapot into the kitchen. The old blue enamel kettle sat on the woodstove, not quite boiling, but very close. Grace said it was good for adding moisture to the air in the winter, but she also used it to replenish the teapot. It was very like the Dickens story, and Heather appreciated it.

While Grace was making more tea, Heather considered her options. She pushed aside the problem of Grace—that would take care of itself, in time; but she decided quickly that what she would do, what she would definitely do, was track down Joe Service and tear his fucking head off. They had heard on the TV that Joseph Humann and his nurse had apparently eloped. That was how it was described. Grace had been surprised but pleased: "Isn't that nice. I knew that Helen woman wasn't for him." The nurse had returned to Butte and had talked to the police, to allay any fears. She said she planned to rejoin Mr. Humann very soon but hadn't revealed where. Heather was indifferent to this news. She'd once thought she was in love with Cateyo, but now that she realized she'd never get close to that sweet body, she just shrugged it off.

Thinking about Humphrey DiEbola, Heather felt that the man owed her money; she determined to contact him, no matter how dangerous it might be. A swine like Humphrey could be deadly, but she had a contract, and a contract was a contract. She'd just have to be careful.

The wind howled, the stove huffed. Heather put all those troublesome thoughts out of her mind and snuggled into the warm comforter. When the tea was ready and they had both sipped at it, with honey to make it sweet, Grace picked up the book and read: "The Dutch clock in the corner struck Ten . . . "

Grace read well. She practically knew the story by heart. The book had belonged to her mother, who had often read it to her and her brothers and sisters on winter nights like this in these very same mountains. But that was a time of isolation, of horses and heavy sleighs, few or no telephones, an uncertain old Philco radio that crackled with ethereal static, and certainly no television. It was, Grace felt, a better time. But a night like this, with the blizzard blowing up again, why it was almost the same as the winters of her youth—at once bitter, isolated, uncomfortable, and arduous, but also homey and snug. It wasn't so easy to win your bread, but the bread was a lot better.

9

Innocent Diversions

Colonel Vernon Tucker, USAF (retired), ushered Joe Service into the kitchen of the house next door to the house on Main Street that Helen Sedlacek had leased. He introduced his wife, Edna, a not very talkative woman much younger than he, a slim brunette who provided them with coffee and then withdrew from the kitchen. Joe had a feeling that she hadn't gone very far. He had other strange feelings about this couple, but he didn't dwell on them for the moment. He and Colonel Tucker sat at the kitchen table, on which the colonel had laid the .45, with the barrel pointing at Joe. They sat by a window through whose gauzy curtains one could see the house next door.

The colonel didn't seem to be in a hurry and Joe didn't mind. He knew he would find out what the deal was whenever the colonel got ready. In the meantime, the colonel hadn't called the cops, which was encouraging.

"So what's your name, pardner?" the colonel said, sipping his coffee.

"You can call me Joe."

"No last name, Joe?"

"Last names get confusing. People are always changing them, the ladies especially. I bet Edna used to have a different name before she married you . . . although I did once know a lady who married a man with the same name. Are you really Colonel Vernon Tucker, USAF?"

"Used to be, Joe. Put twenty-two years into that, before they told me to go home."

Joe could feel a story coming up. He sensed it was his duty to help it come out. "They sent you home?" he said. "Vietnam?"

"Oh yeah," the colonel said, an edge of bitterness in his voice.

"But no pension," Joe surmised, "or not enough of a pension."

"Well Joe, you fly over a hundred missions to Route Pack Six and you're bound to get in a situation which—if you survive—ought to be worth a full disability." The colonel looked grim. He sipped his coffee.

Joe glanced around the kitchen. He'd already taken in the sparse decor, but he just wanted to solidify his impressions. Simple and clean. One electric range, one refrigerator, one new-looking coffee maker, stock veneer cabinets over the sink and the working area. But no chopping board to protect the Formica work surface, no spices, no cute little stirring spoon rest, no matching dish towels. A small plastic container of liquid dish detergent sitting on the drainboard, another cup (belonging to the missus, no doubt) drying on a paper towel on the drainboard. What else? No notes under cute magnets on the refrigerator; no magnets.

"Route Pack Six," Joe said, refocusing on the story.

"Hanoi," the colonel said. "Lot of people don't realize what the air war was really like in Vietnam. They saw stock footage of B-52s unloading tons of bombs at high altitudes, out of the range of the poor, helpless peasants below. That's what they saw on the news, but it wasn't that way, Joe."

Joe liked the sound of this story. He nodded encouragingly.

"Every day we took off from Korat—that's in Thailand. Flights of F-105s—'Thuds'—and F-4 Phantoms. On Route Pack Six, you go up north of Hanoi and turn south down Thud Ridge, which is a mountain ridge leading into the city. It's the only way to get into the city without getting shot down by the SAMs and the Fan-songs—those are radar-controlled anti-aircraft guns, Joe—and the Firecans—heavier anti-aircraft shells that detonate at preset altitudes . . . they knew our altitudes, Joe. You see, the ridge gives you at least a partial shield. So you run the same pattern, day after day. They're all set up and dug in and waiting for you. For them it was like pass shooting at ducks on a flyway: the ducks fly down the creek to the pond and the gunners are in the blinds, waiting. It was the most heavily defended aerial target in history, Joe. In the city they even had militia—just boys and girls, really—lying on their backs in the parks and on the tops of buildings, firing rifles into the air. You think a thirty-caliber bullet can't bring down a Thud? All it takes is hit a hydraulic line, a fuel line . . . one minute you're flying the most sophisticated piece of machinery in the world, the next you're riding a brick, a piece of junk."

"You did this a hundred times," Joe asked, trying to help, "this Route Pack Six?"

"We called it 'goin' downtown.'" The colonel emphasized the first syllable: *down*town. "You're rolling in about four thousand feet, see, maybe seven hundred knots, and you have to jump up to twelve thousand before you make your dive on the railroad tracks or the steel mill. The Wild Weasels lead you in."

"Wild Weasels?" Joe said.

"Thuds. Two-seaters loaded with electronic gear. They run in to get the Fan-songs and the SAMs to key on them. They have Shrikes—anti-missile missiles. When the enemy radar locks onto them they launch the Shrike, which hopefully takes out the SAM, or better yet, if the SAM wasn't launched yet, it takes out the launch site. Also, the Weasels divert the MiGs on the breakaway, when you haul ass down the Red River. The MiGs were very good, Joe. They shot down more of us than we did of them . . . Colonel Kong took out thirty of our guys."

He went on in this vein for several minutes and Joe let him. Joe was interested, but he was alert to the rest of the house, as well. He could sense that the woman was nearby, but he also picked up some other sounds. There was at least one other person in the house, perhaps two more . . . upstairs, he thought.

"You were a Wild Weasel," Joe said.

"Yeah," the colonel said, offhandedly.

"So . . . you went downtown once too often." When the colonel just stared at him, Joe said, "And you got picked up but not by a rescue chopper. You spent some time in the Hanoi Hilton."

"There's guys still there, Joe."

"That's what we hear, but it's been a long time, Colonel. Why would the Vietnamese want to hang on to these guys? They want to trade with us. It has no advantage for them now."

The colonel shrugged. He got up to fetch the coffee pot, taking the .45 with him. He brought the pot back to fill his and Joe's cups. The coffee was not bad, Joe thought, probably Colombian.

"They're zips," the colonel said as he poured, evidently referring to the Vietnamese. Joe had heard the phrase. "They're not white people. They hate us. They want what we have, what we built."

"Mud people," Joe prompted.

The colonel smiled, gratified, and put the coffee pot back under the hood of the maker. "You got it, Joe. Mud people. Not hardly the same species."

"Mud people didn't treat you too well, I guess," Joe said.

The colonel lifted his brows and rolled his eyes in amazement that anyone would ask such an obvious question.

"But now the air force says that you aren't disabled," Joe said. "Are you disabled?"

The colonel said, "I'm not going to strip to show you, Joe, but if I did. . . . And then, there's the mind-fuck." He looked mean now, bitter.

Joe nodded, understandingly. "And your wife," he asked, "how does Edna feel about the mud people?"

"Edna's a good woman. She stood by me. She believes what I believe."

Joe figured the colonel for about fifty. The woman was more Joe's age. She hadn't been married to anyone in 1968, when the bombing was on, or for that matter, 1974, when the war ended. She'd have been about ten at the most. He saw that a question was being solicited here. He obliged: "So what are you doing about your gripe, Colonel?"

The colonel almost imperceptibly relaxed. "We have a little group. Guys like me who have been shafted by the government, sympathizers. We've been, ah, studying the situation."

"The mud people situation," Joe said. When the colonel nodded slightly, Joe speculated on this scenario. Was this really the situation? Was this guy really an invalided fighter-bomber jock, enraged at his mistreatment by the Vietnamese, and then the Veterans Administration, the government, the air force? Was he really involved in some racist organization, probably underground? Joe knew that there were groups like this, drawn to the relative isolation of the Mountain West, particularly. Aryan Nation people, skinheads, survivalists, the so-called militia movement. They made a lot of noise and alarmed plenty of people, including the government. There had been the shootout at Weaver's cabin in Idaho, the siege of the Branch Davidians in Waco, the incidents at gatherings of Aryan Nation encampments in the mountains, reports of the Church Universal and Triumphant in Montana stockpiling tons of automatic weapons. In Montana's Bitterroot Valley a group of militia types had freaked out when a National Guard helicopter accidentally wandered by one of their strongholds. And, of course, the Oklahoma City bombing had given them even more publicity. He thought the colonel's story sounded plausible.

"When I was knocking on the back door," Joe said, nodding toward the window, "you said something, I think it was 'I was wondering which of you would be back first.' "

"Good memory," the colonel said. He looked alert.

"It's improving," Joe said. "But when I asked 'Which of which,' you didn't answer."

"Which of which?" The colonel looked annoyed. "I just meant . . . there's been other folks nosing around my neighbor's house. The lady who lives there is on the road a lot. A good neighbor keeps an eye on a neighbor's house. We don't want any breakins around here. But I didn't notice you were knocking on the door, Joe. It looked more like you broke into the back porch."

"But you didn't call the cops," Joe said.

"I'm not exactly fond of cops. I think you understand. But I'd like to know what you were up to. The cops can still be called, if necessary. But I figure a white boy gets a chance to tell his side of the story, first. Maybe you're a friend of my neighbor."

"What's your neighbor's name?" Joe asked.

"You tell me, Joe, if she's a friend of yours."

"Who's been poking around?"

"Mud people," the colonel said. "Big mud people. I think they call them Tongans. There's some Tongan gangs in Salt Lake."

"Really? Aren't the Tongans some kind of islanders, from the South Pacific? Sweet hula dancers, something like that? Or, I guess

I heard they were missionary people. They don't sound like gangstas. Don't you like church folks?"

"Some of them, maybe most of them, are good folks, church folks. Like you say. But there's these gangs, too." As if answering his own contradictory comments, the colonel added: "Some mud people are okay, if they're docile, don't act up. They have their uses. But too many are against white people. They come here because they want what America has, but they don't have any respect for this country. They want what our advanced technology has won for us, our hard-earned abundance, the good life that comes from hard work; but they don't want to work themselves and they aren't smart enough to figure out how to do it on their own. And then there's white people who like them, who work with them. Race traitors. You aren't a race traitor, are you, Joe?"

Joe looked horrified. "Not me! Screw a bunch of Tongans." Joe recalled with a twinge that he'd said much the same to Cap'n Lite some long hours earlier.

The colonel seemed satisfied, but he asked, "So what do you know about the lady next door?"

Joe shrugged. "I thought it was a babe I knew, named Georgia Johnson. I went out with her a few times. She gave me an address. Maybe I got the wrong address. We had a, uh, nice time. I thought I'd look her up."

The colonel considered all this, then said, "Do you have some identification, Joe?" When Joe produced his wallet the colonel looked at the Montana driver's license, then he called out, "Edna!"

The woman entered immediately. "Keep an eye on Joe, here," the colonel said, handing her the gun. He went into the next room while the woman leaned against the sink, casually holding the .45. She didn't say anything, just watched Joe. When Joe gestured with his empty coffee cup she just shook her head. Joe smiled at her. He wondered why a housewife would lounge around in jeans and a Patagonia jacket. She looked like she was ready to go out at a moment's notice. She looked very fit and alert. She didn't look like she was planning to bake some Christmas cookies.

"Got all your shopping done?" he asked her. Edna barely emitted a snort of amusement, but didn't answer. "Me neither," Joe said. "I didn't even send a single card. Just didn't have the ol' spirit, I guess."

The colonel was gone for ten minutes. Joe could hear him talking in another room, but too faintly to make out the conversation. It was a telephone conversation, though. No other voice audible. When the colonel returned he handed the wallet to Joe. The license was back in the plastic holder. Nothing seemed disturbed, including the few hundreds that Joe kept in the bill compartment.

"I guess you're all right," the colonel said. "I had to call some friends who know about licenses. You understand. We have friends everywhere." He took the .45 from the woman and stuck it in his jacket pocket. The woman left the room without a word. The colonel poured coffee and sat down to chat a little longer about mud people and the grievances of vets. But after another ten minutes he stood up and held out his hand, saying, "Sorry to inconvenience you, Joe. No hard feelings, I hope. You can go. Like to talk to you again, though, if you are interested in our group. Where are you staying?"

"I'm not staying," Joe said. "I'm just on my way through town. I'm headed back to Montana." He shook the proffered hand. "I'm not complaining. You're a good neighbor. We need to look out for each other," he said, hoping the ambiguity registered.

"The lady next door isn't named Georgia," the colonel said. "But maybe she gave you a phony name. What does Georgia look like?"

"Blond," Joe said, "stacked, about twenty-five." He was thinking of Cateyo.

The colonel shook his head. "Georgia gave you a fake address, Joe. Well, sorry about all this, but you shouldn't have popped that door."

"Hey, I hardly touched it," Joe said. "The damn thing practically fell open."

The colonel shrugged. Presumably he bought it. He let Joe out the back gate and looked approvingly at Joe's Cadillac. Joe waved and called out, "Merry Christmas to you and Edna!" The colonel didn't respond.

Joe drove away. Within a few blocks he had picked up the tail. It was a plain blue Ford. Joe turned toward the interstate. The blue car dropped him, but another plain car, a Chevy, followed him onto the northbound freeway. Within a few miles it exited, but was soon replaced by another Ford, or it may have been the first one, which lay well back in the early morning traffic but closed up whenever Joe neared an exit. Joe stayed on the freeway, up past Morton Thiokol, the chemical plants, the air base, headed toward Idaho. In a period of an hour he thought that he had identified no less than four different vehicles. He didn't try to shake them. No doubt they would soon tire of his unsuspicious behavior.

It was still early morning, but the southbound lanes into Salt Lake City were filling up with commuters while the northbound lanes were vacant. The sun had fully risen, spreading across the frosted flats of the north lake. It was a lovely drive with the mountains towering to Joe's right. Somewhere around the climb up into the mountains, not far from the border, Joe looked back and realized that there was not another passenger car visible, just semis and pickup trucks. He drove on for a while at a steady seventy before pulling off at a truck stop in Idaho. He gassed up, then sat in the coffee shop for ten minutes, sipping at a Coke, watching every car that pulled in. At last he returned to the car and started back to the freeway, just a few hundred yards away. He was about to pass the northbound ramp and head back south when he spotted a car with its hood up, parked under the freeway bridge. A man leaned on the fender, looking at the engine but not doing anything to it. Joe swerved abruptly onto the northbound ramp. He had to drive all the way to the next exit, another six miles, before he was confident that the disabled car had not followed him onto the freeway and that no other vehicle had taken up the chase.

On his way back to Salt Lake City, now an hour and a half away, he speculated on the resources that could mount such a tail. And suddenly it occurred to him that he'd screwed up. He exited at the truck stop and, sure enough, there was the "disabled" car parked near the underpass, the hood down now and the driver sitting in it. Joe drove directly to the truck stop, parked in front of the coffee shop and stuffed his wallet into the sleeve of his down jacket. He walked briskly into the place. He asked the waitress in the coffee shop if she had seen his wallet. When she said no and they went to look in the booth where he'd sat, he reached down under the booth and let the wallet slip onto the floor. With a show of great relief he picked it up and thanked the waitress. He gave her a five-dollar tip for helping him find his lost wallet. When he came out of the shop to get in his car he saw that the "disabled" vehicle had now pulled into the parking lot, although the driver had not gotten out. Joe jumped in his car, fastened his seat belt and drove back onto the northbound freeway. He observed that the driver of the "disabled" car had gone into the restaurant.

Good lord, he thought, how long can they keep this up? He figured they must have radio vehicles well up the line, checking to make sure that he didn't get off the freeway and ready to signal the distant tag team when he did. Did they have planes? Choppers? Why not? It was a big operation. And it spelled one thing: Feds. But why would the Feds be this interested in him? The New World Order, he thought, derisively. Maybe the colonel was on the other side and thought Joe was a militia man. But no, obviously it had to do with the house on Main Street. That was where they had picked up his trail. The colonel had preferred to let him run, for some reason. He couldn't imagine why, but he thought that as long as they were letting him run, he might as well run . . . for a while anyway, just to see how far they would pursue him.

He sailed through the snowy hills on the sweeping highway, pondering. Who the hell were these guys? He was a little disappointed in the colonel. He had enjoyed the earnestness with which the man had spun out his tale of the bitter ex-warrior, the grim racist. The guy was probably a liberal, in reality—although if he hadn't been a pilot in Vietnam someone had certainly briefed him well. And then the picture cleared: it was Helen. They had got onto her because she had smurfed a lot of the money she had stolen from him. They would have been alerted by one or more of the banks she'd frequented. Once alerted, it would have been easy to track her back to the house. They would be DEA, he supposed. Possibly IRS or Immigration, or whoever was concerned with large amounts of money being smurfed. Maybe it was a joint operation. And they would be after the money primarily, not the smurf. So why hadn't they raided the house and confiscated the money? Well, perhaps they had. And now they would let the smurf, and/or her accomplices—himself—run, to show them the rest of the smurf gang, the operation, perhaps more money houses. Who knows? If they got lucky the smurf might lead them to the actual drug boss. (In their dreams, Joe thought.) But after a while, they would tire of this running and then they would pick him up.

Joe knew about smurfing. He had done a bit of it himself, but then he had tired of the process. It was too time consuming and it constantly exposed you. That was why he had turned to more elaborate schemes, his so-called "Gogol scam," where a lot of money could be washed with much less exposure. He reflected briefly on the AIDS house scheme, the Last Resort; that seemed promising.

This pursuit crap was making Joe agoraphobic. He was getting way too popular, he felt. He had Mulheisen after him, Tongans, now the Feds. What next—the Fat Man? Oh yes, to be sure. The mob would join the posse. In fact, they had been first out of the gate, sending their hit man after him. They wouldn't give up now. He was sure that Heather had been the second hitter. At least *she* was taken care of. But there would be a third, no doubt—and a fourth, a fifth murderer. And maybe the Colombians would get in on it, too. Hell, why not the Marines? Maybe the Montana Militia would like to ride against him as well.

It seemed a bit much, he thought. All he'd done was advise Helen on how to get the revenge she so desired. She had done the number on Carmine, not he. Once upon a time he had been an invisible man, but no more. One little helping hand. . . . No good deed goes unpunished. Now it looked like Joe Service was going to have to take a fall. Not, he told himself, likely.

Helen! Oh, dear. She would be on the case, too. If she got out of jail in Butte. . . . Joe realized that he had to get back to Salt Lake fast, Feds or no Feds. He wanted his money—if the Feds hadn't already copped it. Helen would be after it, too, and she wouldn't know that the Feds were waiting and watching. There was nothing for it: he had to slip in under their noses and get his money back.

The problem was this damn freeway. It was too easy for them to monitor his progress. It was a long, wide-open trail with only a few exits. Too easy to monitor. He pulled off at a rest stop and got out. He went to the bathroom and relieved himself. He was tired. He came out into the refreshing air. His was the only car. A couple of semis sat muttering. The countryside was open. Distant agricultural structures, distant mountains, a world of snow-dusted sagebrush, and high above, the dissipating ribbons of contrails. Probably spy planes, he thought. He looked at the Cadillac and wished he had a less conspicuous vehicle. But then a thought occurred to him. He knelt and peered under the car. Before long he found the magnetized transmitter, tucked into the rear wheel well. This was how they tracked him. He stood up and looked around the sky. No choppers, no planes . . . could they be using satellites? Why not? He decided to leave the transmitter in place.

He took the exit at Pocatello. It wasn't a big town, but it was a town. It had a university, it had people. He was tired, anyway. He drove to a Best Western motel, a big one downtown, and checked in. He parked the car where it could be easily observed, confidently transmitting his location. Then he went into his room and right out the bathroom window. No point in giving them time to set up a surveillance team. They wouldn't bother that room for a while.

A few minutes later, a few blocks away, he had found the car he wanted: an older model Chevy in a large post office parking lot. It was parked among several other cars near the employees' entrance, so there was a good chance that it belonged to someone who wouldn't be getting off shift for several hours. He was very familiar with this model of Chevy and he was grateful to be in the trusting Mountain West, where so few people bothered to lock their car doors.

Within ten minutes he had filled the tank with gas and was rolling pleasantly south, back to Salt Lake City. It was a lovely drive and he reflected on the notion that an electronic monitor had an interesting aspect, in that it continued to advertise his presence in Pocatello and the very reliability of its constant signal must have a tendency to lull the trackers into a false confidence. It was nice when irritating things could be turned to one's advantage.

10

Jolly Season

Christmas morning was bitter cold, the wind howling about the Garland ranch house. The first thing Grace did was make up the fire in the living room. A few years before Cal died they'd had electric baseboard heaters installed, just as a backup, so they wouldn't have to stoke up a fire to keep the pipes from freezing if she and Cal went off for a day, or even overnight. It had made a big difference in their freedom in the winter and a blessed relief from the annual struggle with frozen pipes. And, of course, the house wasn't quite as frigid in the morning as when Grace and Cal had been newlyweds. Still, habits of frugality die hard; the thermostat was never set above fifty-five degrees.

After the fire was made up and roaring along, she cleaned up the mess from last night. She'd left the tea things out and now she straightened the comforter and pillows on the couch, where Heather had lain during the evening. She pulled up the comforter from where a fold of it had been stuck down behind the cushions and she fluffed it out, then folded it up. Next she turned over the cushions. And that was when she found the bullets. Six .30-.30 cartridges, lying under the cushion where Heather's upper body had rested while Grace had read from *The Cricket on the Hearth*. Grace glanced at the rifle, the sturdy old Winchester model 94 standing by the kitchen door, then at the closed door to Calla's room, where Heather was sleeping.

What to do? What did it mean? Why would Heather remove the cartridges from the rifle and then hide them in the couch? There was something terribly wrong. A chill went through her, then a feeling of sadness welled up. So this, too, was not going to turn out? She'd been happy, reading to the young woman. She could see that Heather had genuinely enjoyed it. She had begun to believe that they would have a real jolly old Christmas of it, after all.

She couldn't make up her mind quite what to do next. Call Jacky Lee? What could she say? This young woman took the bullets out of my rifle? No, no. It was, as yet, too much of a puzzle. It never for a moment occurred to her that Heather had anything to do with the fire at Joseph Humann's cabin. She just didn't connect it. But she knew something was seriously wrong. She knew she had to be on guard. She started to put the bullets in her pocket, then decided against it. She replaced them under the cushion.

She made coffee and chewed on a bit of toast with service-berry jam while she thought of what to do. It occurred to her that Sally would be along in a bit. Sally would surely stop by. She should have picked up her check yesterday, but hadn't. Grace would ask Sally what she thought. In the meantime, when she went out to do chores, she would take the rifle, just to be on the safe side. She had plenty more cartridges in a box in the pickup, which was parked in the barn.

Heather burrowed deep into the down comforter. She would have to get up soon, but for now she was pleased to be able to snuggle into this delicious warmth. But after a while, when she heard the old woman stoking the wood stove and then puttering about in the kitchen, she became discontented. It seemed that she could never really rest. Something was forever calling, demanding that she get up and get going, do something, make something of yourself, quit lollygagging. And even when there was no actual call, no accusation of laziness uttered aloud, there was always the silent accusation, the long pregnant waiting for her to act. Oh, how she hated it.

Heather heard the kitchen door open and close and the faint sound of Grace Garland's boots breaking through the stiff meringue of wind-hardened drifts. Reluctantly, she crawled out of the seductive warmth of the bed, into the chilly air of the bedroom. In the living room the stove was briskly ticking, pulsing a marvelous heat. She stood by the stove in the flannel nightgown that Grace had given her, shivering until the delicious heat penetrated. This was splendid. She thought of herself as a snake, stiff from the night, warming in the sun.

When she felt flexible again, she went to the phone in the kitchen and dialed. A woman answered in that brisk business way of a secretary and when Heather asked to speak to Humphrey, the woman explained that Mr. DiEbola was not available, but that she would take a message. The tone implied that the caller would be very lucky if she ever heard from Mr. DiEbola. But Heather simply gave her name and number and hurried back to the stove. Humphrey rang back within two minutes.

"What is this, you're still in Montana?" Humphrey asked.

"Where am I supposed to be?" Heather answered.

"So what is this number? Is this a good number? Why am I even talking to you? You took my money and then you didn't do the job."

"This number's all right," Heather said. "It's a good number." They both understood this to mean that it was a safe number, not a number that would be tapped. "I didn't do the job," she said, "because you and your guys butted in. I had the job made, but then you kept sticking your nose in."

"You were at the cabin?" Humphrey said.

"Hell yes, I was at the cabin."

"But you didn't get burned. Hmmm. How did you avoid the cops?"

"I just avoided them," Heather said. "I'm secure, nobody even knows I exist."

"So now you're sittin' and wondering." There was a long silence. "Okay," he said, finally, "what do you want?"

"What do *you* want?" Heather said. "You want me to follow through?"

"You still want to do it?"

"Why wouldn't I want to do it? I contracted to do it. The only thing is," she said, "I don't know where to go. I mean, where is the prick?"

"I was kind of hoping you knew," Humphrey said.

Heather thought about that for a minute, then she said, "If you want me to find your guy, I'll find him. Only it will cost you. Your guys barged in and blew my operation just when I was about to come down on the little prick. I mean, like within minutes. So now, I have to find the guy, too? I thought I was just supposed to do the number."

This wasn't an accurate description of how things had gone, but Heather wasn't about to tell Humphrey that she had botched the job. She had seen the TV version. The so-called burglars were obviously Humphrey's boys. It was important that Humphrey should believe that she had been interrupted in the nearly successful accomplishment of her assigned task. Humphrey seemed to buy it.

She stood by the window, watching the barn. It was bitter outside, the wind whisking snow across the stiffened drifts, swirling about in the lane between the house and the barn. She didn't want Grace to catch her talking on the phone. But then she realized that was a foolish thought. It would make no difference whatever.

"So do you know where he is?" she asked Humphrey.

Humphrey was not inclined to let on to Heather that he had lost contact with Joe Service. He considered the value of keeping Heather on contract. It sounded to him like she was secure, had somehow gotten out of the trouble at the cabin, but for all he knew she might be talking on a police phone, trying to entice him into an incriminating situation at the connivance of the Butte cops or, worse, Mulheisen. But . . . he thought, why limit your resources?

"Don't get your tights in a tangle," he said. "We got a line on him. How about you? You okay? You need anything?"

"I'm okay for now, but I'm going to need more money soon. Just point me in the right direction."

What a refreshing attitude. Humphrey liked this. Everybody else seemed to need something. Mostly money. Well, *always* money—and up front. He hadn't liked Heather. He'd thought it wasn't a good idea to hire her in the first place, but this response was encouraging.

"Salt Lake," he said. "That's what I'm hearing. I don't know exactly where the man is, but it sounds like he's hanging around there. He's got some kind of business, something he's up to."

"Is he alone?" Heather wanted to know. She was thinking about Helen.

"He had some kind of little blond bimbo with him, but apparently she split. That's all I know."

"You want me to go to Salt Lake?" Heather asked.

"If you're gonna do the job," Humphrey said. "For all I know, he ain't there anymore. But he was there. By the time you get there I should know more. Call me when you get in." He hung up.

Heather was happy with this exchange. Humphrey wasn't pissed, or not too much, anyway. He bought her explanation, such as it was. She was still on the job. She wanted the job. There was nothing she wanted more than to wring Joe Service's neck.

But first, there were other necks to be wrung. Only safety measures, but just as fatal. She crept back to the stove. It was so warm. She turned her back to the stove and hiked up the flannel nightgown, rubbing her naked buttocks. What could be nicer? But it made even more unpleasant the next step in her morning plans. She had to get dressed now and go out into the cold.

She was feeling pretty good. Her wound was healing nicely and, except for a little stiffness, she could move without any pain. She would have liked to have rested a few more days, but she knew better. So far, no one had come around to inquire about her, but how long could that last? Even if Cateyo didn't mention her to the police, someone would say, "Whatever happened to that young woman, that Heather?" Somebody eventually would seek her out. It was inevitable. And it might be happening at this moment. Even on Christmas morning a sheriff's deputy could be driving toward the Garland Ranch, looking for her. And there was the ditch rider. Through the kitchen window she could see the ditch rider's pickup truck up on the ditch road behind the house, a quarter mile away. She was feeding cattle. Apparently, even on Christmas day the cattle had to be fed. The ditch rider hadn't been a problem, yet. But the ditch rider knew that someone was staying at Grace's place. It was a problem . . . maybe. Heather had seen a check lying on the kitchen counter near the door, made out to Sally McIntyre.

So Heather had to leave. She was healthy enough. To stay any longer was begging discovery. Heather resented it, though. She was pretty sure that Grace was planning something special for today. She would have put together some kind of gift for her, Heather was sure. And her daughter was expected to come over from Bozeman. Grace would be planning a special dinner—there was a turkey thawing on the kitchen counter. In the evening she would read again from Dickens's *The Cricket on the Hearth*. Heather felt a slight pang. She had enjoyed the story. She wanted to hear the rest of it, about Dot Peerybingle and Tilly Slowboy and . . . oh well, one day she would buy the damn book and read it for herself.

Heather considered her plans while she dressed in jeans and a sweater, clothing belonging to Grace's daughter, stored in a dresser. They fit well enough. Should she wait until the ditch rider came by for the check, even if it meant having to meet the woman? The ditch rider could always identify her. But there was no telling how long it would be before the ditch rider came down to the ranch house. With luck, she could be gone by then, and it would look like she and Grace had driven into town, perhaps to church. The old lady had said something about going to Christmas services.

She pulled on her boots, found an old down jacket and some gloves, and stepped outside for the first time in days. It was a bright, sunny day, but the cold and the wind took her breath away. It was just about too damn cold for this business. But business was business. She stepped into the deep holes in the drifts made by Grace and huffed the fifty feet or so to the weathered wooden door of the barn.

Inside, it was surprisingly warm. Or, if not exactly warm, it was noticeably warmer, chilly but endurable. You could see your breath. Dust and chaff drifted in the shafts of light that slipped through the cracks between the siding planks. There was a great roaring of wind in the high space of the main chamber and the rich aroma of cows and hay. The milk cows were all crowded together at one end, and there it was quite warm. Grace had evidently already milked the cows and done something with the milk, probably put it into the gleaming metal device in another room beyond, a room that was spotlessly clean and was kept heated electrically. Grace was not present here, either, however. Heather supposed she had gone on to the henhouse, which was a small, more weatherproof building just behind the barn. Grace had already cleaned the cows' stalls, however, hosing down the manure gutters. The cows looked up placidly, munching on the remains of the hay that had been forked into their mangers yesterday.

Heather went back out into the main space of the barn. A tractor and a truck were parked there, and above, in the lofts, there were great stacks of hay bales, piled nearly to the roof. She could hear pigeons gently cooing. The wind rattled around the barn, but despite the great amount of light seeping through and the huffing of the wind, it was quiet and warm. It was a peaceful place. Heather could not recall ever being in a barn, but it seemed familiar, somehow.

"Heather!"

Heather spun around. Grace had come in through another door and was staring at her with surprise. She was carrying a basket of eggs. "Honey, should you be out?" the old woman asked solicitously. "Well, you look all right." She smiled. She was wearing a wool hunting cap with the earflaps pulled down over her short wiry hair. Her eyes sparkled and her nose was red. "I guess it's time for you to be up and about, but it won't do to get chilled. Here, honey." She handed Heather the eggs. "Why don't you carry these back in to the house and I'll be along as soon as I throw down some more hay."

Surprised and incapable of responding, Heather simply stood holding the basket of eggs. The old woman, dressed in brown duck overalls, walked with a rolling gait over to the ladder and climbed stiffly and clumsily in her heavy pacs up the rungs. It was a home-made ladder and whoever had built it had set the two-by-four cross-pieces rather far apart for the short legs of Grace, but she hauled herself up. "Watch out below!" she called out cheerily, as she began to heave bales of hay onto a chute that led down into the cow byre. When the chute was full of bales, she clambered down and went into the byre, trailed by Heather. She took a utility knife from her pocket and cut the orange plastic twine that held the bales together, then she began to fork fresh hay into the mangers.

Heather dropped the eggs onto the floor. Grace turned, staring in horror at the broken eggs. Heather punched her in the face, knocking her down. But the old lady clung to the hayfork. Sprawled on the wet concrete floor of the cow byre, she lashed out with the fork and it ripped through the left leg of the jeans, biting into Heather's flesh. Heather hissed with pain and danced back.

Grace tossed the hayfork aside and scrambled with surprising agility on all fours toward the doorway. There she snatched up the .30-.30 and turned triumphantly toward Heather. To her surprise Heather stopped and laughed, then came forward.

"Honey, I will definitely shoot," the old woman said. Her voice was so convincing that even though Heather knew that the gun was unloaded, she stopped. "What is it you want?" Grace asked. "What do I have that you want?"

Heather looked at her with contempt. "You don't have anything I want."

"Then get the hell out of here, before I pull the trigger on this thing."

Heather laughed and took a step forward.

The rifle made a surprisingly flat noise in the confines of the byre. The cows shifted uncomfortably, but didn't stop chewing. Heather was shocked and stunned. She looked down at herself. She hadn't felt an impact, but she expected to see blood. Then she realized she hadn't been shot. The bullet had missed. She started forward and stopped, staring in surprise.

Grace was sprawled on her back, the rifle lying to one side. She seemed to be staring at the dusty boards that formed the ceiling of the byre. Heather kicked the rifle aside, then knelt by the old woman. She was breathing faintly, a slight haze of breath hanging in the chilly air. Then that dissipated. The old woman was dead.

Heather was astonished. A heart attack? It must have been. How very, very fortunate. The body lay quite close to the spilled basket with its broken eggs. It would look completely natural. Heather picked up the rifle, intending to take it back to the house, where it belonged. But as she started out through the weathered wooden door, the ditch rider's pickup truck came into the lane, driving slowly through the snow. Quickly she set the rifle inside the door and stepped out.

The ditch rider pulled the truck up next to Heather and leaned out the opened window. "Hi," she called. "You must be Red's cousin, eh? I'm Sally." She stuck out her hand. Heather smiled and shook the gloved hand. "Where's Red—er, Grace?"

"She's in the barn," Heather said. "You want to see her? Come on in."

"Oh, I just stopped for the check and to drop this off," Sally said, handing a brightly wrapped Christmas present through the window. "I got to get back to the kids. Christmas morning, you know. Tell Grace I'll stop by for the check tomorrow."

"Oh, no, wait!" Heather said. "The check's on the counter. I'll get it. I'm sure Grace would love to see you. C'mon in for a minute." She took hold of the door handle, as if to open it.

"Aw, I can't cash it till tomorrow, anyway. Hey, what happened there?" Sally pointed to the other woman's torn pant leg. Blood had stained the jeans.

Heather looked down, dropping her hand from the door handle. "Oh. Oh that. I'm such a klutz! I scratched it on some barbed wire, helping Grace. I was just going in to take care of it. I can get your check. Why don't you wait here, or go in and visit with Grace."

"Sorry. Gotta run! You take care of that, now. You don't want to get blood poisoning from some old rusty wire. Merry Christmas!" Sally gunned the engine with a wave and drove on out the snowy driveway, her big four-wheel-drive tires blasting a nice path.

In the mirror she caught a glimpse of the woman standing in the drive, waving vaguely. Klutz, she thought. Flatlander.

After he hung up from Heather, Humphrey buzzed for Pepe. Five minutes later, Pepe sauntered in, still wearing his apron. "Pepe," Humphrey said, "do we have some salsa? Anything."

"Boss, I got salsa, I got some jalapeños stuffed with hot cheese . . . you want me to do the jalapeños? I got a turkey with corn-bread pepper stuffing for dinner. How many we got?"

"Has Miss Helen had breakfast?" Humphrey asked. "Bring me the salsa, then I want to talk to you. But be sure that Miss Helen is taken care of."

The beauteous Caroline brought the deep-fried jalapeños, stuffed with hot cheese. Humphrey devoured three of them, then stopped. The cheese was too fattening, he thought. That morning he had discovered that he weighed only 219 pounds. He hadn't weighed 219 pounds since he was fourteen. He didn't want to weigh less, or more. He felt terrific. He owed it all to the pepper diet and Pepe. He imagined that Caroline looked at him with desire. He nibbled on the salsa, dishing it up with Pepe's own oven-baked chips. It was incredible. Hot, totally vegetable, almost no fat. When Pepe came back Humphrey asked him about the chips.

"They are tostados," Pepe explained.

"I can see that," Humphrey said, "but why do they taste so good?"

"I bake him. I don't fry. Also, I put a little ground pepper, a little salt . . . you like, eh?"

"They're very good, Pepe. And they aren't greasy."

"Almost no fat, boss." Pepe smiled broadly. "You like, eh?"

"Pepe, when I tasted my first potato chip I didn't know if I liked it," Humphrey said. "But it was salty. I ate another. Within a few minutes I was hooked. But I shouldn't have been. I make chips for a living, you know. Corn chips, too, but they don't taste like this and they aren't good for you."

Pepe knew about Krispee Chips. It wasn't exactly Humphrey's "living." But he nodded.

"Pepe, you are going to make these chips for Krispee. They'll be famous. The day after tomorrow, we'll go down to the factory. You'll be the boss. You'll still cook here, but you will become . . . mmmm." Humphrey thought for a moment. "Production manager. Starting now, your salary goes up. Way up. Now get out of here."

Humphrey felt great. It was Christmas. He enjoyed doing things for people, especially competent people like Pepe. Good people. You had to have good people or you were nowhere.

After a while, Helen came in. She looked rested and very lovely. "Merry Christmas," she said, without any warmth.

"Merry Christmas," Humphrey said. "Listen, I been talking to some of my people out west. They're on to Joe. Can you give me a line on him?"

"Where is he?" she asked eagerly. Caroline came in with a Bloody Mary, the glass stuffed with celery and olives.

"A guy I know, an old friend, says he's in Salt Lake," Humphrey said. He was wearing a black silk jumpsuit. He looked almost elegant in it. His great round face had become almost lean. He was actually not too bad looking. He still had all his hair and it was still black. His eyes looked larger, almost glowing. He got up to poke at the fire in the fireplace. Near by was a Christmas tree, which Caroline and one of the guards had decorated. Humphrey picked up a wrapped package from under the tree and tossed it onto the couch next to Helen. "Merry Christmas," he said. Helen tore off the wrapping and found an antique jade necklace. It was beautiful.

"Unca Umby," she said, "thank you. You're so sweet." She held the necklace to her breast.

Humphrey smiled. He loved giving gifts.

"Salt Lake," he said. "What is Joe doing in Salt Lake?"

"It's a place," Helen said. She laid the necklace aside. "I'm sorry I didn't get you something."

"Forget it," Humphrey said. "What do you mean, 'It's a place'?"

"Well, there's no place in Montana, for instance. It's all country. Do you know where he's staying?" She sipped the Bloody Mary.

"He was staying in a hotel," Humphrey said, "but now he's split. But we think he's still hanging around."

Helen shrugged. "Who is this guy you know?" she asked.

"Just a guy. An old friend. I tried to get hold of him a little while ago, but no luck. He'll call back." Humphrey sat and looked at her. She was draped in a silk dragon kimono. She looked like the child he had never had. Tiny, pretty . . . her black hair shining.

Humphrey got up and rummaged through some CDs, finally selecting one, which he put on the stereo system. "God Rest Ye Merry, Gentlemen," spewed forth, sung by a choir. He returned to his seat to sip at a cup of English Breakfast tea.

"Do you think you could find him?" he said. "You've spent some time in Salt Lake, haven't you?"

"I've been there," she said. "But I don't know too much about the place. It's kind of bland."

"Were you there with Joe? Do you have any idea where he might hang out?"

"Maybe," she said, sucking up the last of the Bloody Mary. "Do you want another?"

"Not so peppery," she said. She went to the hearth and knelt down, hugging herself. Within a minute another Bloody Mary was brought, although she hadn't seen Humphrey order it. It was less peppery.

"Joe screwed us over," Humphrey said. "Some people want him dead. Well, you know that." He sipped his tea and gazed at Helen. "I hate to tell you this, honey, but some people want *you* dead."

She looked over her shoulder, calmly. "But you don't, Unca Umby."

"No, no, of course not, baby. But some guys . . . "

"But I have to find Joe," she said. Her eyes were piercing, blue-black, nearly obsidian.

"*We* gotta find him," Humphrey said.

"And the money," Helen said.

"The money would be good," Humphrey agreed.

She stood up. "The money is mine," she said.

Humphrey smiled and shook his head fondly, as at a child's silliness. "The money isn't yours, baby. The money belongs to the organization."

"Dad's money," she said. "It belongs to me."

Humphrey gazed at her fondly. "Big Sid stole that money from me, us. But I don't give a shit about the money, baby. I got plenty of money. The organization, they care about it. You know how this is. The organization can't ever let someone rip them off. Maybe I could get you a deal."

"Joe for the money," she said. She bit her full lower lip provocatively.

"Not for *all* the money," Humphrey said.

"Half the money," she said.

Humphrey shrugged, then said, "Who knows how much money there is, even? Half the money, a third of the money, a million, anyway?"

"And the rest is yours?" she said.

"Belongs to the organization," Humphrey said.

Helen slumped onto the couch. "What about Joe?"

Humphrey picked a cigar out of the humidor. He clipped it and lit it. The rich odor of tobacco floated in the air. The music had changed to a Bach cantata, "Sheep may safely graze."

"I like Joe," he said, after a while. "He's resourceful. If Joe can survive this, I want him on my side. But if Joe has to go, why Joe has to go. You get me?"

Helen picked up the jade necklace and let it run through her fingers. She said, "Joe is too good. He'd kill me."

"It's not your job," Humphrey said. "I have people. You just have to find him."

Helen sat and fingered the jade. "I can't do it," she said, finally.

"Well, yes," Humphrey said. "You can do it."

She didn't look up. She heard the tone. She could do it, or she could die. She loved the necklace. "Put this on me," she said. She knelt by Humphrey. He fumbled with the clasp, but he got it on her neck. She was like a little girl, with her slight neck. Or a girlish boy. He was aroused.

"I think I better go to Salt Lake," Helen said, pirouetting away to cast herself dramatically on the couch.

"Is it necessary?" Humphrey said. "Can't you just give us a lead? I got people there. They'll deal with Joe."

"No, I better go."

Humphrey blew out air through pursed lips. "All right," he said. "You can take the jet. Only one thing: don't try to take him yourself. You're right: he's too good. Besides, I want to talk to him, first."

Helen laughed, looking him full in the eyes. "You love this dick! You love him!"

Humphrey was affronted. "Joe's clever. He might be able to figure something out. Save us all a lot of trouble."

"He's your boy," she accused. "You love him." She eyed him carefully, then said, "Do you love him more than me?"

"Honey, honey," he crooned. He came to the couch, dropping to his knees. "It's not true. I always liked Joe, but—"

"You love him more than me," she said, stubbornly. Tears started from her eyes.

Humphrey was appalled. "No, no, honey. I love you." She let him take her into his embrace.

Humphrey patted her on the back. "It's all right, s'okay," he said, over and over. After a while, she snuffed and sat up. He crept back to his chair.

"Okay," she said, in a little child's voice. "I'll go find him for you. But you can't hurt him."

"Oh, honey," he said, "I don't want to hurt Joe. It's up to him. Maybe he can come up with something."

"And I can have Dad's money?" she said, pouting.

"Well, honey, we'll have to see how it goes," Humphrey said, "but I don't see why you can't have some of it, anyway. A finder's fee, maybe." He figured something could be worked out. Something could always be worked out.

11

Kill or Be

When Mulheisen awoke he was still sitting in the easy chair by the telephone. In fact, it was the phone that woke him. It was Jacky Lee. Apparently, nothing had happened concerning Sally and her ex-husband. As far as Jacky knew, her kids had gotten off to school—the last day before Christmas vacation—on time. The ex-husband was not in evidence, according to the Tinstar deputy; at least, there were no other vehicles at the mobile home. Carrie Conlin had cruised by there but had not attempted to contact Sally, on the premise that it would be seen as unwarranted meddling. If Sally had been abused she was enough of a woman to complain. It was reasonable to assume that there was no cause to interfere.

Mulheisen had a feeling that the deputy was right. He'd worried needlessly. If Sally wanted to sleep with her ex-husband it was none of his business. He felt a little sad, that's all. But then he felt sour. Her life struck him as tacky, suddenly. What the hell did he have to do with this crap? It wasn't his style. He thanked Jacky Lee and apologized for making a fuss.

Jacky was easy. He said he understood. Mulheisen could practically see his impassive face. Jacky moved on to other things. He asked if Mulheisen had heard anything about this new heroin,

"China White." It was supposed to be much purer than the tradi-
tional stuff that came out of Turkey. You could snort this stuff, or
drink it in solution. That it was easier to use made it potentially
much more dangerous: middle-class and upscale people, to say nothing of kids, didn't like to inject needles. This was more like cocaine.
But it could be deadly. Very high-quality stuff. If you did inject, you
could overdose. Apparently, it came out of Hong Kong.

Mulheisen had never been very interested in the narcotics
trade, except as a source of income for the mob. In some ways he saw
it as a victimless vice—not quite victimless, to be sure, since it caused
a lot of human grief, and then there was the aspect of people getting
hooked before they realized what they were about. But using drugs
was something that people chose to do, at least initially. He chose
to drink whiskey, knowing that it was bad for him. It was very bad for
him. Maybe it was worse than heroin. He knew heroin addicts who
had gotten over their addiction. He knew alcoholics who had gotten
over theirs, although they often said that you never really got over
the booze, you just held out against it as long as you could. He knew
one so-called "abstaining alcoholic" who said he was just waiting until
he found out that he was dying and then he would go on one last
great bender. It sounded like he was looking forward to it. In the long
run, the bottle got you back. That's what they said.

Another aspect of this new strain of heroin that bothered
Mulheisen was the casual racist hint: China White, a replay of
America's historical fear of the Asian hordes? A thin whitewash of
the Golden Horde? He asked Jacky if Johnny Antoni, the Silver
Bow County attorney, was on to this new threat.

"Like an eagle on a spawning salmon," Jacky said. "It's Yellow Peril time. Or maybe this is White Peril." He laughed, a short,
humorless bark. "He already called a meeting of the Task Force.
He's sure this stuff will be showing up in Butte, soon. You'll be
getting a call."

"Forget it," Mulheisen said. "I'm not on the Task Force, remember? I'm a Detroit cop. With all due respect, Jacky, I don't think you guys know what real crime is."

Jacky snorted. "Crime is crime, Mul, wherever it is. But maybe you're right. Hey, don't let me keep you. I know you're busy, up to your neck in real crime."

"Jacky, I don't mean that you don't have crime. Sure, you've got crime. Serious crime. Okay? It's just that what we've got here is a *world* of crime. If you haven't been here it isn't easy to imagine. We've got a situation here where a lot of people *have* to break the law in order to survive. Look, I'm sorry. It's just that I can't be dashing off to Butte every time Johnny changes his mind and decides that he can make some political hay out of crime. The last time I saw him he just wanted me gone, because I was an emblem of crime. You remember. It was 'Take your thugs and get out of my county.'"

Jacky laughed. He understood. No hard feelings. He rang off.

Mulheisen felt like hell. It wasn't just sleeping in a chair, worrying about a woman who was none of his business, telling Jacky that he didn't understand the true nature of crime; it was . . . well, what was it? It was jet lag, a feeling of disconnectedness, annoyance at the changed situation in the precinct, frustration at not getting further with the Joe Service investigation. The Christmas season. He hated Christmas, he decided. The American way of Christmas was so crass, so vile, so obvious a violation of genuine feelings of humanity and, and. . . . Ah, to hell with it. And yesterday he had been so up. So intense. Standing on a cold street corner in Salt Lake City, he'd felt good. The scent was up, he could almost taste it. He'd felt that he was getting close, at last, to his nemesis. But then Jimmy Marshall had brought him down to earth. And Christmas. The damned lights, the incessant caroling, the buying, the senseless giving just to be giving, the pressure to give something, anything, instead of giving because you cared for someone and had found something that you thought they might like. He felt that the culture had taken something good and run it into the ground. He was sick of it. Christmas had become a plague, something to survive rather than enjoy.

He decided to rest today, to read a book, catch up on the mail. He called the precinct and told Jimmy that he wasn't coming in, he was too exhausted. Jimmy said it was fine, not to worry. Take a day off. Take the whole weekend. They had made an arrest in the shooting case.

Mulheisen showered and shaved, had coffee, then went for a long walk down by the river. Although it was December he saw a great blue heron. Well, it wasn't very cold for December, just the usual gray overcast. It was weather that he liked, in fact: a good gray day. He hiked along the river path until, without thinking about it, he ended up at Ozzie's marina, a hangout since his youth, no more than a mile from the house. It was run by Gary Oswald, a burly man with a huge, drooping mustache. His mother used to call Ozzie's an "attractive nuisance," since Mul and so many of his pals would spend endless days there, summer through winter, puttering about the boats, pestering Oz. For most of them it was where they had gotten their first paying jobs, hauling out boats, putting them in, fueling them, painting them, minding the store. In some ways, the winters were better than the summers, because there were fewer boaters around, fewer summer people: one could think of oneself as an old salt, a wharf rat, an insider.

To Mulheisen's delight several of his old pals were present. They were messing about with boats, that pleasurable pastime mentioned fondly by Ratty in *The Wind in the Willows*. They were still putting up boats for the winter. It was very nice in the marina. The guys helping each other, speculating on what should be properly done, drinking coffee with "a little something" in it. Before he knew it, he was having a shot of whiskey in his coffee and chatting with

Vito Belk, who was taking a break from his job to get his gaff-rigged catboat put securely away. They talked about the baseball strike, the hockey strike, about the Tigers, the Red Wings, the Lions, the Pistons. All the Detroit teams were doing poorly—it bothered the guys, but it was the kind of bother that you didn't mind too much. Mulheisen had long opined that this was the essential value of big-time sports: it provided an inexhaustible topic for idle conversation.

They looked over Fred and Jim's *Searay*, which had a bad bash in the bow from something, maybe a floating bottle. A bottle could bang you up if you were hauling ass like Jim always did. "Another example of the dangers of hitting the bottle," Mulheisen observed and found himself foolishly pleased by the guys' laughter. He even overheard one of them telling it to another, later.

And somehow the subject of satellites came up. Vito knew something about this. He said it was true—sort of—what they wrote about in spy novels, about the Russian peasant taking a piss in the snow, unaware that an American satellite was watching him. But, in fact, it was more likely that a satellite would observe an American taking a piss in the woods. More satellites here than over Russia. Mulheisen was fascinated. He'd had no idea that there were so many satellites.

Later, when he got home and had made lunch, he shuffled through his mail, tossing aside anything that looked even remotely like a Christmas card. The rest of it was quickly dealt with: a few bills, a few catalogs, some new books from the History Book Club that he didn't remember ordering. He had never been very interested in the American Civil War, although he had read Bruce Catton, which seemed enough. Why would he have ordered a book on the Golden Horde, and one on Patagonia? Well, perhaps. He looked about his shelves for something more familiar, like Plutarch, or Caesar's *Gallic Wars*, perhaps even old Parkman on Pontiac's

Conspiracy. It conjured up the prospect of a pleasant afternoon indoors, quiet, reading, pondering something remote from himself, but still somehow relevant. He happened upon Morison's *Maritime History of Masssachusetts*, a book he didn't so much remember as recall its pleasures. He sat down to it with gratitude and he read at least twenty pages before his mind began to wander to Vito's satellites. It was something in the text about spies.

There was a romance about spies. Auden, one of the few modern poets for whom Mulheisen had any regard, had a notion of the spy, the loner parachuting into a strange land. And there was the romance of the so-called "Indian princess" who had betrayed Pontiac's conspiracy to the British at Detroit. From his own youth there was the thrilling episode of the so-called Nazi sympathizers in Detroit helping an escaped Luftwaffe pilot. In the press of the time it had been darkly hinted that these people were spies; even the pilot was sometimes said to be a spy. These stories almost always turned out to be fiction, he thought. Real spies were different. Real spies, perhaps more like Graham Greene's or John le Carre's inventions, were less romantic—troubled men and women with conflicting loyalties, or ideologically obsessed. Today, the real spies turned out to be satellites.

And thinking of that, he called Vito at home. Was it really possible, he asked, that a satellite might routinely record an event that would certainly otherwise not have been witnessed? That something one might have thought was lost to history could be miraculously recovered in some archive? Such as a murder on a lonely highway? A killing by a remote hot springs? Vito said it was certainly possible. The problem was that there was so much data, an absolute blizzard of data, that one had to know where to look. Computers were essential, but even with the help of a computer, if one were to look only at possibilities . . . if the time frame was not precise, the geographical area too broad or not accurately located . . . it would take a long time. But sure, it was possible. Vito himself was pretty good at finding data.

Mulheisen suggested some times, some places. Vito said he would take a look. He agreed to let Mulheisen know if he turned up anything interesting. It seemed like an amusing thing to try. Mulheisen went happily back to his book.

The day after Christmas Vito called back. He'd been lucky, he said. He thought Mulheisen owed him lunch. Pinky's seemed like a good place.

Mulheisen was feeling much better after Christmas. It was such a relief to have this annoying holiday behind one. Months and months of non-Yulishness stretched pleasantly ahead—he fleetingly wondered what a winter would be like in some non-Christian country: a pagan peace, he supposed, celebrations of the solstice. At the Ninth Precinct he went over the shooting case with Jimmy Marshall and cautioned him about the suspect: she was the victim's husband's lover, it seemed, but she legally owned the gun, she lived in the neighborhood, and she had a reasonable excuse for being in the supermarket. He didn't think it was as open and shut as it looked.

He also coordinated all his Salt Lake City plans with Lieutenant Marshall. He talked to detectives in Salt Lake City, explained his needs, promised reciprocity, faxed pictures and fingerprints of Joe Service, made inquiries about Helen Sedlacek's current whereabouts. She was in Detroit, apparently, but not at home, not at her mother's home, although she had visited on Christmas Day. Not the Serbian Orthodox Christmas, however, which came a few days later. Mulheisen shuddered. Another Christmas Day! One yet to come.

He went to lunch at Pinky's. When he returned to the precinct he was pensive, not sure how to proceed. It appeared that he had sufficient reason to interview Helen again, but there was still no word on where she was.

There was a message from Jacky Lee. He was calling from a number that Mulheisen didn't recognize. It wasn't a Butte number. It had the same three-digit prefix as Sally McIntyre's number, in Tinstar.

"Oh no, oh no," Mulheisen thought, as he dialed back. He hadn't called Sally after the foolishness a few nights earlier. He had thought about it, but he hadn't done it. He'd had an irrational notion that somehow Sally had heard about his panicky call to Jacky. He should have called. Instead he had shut her out of his mind. Now his mind was racing with thoughts of mayhem, of slaughter in a trailer house. Christmas was notorious for these hideous acts. With a premonition of disaster he listened to the phone ring.

As he had feared, Deputy Lee had serious business to report. Grace Garland's daughter had gone to visit her mother earlier that day. She had meant to visit on Christmas, but instead she had called around noon, intending to tell her mother that she would be over the next day. When there was no answer, she didn't think much about it. Her mother was probably out doing chores, or perhaps she had gone to the church or was visiting neighbors. The daughter, Calla Garland, had gone to dinner with a man she was seeing in Bozeman and she had gotten home too late to call again. The next morning, this morning, she had driven over to the Ruby Valley.

Mulheisen couldn't bear this tedious description of Calla Garland's Christmas plans. "What about Sally?" he demanded.

"Sally? This isn't about Sally."

"Why are you calling from Tinstar?"

"I'm calling from the Garland ranch. Calla Garland found her mother in the barn. She was dead. It looked at first like she had a heart attack, but there's some problems. For one thing, the car is gone. Old Mrs. Garland had a 1989 Oldsmobile, which she kept in the garage next to the barn. She never drove it, hardly, except to church. She usually drove the pickup, but it's still parked in the barn."

Jacky's matter-of-fact police manner was driving Mulheisen crazy. The man was normally so phlegmatic, he hardly said a dozen words all day, it seemed. Now he was droning away.

"So what's the problem?" Mulheisen asked.

"I'm getting to it," Jacky said, unperturbed. "The daughter didn't find her mother in the house, so she went outside. She noticed the door to the garage was open and the car was gone, so she figured the old lady went visiting, but then she heard the milk cows bellowing in the barn. So she went in and found her. Dead. But where was the car? And why was the old lady's face bruised?"

"Have you talked to Sally?" Mulheisen broke in.

"Mul, this is not about Sally. This is about Grace Garland, the woman who owns—owned—the ranch next to Humann's. She may have been murdered. I thought you would be interested."

"Sally worked for Mrs. Garland," Mulheisen said. "She fed the cattle, or something. Have you talked to her?"

Jacky hadn't known that. He said he'd call back. It took twenty minutes, during which time Mulheisen paced back and forth, into the squad room for coffee, back to his office, back for more coffee.

"Sally may have seen the killer," Jacky said.

"She's all right?"

"Yeah, she's all right. She was just leaving for the Garland ranch when I called."

"You said killer," Mulheisen said. "Is this just on the basis of a bruise and a missing car, or do you have more?"

"There's also the problem of a rifle," Jacky said, "and the presence of a stranger."

"What about the rifle?"

"The old lady's .30-.30 carbine was found in the barn, standing next to the door. It had a spent cartridge in it. Grace Garland may have fired it, maybe in self-defense, but she didn't get a chance to work the lever action, which would have ejected the shell and brought a fresh round into the chamber. That's the way it looks."

"And Sally saw this stranger?" Mulheisen asked. "Was it a woman?"

"Yeah. How did you know that?"

"Was she tall? Short hair?"

Jacky was suspicious. "What do you know about this?"

"Tell me what Sally saw."

"Yesterday morning, after feeding the cattle, Sally drove down to the barn just to say hello and deliver a present. She met a woman—tall, short hair, about thirty—who was coming out of the barn. This woman, who she didn't know from Adam—or Eve—said Grace was in the barn. She invited Sally into the barn. Sally didn't have time, she had to get home. It was Christmas and the kids were home alone. The woman urged her to come in and talk to Grace, but Sally said she'd see her later. She gave the woman the present, a scarf she'd knitted. Sally says she'd talked to Grace a couple days ago and Grace told her she had a cousin visiting. Sally figured this was the cousin.

"She feels pretty bad about this, Mul," Jacky said. "She has an idea that maybe if she'd gone in the barn, she might have . . . you know. But I told her it was a good thing she didn't go in. It looks like this woman is our killer."

Mulheisen shuddered. "Where is she now?"

"We're looking, Mul. We put out a four-state alarm on the car."

"No, no," Mulheisen said impatiently. "Where is Sally?"

"She's on her way up here," Jacky said. "Somebody has to feed the cattle. Carrie's up here. Carrie'll bring her down to the house soon as she arrives."

"But she's all right?" Mulheisen asked. "What was that—the woman kept asking her to come into the barn?"

"Yeah. Sally said she asked two or three times. Also, she said the woman was bleeding. Which is another reason to think it was murder. Not much blood from a heart attack. But the autopsy will tell us for sure."

"Bleeding? The woman was bleeding? Wasn't Sally suspicious?"

"She said the woman had a torn pant leg and she was bleeding. The woman said she'd gotten tangled in some barbed wire. Said she was just going to go fix herself up, but she said it wasn't anything and Sally should come with her to the barn."

Mulheisen muttered several semi-Christian oaths under his breath—or perhaps they were not so much Christian as blasphemous and obscene.

"Jacky, get her down to the house as soon as she shows up, get her on the phone."

"Mul," Jacky said, calmly, "I'm on the case. You can talk to her. I've got one upset woman here already. I'll call you back." He hung up.

Mulheisen stared at the phone, enraged. But then he sat down. Jimmy Marshall came in and asked him what was up. Mulheisen gathered himself, calmed himself, and gave a brief reprise of what Jacky Lee had told him. Marshall wanted to know if this had anything to do with Joe Service, with Helen. Mulheisen said he wasn't sure, but it looked like it. He sensed that Marshall wasn't too keen on this complication.

Mulheisen sighed. "I don't know what the hell it means, Jimmy. Maybe it's just coincidence, but—"

"Murder next door to a killer is never coincidence, Mul," Jimmy said. "You taught me that. It's like the woman in the supermarket. Not a coincidence that her husband's girlfriend is there."

Mulheisen nodded. He didn't care about the woman in the supermarket. He got up and stepped to the door of the office, looking down the hall to see what time it was on the precinct clock. He never wore a watch. Watches died on his wrist. It was almost three o'clock. He came back and sat down. He wondered if he should tell Jimmy about the satellites. He didn't want to compromise Vito. He decided he didn't have any secrets from Jimmy, so he told him. Twice during the telling he got up to look at the clock. A half hour had passed.

"I think I better go out there," he said.

"You think so?" Jimmy said, noncommittally.

Mulheisen dialed the number again. Another deputy answered. He got Jacky on the phone.

"She's feeding cattle," Jacky said. "She was already late. The cattle have to be fed, the cows have to be milked, the hens have to be fed. Sally'll be done in a little bit. I'll call you." He was curt.

"They don't seem eager to see you," Jimmy observed.

Mulheisen frowned. "Jimmy," he said quietly, "you aren't suggesting I shouldn't go?"

Jimmy shrugged. "Just an observation, Mul. If you want to go, go. Maybe it's relevant."

Mulheisen nodded. The phone rang.

"Hi Mul," Sally said. She sounded tired, sad.

After all the "are you all right?" exchanges, Mulheisen said, "What did Mrs. Garland tell you about this woman?" He had a vague notion of Grace Garland. He had spoken to her once, he thought, perhaps twice. Sally related all that she knew. It wasn't much. Apparently, Grace Garland had gone out of her way to let Sally know that she was enjoying her visit with this relative, although the daughter denied that there was such a relative.

"Grace was really happy to have the woman for Christmas and when I met her the woman seemed all right," Sally said. "A little excited maybe, but then she'd cut herself, torn her pants. She said she was a klutz. I figured she wasn't from around here, but she seemed friendly. She was eager for me to go in the barn and see Grace."

There was a long silence as both Mulheisen and Sally thought about that. But Mulheisen went on to say that he was coming out there, that he would see her. He hinted about the husband—"You'll be home with the kids, I suppose?"—but Sally didn't rise to that bait. She just said she'd be home and she sure would be glad to see him.

"She killed Grace," Sally said. She was angry. "Grace took her in, nursed her, and then she killed her. What kind of woman would do that?"

"Nursed her?" Mulheisen asked.

"That's what Grace said, when I talked to her on the phone the other day. She said the woman was feeling a little poorly but was settin' up and taking nourishment and she'd have her out helping with the chores before you knew it. And now she's killed Grace, who never harmed a—"

"Sally, Sally . . . it's not certain—" Mulheisen tried to interject.

"They found my present lying in the snow. She waved me out of sight and then just threw Grace's Christmas scarf into the snow. She killed Grace."

12

Late Lite

They brought Cap'n Lite into the room, two big men on each side, holding his arms firmly. They were his closest associates and he knew by the firm way they held him that this was not a good thing. If you are being ushered into an interview for, say, a new job, the ushers don't hold you firmly by the upper arm. He was bothered about his hat, a green felt Tyrolean affair that had gotten dislodged slightly in the process of entering the room, the turning and bumping. The hat was atilt and some of his bald head was exposed. It felt silly and yet he didn't think he could complain or ask them to straighten it. But it unsettled him. He'd lost hair from his treatments and while he wasn't exactly vain, he was self-conscious about it.

Also, the interview room wasn't encouraging. Cap'n Lite had been driven south from Salt Lake City for about an hour, to meet "someone big." His associates had never mentioned such a person to him before, although they had sometimes intimated that there were higher powers somewhere, to whom they were beholden. Presumably these powers were back in Tonga—or Los Angeles, where there was another large enclave of Tongans.

The Tongans had recruited Cap'n Lite as their leader off the streets of Salt Lake City, a couple of years earlier. He hadn't been in Salt Lake City for very long, but he had gained a reputation as a man "who knew heavy people." Well, he knew Humphrey, the Fat Man; he was heavy, all right, but it was Humphrey who had told him to take a hike, although the Cap'n had never given up hope that he'd be asked to come back. Presumably it was because of this tenuous attachment, however, that the Tongans had picked him to be their leader. Well, not leader, but more like an executive. The arrangement was informal in the extreme. These people weren't articulate, not in English, anyway. They indicated that he should get them into various kinds of illegal operations, using his boasted contacts. He felt that he had earned their trust, gradually, as was demonstrated by the substantial amounts of money they allowed him. It was a hell of a comeback for Cap'n Lite. He hadn't had access to this kind of money since he had worked for Big Sid Sedlacek, mostly in the numbers racket in Detroit, in the 1950s and '60s. This was much more money. He'd done well in Detroit, but he'd had to leave when his old sponsor got into trouble.

The Cadillac had turned off the highway and driven several miles on a private road before approaching a large, modern house, a spectacular house made of huge logs, with lots of stonework and lots of glass. But the Caddy hadn't stopped at the house. They had driven on past the corrals and barns for a half mile on a more bumpy road, just a dirt track winding around low hills covered with sagebrush, to an old and weathered log house of just a couple rooms. This had probably been the original homesite, perhaps a hundred years old now, but it hadn't been kept up. Cap'n Lite wasn't exactly conversant with pioneer architecture, but he had an idea that this old homestead was itself worth something, the logs probably hauled down from the low mountains nearby and roughed into this well-made structure. But his architectural musings didn't occupy him for long. He was infinitely more curious about why they were meeting the Man here, instead of at the fancy house. But there was no point in asking the guys, he knew. They were never much for talk.

There was nothing in this house. It had a dirty wooden floor with cracks between the planks through which the cold wind huffed rills of old, tired dust. The walls of the cabin were darkened by cooking smoke and there were a few tattered remains of pictures that had been thumbtacked to the logs, pictures cut from magazines that no longer existed. One of them was a Norman Rockwell cover from the *Saturday Evening Post,* depicting a cowboy placing a child on the back of a pony.

A chair had been placed in the middle of the room. It was a large, modern chair of steel and leather, and it had obviously been brought in to provide ease for the very large man who was sitting in it. No doubt it would be removed when he left.

The Man was not just very large, he was easily the largest man that Cap'n Lite had ever seen. He actually made Cap'n Lite's lumbering bodyguards look normal. He was probably six feet and ten or eleven inches tall and weighed as much as four hundred pounds. He had, like the bodyguards, a huge, blank placid face, reddish brown in color, but with more delicate features and more intelligent eyes. No emotion was visible on this face, though perhaps his own people could detect emotion. They seemed tense.

"Bring him closer," the Man said. His voice was quiet, almost inaudible, but it was articulate and he spoke English easily. Still, he spoke so softly that one had to strain to hear. Cap'n Lite thought it might be part of his style: the Man didn't have to speak up; it was for others to listen intently. Cap'n Lite was chilled by the Man's manner. It portended no good thing. Tonga-heart, he thought.

"What is your name?" the Man asked, almost without interest.

When Cap'n Lite got his nerve back, he rasped out his real name: "Clarence Woods." And when the Man asked why he went by such a foolish name as Cap'n Lite, he found that he couldn't answer. But no answer was really desired. The Man didn't care.

"You let this man Service go," the Man said. "Why?"

"I talked to the guys," Cap'n Lite said. "They agreed to it. He was onto some money." He was annoyed to hear the weakness, the pleading tone in his voice.

"You weren't supposed to let him get away," the Man said. "Now we don't know where he is." It was said casually. The Man turned his chin slightly and rubbed an itch.

"We'll find him," Cap'n Lite said. "We know the house where his woman went."

"Not the blond woman," the Man said. "She's gone. You mean the woman he told you about?"

"Right. We just watch that place and he'll show up."

"He took the blond woman back from you. He even took her car," the Man said, petulantly. He sighed and looked at the floor. "But that isn't the worst. You talked to the people in Detroit. You told them about Mr. Service and the money."

Cap'n Lite was frightened now. He was also shocked. How did they know he had called Detroit? "I only wanted to find out if Joe was telling the truth. I got old friends in Detroit, friends who could find out if he was screwing us over. Hey, that's how I found out that there was more money than he was telling us . . . and about the other woman. I had to find out somehow, didn't I?"

He was frankly pleading now. He hated the desperate tone, fearing that in itself it would somehow contribute to the situation. But he knew he had to get this notion across. It was no more nor less than what his life was worth. The Man's face had darkened.

"It's good to find out things," the Man said.

Cap'n Lite was relieved. "That's all it was," he hastened to add. "I was just trying to figure out what was going down. The way Service was talking, it was only a few hundred grand—nothing, really. But my friends back in Detroit, they tipped me off. There's a lot more. Millions! And now that Joe has split, we don't need him. Right? It's all ours. Yours. I mean, we know where the house is, where the woman took the money. So it was good I called Detroit. Right?"

"To a degree," the Man said. He looked pensive, stroking his chin.

Cap'n Lite felt emboldened. "Well, who else could have found out for you? I mean, that's why you hired *me*. Right?"

The Man nodded vaguely. He was thinking of something else, it appeared. He didn't say anything for a long moment, just gazed at the dirty window, through which one could barely make out a snowy field, perhaps a hint of a distant mountain range. The Man shivered. "It's cold here," he said. He adjusted his heavy overcoat.

"Well, yeah, it is cold." Cap'n Lite was eager to agree. His head was cold. He wanted to say something about his hat, but it seemed an impossible subject. "Too cold. Maybe we could go back to the big house, or someplace warmer. We ought to be thinking about getting into the chick's house on Main Street, get the money. I been keeping an eye on the place, I got kids moving around there. A place like that, you don't want to rush in without you case the layout, make sure it ain't a trap, or something. Look, I got a lot to do, I . . . "

He was babbling, he knew, but he was relieved. It was going to turn out. It was good, he began to think, that he'd finally met the Big Man. It suggested that they trusted him.

The Man waved his hand to shut him up. "But now, also, these Detroit people know about the house, about our interest. They will want the money for themselves," he said. "That isn't good."

He held up an immense left hand and with his right forefinger he ticked off items of interest. "It's good we found out about the money. It's bad."—he ticked another finger—"that they know about it, about our interest." He ticked another finger. "And then there is you. Are you any good to us? You are *their* man, it seems. They have a contact in you. Now we will never know if you are working for us, or for them."

"But I work for you," Cap'n Lite almost shrieked. "You know that! You picked me up, gave me a job—"

The Man nodded. "That is true. You were nothing. But you had useful knowledge. We thought you would be grateful, loyal, because you had been rejected by your own people."

"I *am* grateful! I *am* loyal! How can you say that I'm not?"

"But now," the Man said, tapping the fourth finger forcefully, "you have made your way back into the good graces of these Detroit people, you see. They will no doubt appreciate your loyalty to them. They will see that you are useful after all, that you have made amends for whatever it was that offended them. It was something to do with skimming, was it not? It couldn't have been too serious, or they would have killed you. But you were no longer trusted. They were content that you should just run away, go into exile. So you were useful to us. But now you have won your way back. And you are no longer useful to *us*. It is ironic, is it not?"

The Man lifted both hands as if demonstrating an obvious truth and he looked at the two men who held Cap'n Lite, but not at Cap'n Lite. He wasn't really talking to him, it seemed. He was explaining the situation to them, but explaining it in English out of deference to Cap'n Lite.

"When a man is of no use to our competitors, he is useful to us. When he becomes useful to them, he is useless to us." He dropped his hands to his knees, sat in thought for a moment, then heaved himself to his feet. "This is a grave situation. It endangers us all. In such a situation, the leader must act. It is his responsibility, his alone."

Now he spoke in the native tongue, his voice low and rumbling. He spoke for several minutes, addressing the two men while they held their captive even tighter. So tightly, in fact, that he cried out in pain. The rumbling stopped. The Man looked at Cap'n Lite in surprise, then said something to the two men in the island language. They immediately changed their grip, moving their hands down to grasp his hands, almost like children, except that they also grasped him by the wrists with their other hands. Also, they stepped away, slightly, so that Cap'n Lite's arms were now more or less extended.

The Big Man approached Cap'n Lite, loomed over him. He stood so close, at last, that he was almost touching him. He looked gravely down into Cap'n Lite's eyes and said something incomprehensible. Then he put his hands around Cap'n Lite's neck and began to squeeze. He was very powerful. His hands completely encircled the scrawny neck. He squeezed. The gesture knocked off Cap'n Lite's hat, exposing his bony skull with its few clinging strands of pale hair. Cap'n Lite started to protest. "I'm a sick ma—" he got out.

The big man squeezed harder, cutting off all sound. Cap'n Lite's tongue protruded, his eyes bulged. He tried to struggle but it was hopeless. The men held his arms; he had no room to move. He knew he was being murdered, that this was it, that there was no argument, even if he were allowed air to speak it, and then he lost consciousness.

When the strangler was confident that his victim was dead, he released him and stepped back. He wrinkled his nose. The victim had fouled his pants. The murderer spoke to the two assistant murderers in their own tongue and they dragged the dead man to one side, holding him still at arm's length. The big man stood, self-absorbed, rubbing his hands together, kneading first one then the other. All the while he gazed pensively at the dirty window. But finally he seemed composed. He took a deep, chest-lifting breath, straightened his coat and buttoned it, turning up the collar. Then he went out the door.

When the two assistant murderers heard the leader's car drive away, they dragged Cap'n Lite out to the Cadillac and heaved him into the trunk like a sack of garbage. One of them went into the cabin and retrieved the hat, tossing it into the trunk before he slammed the lid. They drove back into Salt Lake City and, around four A.M., they decanted the body and the hat onto a quiet downtown corner, 300 South at 400 West, near the Amtrak station. It was discovered about an hour later by a cruising policeman who at first thought it was a derelict. But it was too cold for a derelict to be out. It was the very dead of winter.

13

Music Lessons

Mulheisen was trying to explain to Cateyo why she should talk to him. "A lot of people think that they don't ever have to talk to the police; that's the popular notion, but it's not true." That sort of thing. The problem was compounded by the presence of Ms. Daphne Z. Stonborough, sometime attorney to Helen Sedlacek and now retained by Cathleen Yoder. Since Ms. Yoder was not in custody and was not accused of any crimes, at this point, she had only consented to speak to Mulheisen if the interview took place in Counselor Stonborough's offices. Mulheisen didn't mind this. He liked Ms. Stonborough. She had two invaluable assets: competence and intelligence. He disliked having to deal with incompetent attorneys, which he seemed to meet all too frequently.

The valuable thing about interviewing a witness in the presence of a competent lawyer was that the lawyer willy-nilly aids the detective by not permitting illegal and improper questions, so there is less chance to see a case thrown out of court by impropriety of the investigating officer. Mulheisen appreciated this. Still, there were problems. Essentially, what one had to do was convince the attorney that the client should talk to the police, that it was in her best interests. This is never an easy thing to do. It is well known that the most hideous sound in the world, to a lawyer, is the sound of her client's voice.

As Mulheisen saw it, he had to convince Ms. Stonborough and Ms. Yoder that it was all right to say who the woman was who had accompanied Cateyo to Joe Service's cabin and, secondarily (though most important, in Mulheisen's eyes), where Joe Service was now. Mulheisen started by explaining that he knew another woman had accompanied Cateyo to the Service cabin. He didn't say anything about a satellite, just that he had a witness, but he declared that the witness was ironclad.

"Who is this witness?" Ms. Stonborough wanted to know.

Mulheisen said politely, calmly, but with all the confidence he could muster, that the witness could not presently be identified. The witness had rights, too, just as Ms. Yoder had rights that he was bound to respect. He could not reveal this name; it would be a breach of confidence.

"Well, if you have such a wonderful witness," Daphne sniffed, "why do you need Ms. Yoder? Your witness sounds fabulous."

Fabulous, Mulheisen thought, in the sense of mythical? But he said, "The witness is good, irrefutable. Still, as you know, there is a difference between having a single statement and one that is corroborated by another. Beyond that, my witness is not privy to the kinds of information that we think Ms. Yoder has. My witness doesn't know Ms. Yoder's friend's name, for instance." He turned to Cateyo and said, "Surely, there's no harm in giving a name."

"I don't want to get anyone in trouble," Cateyo said.

Mulheisen glanced at Ms. Stonborough; she was noncommittal. "This woman is already in trouble," he said. "Deep trouble. Is she a friend of yours?"

Cateyo glanced at her lawyer, then said, "If she were a friend of mine it would be disloyal, wouldn't it, for me to betray her?"

Mulheisen brushed this aside, saying, "Loyalty is a fine senti-
ment, but you have to ask yourself who you're being loyal to. There
is nothing ambiguous about this situation, Ms. Yoder. We believe
your friend could tell us something about the murder of an elderly
woman who operated a ranch in Tinstar, a ranch located within two
miles of Joe Service's cabin. But we can't locate your friend, mainly
because we don't know her identity."

As he spoke he observed with satisfaction the expression of
shock on Cateyo's face. Clearly, she didn't know about the murder
of Grace Garland, or at least she hadn't connected it with Joe Service or his cabin. For that matter, even after examination there was
as yet no indication that Grace Garland had, in fact, been murdered.
But she had certainly been intimidated, she had been struck, so the
presumption was still murder. The Butte–Silver Bow coroner was
waiting for the medical examiner's report.

He went calmly on: "I feel that you are a moral person, Ms.
Yoder. You're a nurse, a woman committed to helping people. The
murder victim was alone, a widow. She took in this other woman,
who may have been injured, or at least in trouble. So she was helping this woman out. I don't have to tell you: out here people do this,
it's the custom of the country. But sometimes it's asking for trouble.
In this case, it looks like Mrs. Garland invited a killer into her home
for Christmas. She was assaulted, and the woman she took in has
disappeared. So we need to find this woman."

"You don't know that this woman killed Grace Garland,
then?" interjected Stonborough.

Mulheisen did not display annoyance at the interruption, nor
did he take his attention from Cateyo's face. He said, "We know
she was there, at the ranch, right up to the estimated time of death.
We have a witness who saw her there and talked with her. We have
an excellent description. We need to talk to her. *You* weren't there,

Ms. Yoder, so we don't feel that you can tell us anything about the circumstances of Mrs. Garland's death. It doesn't have anything to do with you, directly. But you can tell us something about the woman who was with you at Joseph Humann's cabin. The man we know as Joe Service."

"I don't see that a woman at the cabin necessarily has anything to do with a woman at Grace Garland's," Stonborough said. "That's rather a giant leap, isn't it, to think that they are the same person?"

"No. From the descriptions we have of the woman at the cabin and the woman at the ranch, we're fairly confident that it's the same woman. But we need to nail it down. That's why Ms. Yoder's testimony is so important," Mulheisen said. He kept his eye on Cateyo. He noted that she looked concerned. "Did the woman leave the cabin when you left?" he asked.

"No," Cateyo said. She looked wildly at her lawyer, who only sighed and raised her eyes to the ceiling.

"So you left the cabin with Joe Service, and the other woman stayed behind?" Mulheisen asked.

"Yes." Cateyo's reply was faint, tentative.

"But she went to the cabin with you and Joe Service?"

"Yes."

"So you know her name. You know who she is," Mulheisen said. "She was a friend of yours."

"Not . . . not exactly," Cateyo said. Again, she glanced to her lawyer for assistance, but the attorney only sat forward with interest.

"Who was she then?" Mulheisen asked.

Cateyo sighed and said, "Her name is Heather Bloom. She was my roommate." She went on then to explain how she had met Heather at the hospital and how, later, Heather had come to her home, inquiring about a place to stay. Cateyo had rented a room to her for a couple of months. Heather seemed very nice, she said. She provided a description of Heather Bloom and said she understood that Heather was only temporarily in Butte, that she did some kind of computer work, apparently for the power company, but she expected to move on to another job before long. Heather seemed to have unconventional hours. She had volunteered to accompany Cateyo and Service to the cabin, when Service was allowed an "outing."

"You met her at the hospital," Mulheisen said. "Was she a patient? Visiting someone?"

"No, actually, it was outside the hospital. I'd taken Joe, Mr. Humann—or Service—for a walk, in a wheelchair. She came up to us and started talking about being new in town. Then Joe had an accident—it was my fault, really, I wasn't watching what I was doing—and he fell out of the wheelchair. Heather picked him up and carried him up to the hospital while I brought the chair."

"She carried him?" Mulheisen said. "She must be pretty strong."

"She's quite strong," Cateyo agreed.

"What happened at the cabin?" Mulheisen asked.

"How do you mean?" Cateyo looked tense.

Mulheisen mused for a moment, then said, "Well, I take it that you weren't planning to spend the night. That wasn't the plan for the outing that the doctor had authorized, was it?"

"No, but once we got there and the weather started to turn bad . . . I mean, there wasn't any problem with staying over. I called the hospital. It was all right."

"But you didn't stay over," Mulheisen pointed out. "You and Service left, despite the weather. But Heather Bloom didn't leave with you. Why?"

"Why?" Cateyo looked at Daphne Stonborough. The attorney held up her hand, to stop her, then asked Mulheisen to step out of the office. He only had a few moments to kick his heels in the outer office before he was invited back in.

"You may proceed, Sergeant Mulheisen," the attorney said, "but please go carefully. I don't want to compromise my client's rights here."

"Of course," Mulheisen said, showing his teeth as amiably as he could. "So, Ms. Yoder . . . you and Service left together, but Heather stayed behind. Why didn't she go with you?"

Cateyo still seemed quite confused and uncertain, despite her conference with Stonborough. She knew that she had committed herself to telling about the situation at the cabin, but she was unwilling to elaborate. Mulheisen simply sat and waited. He'd always found it a very good tactic, simply sitting and waiting. The interviewee gets nervous, wants to fill the silence, becomes more and more conscious that only she can break this deadlock.

"I . . . I don't know," Cateyo faltered. "I mean, we weren't planning to go back to Butte, to the hospital. We weren't going anywhere that she would . . . " Her voice faded. She didn't know how to go on.

"You didn't want her to go with you, with you and Joe?" Mulheisen suggested, helpfully. When she nodded agreement, he went on: "But why did you and Joe leave?" Mulheisen relieved her by proceeding to the next obvious move. "Wasn't the weather too bad? Wasn't that why you stayed in the first place? The weather didn't improve suddenly, did it?"

"I believe we might be getting into another area of inquiry here, Sergeant Mulheisen," Stonborough said.

Mulheisen turned to her and asked reasonably, "Do you think so? It seems relevant to the inquiry about Ms. Bloom."

Stonborough considered this for a moment, then said, "Very well. But." She turned to Cateyo. "If you feel uncertain, just say so and we can consider it privately before proceeding."

"You and Joe left together, without Heather," Mulheisen prompted, "even though the weather had not improved. Why?"

Cateyo just stared dumbly at Mulheisen. She was a moral woman, brought up in a strict fundamentalist Christian family. She didn't want to lie, but she had to protect Joe.

Mulheisen recognized the situation; it was the usual problem: the witness was trying to decide whether to lie and then to what extent. He could help the person lie by suggesting something neutral or more or less true to which she could agree, or seize on, as a possible alternative to the whole truth. This would lead to a situation where she must slip into the lie or back out of the muddied water. People don't like to back out; it makes them look as if they'd already lied, when they had not, really. So they tend to take another tentative step into a less tenable, but still not quite false position. Then, once the person has embarked on this not-quite-lie he could let her get deeper and deeper into a morass and then either rescue her or offer her a way out to the blessed firm ground of the truth, or he could confront her and bully her into the truthful admission, or . . . there were a lot of variations on the tune. But the tune was definitely starting. Now was the time to take care. He was reminded of a saying he had heard recently, attributed to the great jazz saxophonist Coleman Hawkins: "I hear a tune, but I cannot play it." He could hear the distant strains of the tune, but not all the changes.

"What time did you leave?" he asked, choosing the neutral question.

This she could answer freely; nothing was involved. "I think it was about ten, maybe a little later. I'm not sure."

"Did Heather object to your leaving?"

This was more difficult, dodgy in fact. Heather had actually attempted to murder them both, but Cateyo was confident that there was no way that Mulheisen could know this. The question could be answered just as Cateyo improvised: "You could say that."

Mulheisen began to get excited. There was something definitely wrong here. He wanted to find out what had happened—had they argued? Had Heather threatened them in some way? But he was patient. "But you decided to leave her there? Did she have a car?" He knew from the satellite pictures that there had been only one car, but it was an opportunity for Cateyo to embroider, to elaborate, to make up a lie. She didn't do it.

"Uh, no," Cateyo said, glancing at Daphne, who bent forward at her desk, fascinated and curious.

"You left her in the cabin without a vehicle? In a blizzard?" Mulheisen's tone was not condemning, but mildly puzzled. It was a distraction. It led Cateyo to believe that he was more interested in her behavior toward Heather than in Heather's behavior, or Joe's.

"It was *my* car," she said, defensively.

Mulheisen shrugged. "So you left," he said, neutrally. He paused for a long moment. He supposed she would anticipate that he would ask where she and Joe had gone, and she would be preparing her response. "Have you seen her since?"

"Hunh? Why no. No, I haven't."

"You didn't go back to get her? You left her up at Joe's cabin, in a storm, and you didn't go back to get her?" He managed to sound faintly incredulous.

"Well, I . . . we . . . we heard there was a fire. . . . I assumed she was all right, people would have helped her . . . "

Mulheisen seemed to accept this lame response, saying, "But you haven't heard from her, you haven't heard anything about her, have you?"

"No, no I haven't. I suppose I should have enquired. . . . I don't know. . . . I didn't think."

Obviously, she hadn't had to worry, Mulheisen decided, because she knew what had happened to Heather. Heather had either gone with them or she had already left, or she had been disposed of in some way. It was also possible that Cateyo only *thought* she knew what had happened to Heather, and (he had to admit to himself) it was possible that she simply didn't care or was distracted by her concern for Joe. But he had a feeling that she knew that she needn't be concerned for Heather Bloom.

He could sense that Daphne Stonborough was bristling, although he didn't look at her. He didn't want to pursue this line at the moment. He opted for neutral ground again.

"You've been back to your house, here in Butte," he said. "Is there any sign that she returned there?"

"Not that I saw," Cateyo said.

"Would it be okay for me to go to the house, to have a look at her things, her room?"

"Wouldn't you need a warrant for that?" Cateyo said, looking to Stonborough for help.

"I'm sure the sheriff could easily obtain a warrant to examine the living quarters of a prime murder suspect," Mulheisen said, "but I just wondered if you had any objection to my coming by the house. No? Fine. And you didn't have any suspicions of this woman? She didn't act strangely toward you? You didn't notice any odd behavior? Hmmm. Did you ever see her with other people, friends, associates? No? She didn't talk about her associates? Where did she say she was from, anyway?"

When Cateyo said "Detroit," Mulheisen almost shivered with excitement. "She had references from Detroit? No? You didn't ask for references when you rented a room to her?"

"It was only temporary," Cateyo said.

"She lived with you for—what—a couple of months? Do you have a camera? Did you ever take a picture of her? No? What kind of person is Heather? I mean, was she fussy? Excitable? Quiet? Athletic?"

Cateyo found it difficult to describe Heather. In fact, the woman had made Cateyo nervous from the start, but she couldn't say just how. "Aggressive, maybe," she said finally. "She was nice, but . . . I don't know . . . she could be a little pushy." What she was quite unwilling to say was that she had become nervous about Heather's way of coming into the bathroom when Cateyo was taking a bath, of offering to scrub her back, of commenting on Cateyo's physical appearance—"You have a great figure," she'd said, more than once. But Cateyo said nothing of this to Mulheisen—it was too embarrassing.

"Let's go back to the cabin for a moment," Mulheisen said. "Did anybody else come to the cabin while you were there? No? Did you receive any phone calls?" Again, no. Mulheisen was stumped. He had been at the cabin himself, some hours later, having tracked Helen there. By that time the thugs had also arrived and apparently encountered Helen, who had fled. Then the cabin had blown up. Joe Service and Cateyo had long since disappeared, as had Heather Bloom. If Heather had not gone with Joe and Cateyo, she must have been in the vicinity, hiding out. Subsequently, she had appeared at Grace Garland's, with fatal results. He had found Helen himself, hiding in the hot springs, but he had been totally unaware of the presence of Heather, until he'd seen the satellite pictures. She had been around, though. Perhaps she had fled immediately after the departure of Joe and Cateyo, to Grace Garland's. But he recalled that the deputy, Jacky Lee, had talked to Grace after the incident at the cabin, to explain the events of the night. Garland had not mentioned anything about a visitor, but perhaps she hadn't made a connection with the incident at the cabin. There was more to it than that, of course: Garland had subsequently told Sally that she was being visited by a "cousin," or some such relation. Why Garland would do this, he didn't know, and he doubted that they ever would know, unless they apprehended Heather and she told them.

"Let's get one thing straight," he said, speaking more sternly now. "Did you part with Heather on friendly terms? Did she consent to stay?"

This was the critical moment. Cateyo made her decision. "Yes," she said firmly. She saw the implication: that if she and Joe had run out on Heather, then Heather's presence at Grace Garland's, *and the murder of Grace Garland*, was their moral responsibility. She couldn't accept that responsibility, for herself or Joe.

Mulheisen recognized this as a lie. He nailed it down. "She agreed to stay, without a car, in a blizzard?"

Cateyo said yes, taking another step into the morass.

"So, she must have been driven from the cabin by the arrival of the men who broke into the cabin and ultimately destroyed it, and themselves," Mulheisen said.

Cateyo shrugged, a kind of agreement. It had nothing to do with her, or with Joe, she felt confident.

"Why would she agree to this?" Mulheisen pursued. "Did she have reason to believe that you and Joe would return?"

"I guess," Cateyo said.

"You guess?"

"There was plenty of food, plenty of fuel," Cateyo said. "She could stay there for days. We didn't know those men would come there."

"So, you and Joe were planning to come back and get her? You told her that?"

"Well, more or less," Cateyo said, unconvincingly.

"Where did you and Joe go?" Mulheisen asked—the ultimate question.

"I don't see that it's important where they went," Daphne Stonborough said.

"You don't?" Mulheisen said. "I think it could be very important. If they just ran into Tinstar, a few miles away, to get cigarettes or something, planning to return right away . . . " He let the suggestion hang. "But it sounds like they actually went much farther, and that Heather Bloom knew it, that she thought her only way out of there was to trek over the hill to a neighbor's . . . " He let that hang, too.

"We went to Salt Lake City," Cateyo blurted out. "We were planning to get married."

The lawyer and the detective stared at her. The young woman looked so innocent, so wishful, that they involuntarily turned to each other with a look of surprised pity. Mulheisen recovered first and said, "Did you get married?"

"Um, no."

"Where is Joe now?"

"I don't know," Cateyo said. She looked defiant.

"Where do you think he is?" Mulheisen asked.

"He's probably still in Salt Lake City, but I don't know where. He checked out of the hotel we were staying in. He said he had some business to take care of."

"You expect to hear from him?"

"Yes." She went on to say, in response to Mulheisen's request, that she would be sure to contact him if Joe called. But Mulheisen knew better.

"I don't know who you think Joe Service is," Mulheisen said, with a tone of sad regret, "but he's not a good guy. He has very close connections with organized crime in Detroit and, in fact, all across the country. He's a contract man. We think he was involved in at least two murders, maybe more. He's a dangerous man, Ms. Yoder. He's very likable, apparently, quite convincing, but he isn't a good guy." The admonition had little effect on Cateyo, he could tell.

"I just hope he's taking his medicine," she said.

They went to Cateyo's house, then, accompanied by Ms. Stonborough. As Mulheisen had feared, there was no evidence there that Heather Bloom had ever been in the house. Everything had been removed from her bedroom. But he still called Jacky Lee and got him to come by with someone who could check for fingerprints. It was always worth a chance.

Cateyo went back to work and Mulheisen took Daphne to lunch. She was admiring of his technique in questioning Cateyo, but seemed annoyed with herself. "She was singing away there, in the end," she said.

"I don't think you have anything to worry about," Mulheisen said. "Johnny isn't going to prosecute her for anything. All she did was run away with a patient. It's interesting, though, to think of a woman like that being so close to the action and yet not really seeing anything."

"Love is blind," Stonborough said.

"So is justice. Well, Cateyo saw more than she let on, but even she doesn't know what she saw, so it's hard to get her to say what it was. I think she's very disturbed about this Heather." He let that drop, seeing that Daphne wasn't going to discuss what her client might or might not know. Instead, he asked, "So, are you still representing Helen Sedlacek?"

"No. She fired me from Detroit. Said to send her a bill."

"What address?" Mulheisen wanted to know. But Daphne couldn't remember. They went on to chat about other things, such as Johnny Antoni and his excessively healthy family, and they ended up laughing at Mulheisen's misadventures fishing the Big Hole River. It was a very pleasant lunch and Mulheisen half-wished he could think of some way to continue it, but the fact was that he was suddenly extremely anxious. He had to get on with this case, now that it was starting to break.

What ensued was several hours of pacing, phone calls, more pacing. He knew he should call Sally McIntyre, make some kind of amends for . . . well, for what? He hadn't done anything to her, but they weren't talking very well. Instead he called everybody else he could think of and paced up and down the Butte–Silver Bow sheriff's offices. He went for a walk at one point, just to get some fresh air, and found himself east of town, at the Berkeley Pit. This was an immense hole in the ground, from which the Anaconda Company had taken millions of tons of copper ore. Now it was just a hole, but a vast hole, miles across and a half mile deep. It was filling slowly with water, obviously not very clean water, either: earlier that fall more than two hundred snow geese had been found dead along its shores, evidently poisoned. He stood on the little viewing platform, feeling the cold wind snapping at his face, while he gazed about at the terraced walls of this monument to man's capacity to destroy. He thought, idly, that if his mother ever saw this . . .

In the afternoon he learned from the telephone company that someone had called a number in Grosse Pointe from Grace Garland's house. Mulheisen contacted Andy Deane, his old buddy at Rackets and Conspiracy. Andy identified the number as Humphrey DiEbola's home phone. Mulheisen asked if Humphrey had shown any signs of activity lately, but Andy said they hadn't been watching. However, he agreed to check on movements of Humphrey's private plane, which was normally stationed at Detroit's City Airport.

Mulheisen talked to a detective in Salt Lake City. The conversation was mainly about Joe Service and his possible whereabouts—nothing had been noticed at the Main Street house—but a curious little tidbit was tossed out. The detective, apparently in association with Mulheisen's Detroit origins, mentioned that they had recently found a local "character" strangled on the street. The detective seemed to think it was just another curiosity, a testament to the evil times we live in, when such a harmless guy as "Cap'n Lite" could be strangled and tossed idly onto a curb. He supposed the guy had gotten into some kind of deal that had gone sour. It happened. The only reason he mentioned it was that this character was apparently an old Detroit hood named Clarence Woods.

At first the name didn't register with Mulheisen, but then he felt a vague prickling of the scalp. "Cap'n Lite, you say?" he asked. "A little guy, kind of beaky?" Mulheisen knew him. He knew him as a nonentity, a gofer who'd been tolerated and supported by the late Big Sid Sedlacek, father of Helen. Many, many years ago, long before the scam that had gotten Big Sid killed, Sid had engineered a milder ripoff that had almost gotten him permanently retired, but out of which he had staged a remarkable comeback. In that affair, one of the people who had taken the heat for Big Sid was little, beaky Clarence Woods, a.k.a. Cap'n Lite. Clarence had disappeared, was thought to be dead, but evidently he'd only been exiled, doing penance for his patron, Big Sid. And now, just a day or two earlier, Clarence was strangled. Mulheisen never was a believer in coincidence.

14

New Kid II

Joe Service was very interested to read in the *Salt Lake Tribune* that a man named Clarence Woods had been found dead on the street the day before. And not very far from where Joe was sitting, in the Rio Grande Cafe, a converted railway waiting station. There were these cafes all over the West—railroad architecture was attractive—but this was one of the nicer conversions. Joe was fond of trains and so he had naturally gravitated toward the Rio Grande. In this case, Amtrak still used the depot from which the much-admired Denver & Rio Grande silver trains used to go racing out across the Rocky Mountains. The cafe featured an upscale Mexican cuisine. Joe had enjoyed the tostada. Now he was enjoying the coffee. But he found himself strangely disturbed by the murder of Clarence Woods.

At first he hadn't paid any attention to the article, and doubtless wouldn't have, but the colorful nickname Cap'n Lite was mentioned. There was no picture, but none was needed. There couldn't be two such characters in Salt Lake City. And this small man had been strangled. Joe could easily imagine it. He couldn't help thinking that he was in some way responsible. Not genuinely responsible, of course; it was clearly the work of the Tongans. But it wasn't hard to see that Cap'n Lite had been brutally punished for his failures with Joe. And publicly dumped, an unsubtle demonstration for other would-be rats. No doubt the Tongans would be redoubling their efforts to nail Joe. He had no idea what kind of an organization they had, except that it didn't seem all that efficient. What kind of gang was this?

He thought back to his own experience with gangs. As a boy in Philadelphia he had admired older boys who belonged to gangs. But when his turn came, for some reason he had never joined. His reasons were vague. The idea of being part of a gang ultimately didn't sufficiently appeal. These older boys were too bossy, forever making the younger boys run and fetch, "do this, do that." Joe wasn't into that. Nonetheless, he had liked to operate around the edges. He had ended up doing things for the gang on an independent, contract basis: things like finding out about someone, where someone lived, who his girlfriend was. He liked it better that way.

This Tongan gang, what was it? Was it mostly adults, mostly kids? Were there colors involved, secret signs, a special language? How many people were in it, he wondered, and were they all Tongans, or were other islanders, other ethnic groups involved? He didn't really care, except that they represented a possible danger to him. It was another reason to get his act together fast and take it on the road . . . out of Salt Lake City.

Still, he felt annoyed, angry even, at this murder. He had kind of liked the raspy-voiced little man who, after all, had given him a break—a calculated break, to be sure, but still a break. Perhaps it was the sympathy that one small man might feel for another in a world of overgrown oafs, especially oafs like these monstrous islanders. Perhaps that was why Cap'n Lite had given Joe a break. For Joe's part, he never thought of himself as small. Not tall, but not small. Cap'n Lite was a little guy, but hanging out with a bunch of Tongans would make even a six-footer feel puny.

It was early afternoon, a nice winter day, cold but sunny. He went into the Amtrak station and inquired about trains. The eastbound Zephyr wasn't due until 4:45 the next morning. He'd been on that train before. In fact, he'd ridden the Zephyr to Iowa some nine months earlier, a trip that had led to his present situation. He had been on the trail of a mob hit man who seemed to have gone astray, had begun to do a little more work than he'd been hired to do. Joe had found the guy, all right, but he'd had to take him out. He'd felt a little bad about it at the time, but he hadn't let it bother him too much. And from that he had become entangled with Helen.

Well, well, he thought, here I am back on the same track—or is it a loop, going around in circles? He wasn't sentimental, not a superstitious type. It didn't bother him. What bothered him was whether he could accomplish what he needed to accomplish between now and four in the morning. He decided he couldn't. He booked for the following day, for a room he had checked out carefully during his last trip on the Zephyr. Room H was a big and comfortable room, complete with a shower. He figured he'd need a little extra space. He paid in cash, using the name Clarence Woods—in memoriam, as it were. He booked straight through to Chicago.

Yes, he told himself, I'm just back on track. Only this time he wouldn't stop in Iowa City. And then he realized with a start that he hadn't even thought about his memory problems all day. He *was* back on track.

Next he called the Utah State Medical Examiner's office and was gratified by the information he was able to obtain there. Based on that, he called around to a few funeral homes until he found the deal he wanted and he made the requisite arrangements.

He drove to Main Street and parked in the alley again, but this time several houses away from the colonel's lookout post. He still had a pair of Glock 9mm automatics that he'd liberated from the Tongans when he'd rescued Cateyo. They were heavy, clumsy things, not the sort of gun he would have chosen, but they had fire-power to spare. He discovered that his down ski jacket had a couple of inside pockets which would hold the guns fairly well and, the jacket being bulky anyway, they weren't obvious. He jammed one in each jacket pocket and walked blithely up the alley, away from Helen's house to a corner convenience store and gas station.

He bought a couple of magazines and a red and white knit wool cap that had the "Utes" logo of the University of Utah foot-ball team on it. He pulled this over his head, down low, right to the heavy black brows, and went outside. It was colder now, breezy. From the pay phone outside he could scan the whole block. He held the phone in his hand and uttered the words to the old tune "I'll Be Home for Christmas" while he carefully examined the street. After about five minutes he was fairly certain that there was no exten-sive observation of Helen's house. To be sure, the colonel and Edna were next door, very likely with a third agent upstairs operating a radio. But it didn't appear that there was a second watching post. No parked vans. No idle walkers, no electrical or telephone work-ers hanging in the air in power-lift buckets, no street workers stand-ing around a sewer access looking aimlessly about.

Other than the house where the colonel was, there didn't appear to be a really good watching post on the block, except for a used-car lot diagonally across the street. From a used-car lot you could see a great deal and you wouldn't draw much attention: there could be lots of traffic in and out, lots of different people coming and going. But there didn't seem to be any of that here. Down the block was a pizzeria that wasn't open yet, some kind of insurance agency that seemed to be either closed or at least not doing much business, a credit union office that had an occasional visitor. Really, Joe thought, there was just the used-car dealer. He decided to give him a visit, though not by walking up. Edna or the colonel, or the guy upstairs, would be sure to make him if he tried to just walk down the street.

He went back to the alley and drove his car around the block, then a few blocks further, just to make sure he wasn't being tailed. It looked clean. He returned to Main Street and simply drove into the used-car lot, making sure to park to one side, where he would be obscured by other cars. He walked into the dealer's office, which was nothing more than an aluminum prefab unit set up as an office. In addition to a secretary—one of those efficient, seemingly anonymous women of thirty-five or forty, diligently working on titles and insurance details—there was only a hefty man of thirty in a sport coat and a tie, not overly bright but nobody's fool, it would seem. Nobody else in the office. No federal-agent types. Nobody just sitting around sipping coffee and watching the street.

"Bob Tyler," the hefty man said, holding out his hand.

"Clarence Woods," Joe said, shaking the hand firmly.

"Lookin' for a good car, Clarence?"

"Not really, Bob. No, I was just . . . Bob, where do you get these cars?" Joe asked.

"Where do I get 'em? They come in. I buy 'em. All good cars, Clarence. I got the greatest mechanic in the Mountain West. He goes over 'em, gets 'em in top shape, and I sell 'em. Can't hardly get enough of 'em."

"You mean these are all cars that people drive in here and sell to you?"

"Sell, trade . . . that's about it, Clarence." Bob was confident, relaxed. "You wouldn't believe the return bidniss I git. Guy come in here—what was it, Lynn?" Bob turned to the woman at the desk. "Two days ago? That old fella from Sandy?"

The woman nodded without looking up and said, "Lewis, James."

"Right. Old Jim Lewis. He bought the sixt' car, I think it was, he's got from me, over the years. Good cars, ever one. 'Pendable cars." The man leaned back against the door jamb, writhing slightly to scratch his back, his belly bulging his wide belt with its cruelly biting rodeo buckle. "You don't git that kinda return bidniss, you don't pervide good cars. Clarence," he added.

Joe nodded enthusiastically. "But Bob, you must have times when the demand outruns the supply?"

Bob stood upright, his brows shooting up. "Can't hardly maintain inventory, Clarence. I like to keep the lot full. It looks like success. Funny, eh? When you figure that real success would be if you *couldn't* keep the lot full. Whudjoo got on your mine, Clarence?"

"Bob, can we talk?" Joe gestured toward the inner office.

"Can we talk? Clarence, you're talking to a auto-*mo*-beel salesman, *the* original motor mouth. Come on in here. You want a coffee? No? Mormon tea—Coke?" he said. He ushered Joe into his office and closed the door, then got a can of Diet Coke out of a small refrigerator. "Whudjoo have in mine, Clarence?" he said, opening the can and setting it down on the edge of the desk. He had a habit, when not talking himself, of moving his lips slightly, as if helping you say what you had to say. It could be disconcerting at times.

Joe refused the chair, preferring to stand and look out the picture window, ostensibly at the lot. "Bob, I've got a bunch of cars. Actually, I've got access to as many cars as you can handle," Joe said. He gazed casually at the street, talking over his shoulder. Nothing was happening. "Cheap cars," he added.

"Cheap," Bob said. "How cheap?"

"What did you pay for that Bronco?" Joe asked. He had to glance away to avoid repeating "Bronco" when Bob clearly mouthed the word.

"I don't know right off," Bob said, cautiously, coming to stand by him. "It was a trade-in. A Mormon bishop from Idaho brought that in, I took it on trade for a damn near bran' new Buick."

"Did you give him thirty-five hundred?" Joe asked.

Bob stood and sucked his teeth for several seconds, then said, "Whudjoo got in mine, Clarence?"

"What I had in mind was you could have given him thirty-five," Joe said, "and you'd still have made a thou."

Bob looked out on the lot, standing next to Joe. "Mmmm," was all he said. Then, "I don't want no rust. Midwest cars gotta lotta rust. They use salt on the roads back there. Folks 'round here won't buy rust."

"Southwest," Joe said. "Arizona, New Mexico. Like that."

"Good titles?" Bob said.

"Solid," Joe said. He turned to look at the man. "I'm talking, say, five hundred cars?"

Bob made a face. "No way I can do five hunderd cars."

Joe shrugged. "Oh well. I thought maybe you had more turnover."

"I tell you what, though," Bob said, earnest now, "I can make some calls. I could prolly fine a place for . . . mmm, three hunderd?"

"You talk," Joe said.

Bob went to the phone. Joe continued to look out the window. The more he looked the more he was convinced that nothing was going on. The colonel had his lookout, but it was the only lookout.

After a while, Bob hung up the phone and said, "I can place three hunderd. If," he emphasized heavily, "you can give good titles, Clarence."

Joe sighed and said, "Can I use the phone, Bob?"

"My pleasure." Bob stood up, shoving the phone toward Joe. Joe sat down behind the desk. He still had a commanding view of the street. "This may take a little while, Bob. I have to call long-distance. Is that a problem?"

"No prob," Bob said.

"Uh, could you leave me?" Joe asked.

Bob was easy. "Hey, it's your office, Clarence. But let me ast one thing. What are we talking, unit-wise? Say a nineny-three Olds, four-door?"

"Bob, how about a ninety-four de Ville? I got one in Pocatello, it has less than four thou on it, run you . . . oh, five bills?"

"A nineny-four de Ville for five grand? Clarence, you can call Spain, I don't care." He went out and closed the door.

Joe sat at the phone for a long moment, thinking. He watched the street closely. Then he got up and opened the door. Bob stood nearby, sipping a Diet Coke. "Honey," he called to the secretary, "what's the area code for Detroit?"

"Three one three," she said, consulting the phone book.

"Clarence," Bob called out, "I don't want no Midwest rusters."

"Rust-free," Joe said. He closed the door and sat down at the phone.

Humphrey answered on the second ring.

"I need three hundred used cars," Joe said.

"You gotta be kidding," Humphrey said.

"In Salt Lake City."

"They don't have any used cars in Salt Lake City?" Humphrey said.

"They don't have enough," Joe said.

"Who'da thought? So, Joe. You're going into the used-car business?"

"I'm thinking about it."

There was a long silence, then a long sigh. Humphrey said, "You know, Joe . . . " He stopped.

"Go ahead man."

"Joe, I got a problem with you. But . . . " Another long silence, another sigh.

"Fat Man, you and me never had any problems," Joe said. "You know that. I had problems with Carmine. I even had some small problems with Mitch. But you and me, we never had any problems."

"I know that, Joe. I know that." Humphrey sat, staring at Lake St. Clair, snow slithering and swirling across the ice. "You know, Joe," he said sadly, "I'm not sure I can deal with you. I mean, there's other people involved, a lot has—"

"Fat Man," Joe interrupted, "I can imagine what the problems are, but they're just problems, aren't they? Problems are what I solve. Everything is a problem. Right? I can talk to Mitch. I can talk to Franco, if I have to. They're just problems. Right?"

"Joe, some problems come with built-in answers," Humphrey said.

"No, no, Fat. Every problem comes with multiple choice these days. The stupid man takes the simple answer."

"Joe. Joe. It isn't multiple choice anymore. You went a little too far."

"Oh, fuck you, Fat. You're living in some kind of dream world. You can't do what you want, because Mitch or Franco isn't going to think you're a good guy? What are we talking about here? Kiss of death? I'm looking out here, Fat, and I'm looking at big lumpy Tongans. You know what Tongans are, Fat? They're big fat kids who got dragged over here from the islands, from the garden of Eden. They're lumbering around in Salt Lake City, trying to figure out where they are, what happened to the fucking palm trees, the surf. These crazy bastards are looking for me, Fat. They want to kill me. We had a little disagreement. But . . . " Joe gave it a good long pause. "They won't kill me, Fat." He almost whispered it. "Before these dickheads kill me, Fat, I'll kill you."

After that there was a good long silence. Then Humphrey said, "You shouldn't call me Fat. I'm not fat anymore. Joe, can you believe it? I lost a hundred pounds."

"Humphrey! You lost a hundred pounds? I love you, man. You're the coolest. I guess I won't kill you. So. Can you get me three hundred cars?"

"Three hundred cars. They're on the way. Where do I send them?"

"Salt Lake City."

"Where in Salt Lake? I gotta know. Also, what kind of price are we talking?"

Joe opened the door and beckoned Bob in. "Bob, I got the man on the line. We're talking three hundred cars. What price are we talking, total?"

"Total?" Bob said. "Geez, I don't know. I'd have to see what I'm gettin'. How many late models? I don't want no beaters, now, but I don't want too many new ones. It's hard to say, Clarence, till I saw 'em, or saw a manifest."

Joe held up his hand to stop him. He listened to the phone, then held up five fingers. "Per unit?" he said into the phone.

"Five?" Bob was incredulous. "What are we talking? Is this all Caddies? I don't want just Caddies, Clarence."

"Bob, the Caddie in Pokey is a one-shot deal, you and me. You aren't gettin' no ninety-four Caddies for five bills from this man. But he'll do all right by you. Wait a minute," he said as Bob started to reply. Joe shook his head to shut him up. "Humph," he said into the phone, "we need late models, but not too new. No rust. What do you say to three apiece?"

"Joe!" Humphrey was shocked. "I got to ship them? I've gotta have ten."

Joe laughed. "Be serious, Humph." He listened, looking at Bob. Then he shook his head and said to Bob, "He's talking five."

Bob did a quick calculation. "I don't think I can do it," he said. "I can't get that kind of capital."

"Can't do it," Joe said into the phone, watching Bob mime his words. "Can we get a deal? Say, half down, half later."

"Joe, Joe," Humphrey said, "what is this shit? What are we talking about? You serious about this? These fucking cars? I can get you some cars, but is this what you called about?"

"What do you mean?" Joe said.

"Don't we have something else to talk about?"

"Yeah, I guess we do, but what about my man, here?"

"Who is this guy?" Humphrey sounded annoyed. "Is he for real? What do you know about him? Hey, I tell you what, Joe. For you, I'll make him a deal. Fifty cars, three apiece. That's a lousy hundred and fifty grand. If he can get that kind of money together, we've got a deal. Payable on delivery, in cash. But it's on your scorecard, Joe. If he's some kind of cop, some kind of ripoff, then you pay. You got me?"

"Wait a sec," Joe said. He turned to Bob and explained the deal. But he could see that Bob, his imagination once fired, was now beginning to have second thoughts. He'd been caught up by Joe's enthusiasm, but now he realized that Joe must be into something much more seriously crooked than he wanted to deal with. Bob was smiling and moving his lips, but he couldn't stop shaking his head. One hundred and fifty thousand dollars was a lot of money to be giving a guy who had just walked in off the street, a guy wearing a wool Utes cap and a ski jacket. Bob's vision of a big splash was giving way to a strong sense of reality.

"I'll have to call you back," Joe said.

"Joe! Don't hang up," Humphrey said. "We can talk. Where are you staying, what's your number?"

"I'll call you back," Joe said, but he didn't hang up. "My man's got cold feet." He looked at Bob with something between reproach and contempt.

"Joe! How about this? Twenty cars . . . " There was a calculating pause, then: "Twenty cars at three apiece. I ship them. I got trucks sitting idle. That's only sixty bucks, but I'll knock it down to fifty. You got some kind of turkey there, I can tell. He'll like these cars, I guarantee it. Then, later . . . " Humphrey permitted himself a low chuckle. "We'll show this yokel how real money is made."

"Fifty bills too big for you?" Joe said to Bob. "Twenty primo cars. Deal?" To the phone he said, "He wants to talk. Here." Joe handed the phone to Bob. He went to stand by the window while they talked. It sounded like progress was being made.

Across the street he saw a large dark-complected man stroll by Helen's house. The man looked at the house, but he didn't pause. Joe smiled. A few minutes later, while Bob and Humphrey continued to seal their deal, another islander came strolling from the opposite direction. He didn't stop either, although he gave the house a good look. Joe thought this was very promising.

He stood and watched for another fifteen minutes while the deal was being discussed and hammered out. No more Tongans appeared, but then he saw something even more interesting. A late model Pontiac pulled up in front of the house and Helen Sedlacek got out. She stood for a second, looking around, then walked up to the front door of the house and fumbled with keys.

"Bob," Joe said, turning to interrupt the lovely friendship that was developing, "I've got to go out for a minute. Talk to you." And he was out the door. He drove his car down the street and turned left at the corner, then left again to enter the alley. He stopped well short of the house and got out cautiously. He reached the alley gate in time to see not only the colonel approaching the back door, but Edna hustling around to the front. Joe understood this situation. It was obviously what the colonel had been waiting for: once Helen was in the house Edna would go to the front, ring the bell, gain entry, and bust Helen; if she wasn't cooperative, the colonel would come in the back. No doubt he had a key, but he would probably prefer it if Edna could let him in. Then they would search. They would have a warrant, of course, but they would probably call for backup, probably get in some expert searchers. They'd make a big show of it, particularly when they found the money. All the better to intimidate Helen, get her to cooperate.

Joe waited behind the fence. It took about two minutes. Then Edna opened the back door and with Helen standing to one side, covered by Edna's revolver, the colonel was allowed in.

As soon as the door closed, Joe raced to the house next door. As he had hoped, the colonel had not locked the kitchen door behind him. He went in quickly and quietly and snuck up the stairs while the phone was still ringing. Someone upstairs picked up the phone and said, "Roger. You got it boss," and hung up.

The agent was about to make his call for backup when Joe entered the room. The agent recognized the authority of the Glock in Joe's hand with no difficulty. Nor did he complain when Joe relieved him of his .38 Chief's Special and handcuffs and shackled him to a water pipe in the bathroom. For that matter, Joe said hardly five words himself.

He walked next door quickly and knocked on the back door.

"That was fa—" the colonel started to say, but stopped when he saw Joe. He started back into the kitchen but Joe made an abrupt gesture with the Glock and he relaxed. "Company," the colonel sang out, and walked in front of Joe into the living room.

Joe kept a straight arm in the man's back and forced him to one side at arm's length so he could cover the startled Edna. Helen was sitting in an easy chair, a look of disgust on her face that instantly was transformed into surprise, then delight.

"Joe!" she cried. "What are you doing here?"

"Easy," Joe said. "That's enough names, enough visiting." But he couldn't resist adding, "Glad to see me, babe?"

"Am I ever!" She got up and came toward him.

"Whoa," Joe said. He gestured at her with the gun. "I said, 'Easy.' I meant it, babe. Sit down. No, on the couch. Edna, just lower that piece to the carpet, okay? Sit next to Helen. Colonel, let's have the .45. Now you sit, next to Edna."

When he had them all seated, side by side, Joe carefully picked up Edna's gun. "All right, now," he said, sitting in the other easy chair, across from them. "Here we all are. Colonel, I'd introduce you to the lady, but I guess you know who she is. No? Oh come on now, you must have had time to identify yourselves. What is it, DEA? IRS? Or are you still just the friendly next-door Aryan Brotherhood?"

"Joe," Helen said, "what's this all about? These people said they were cops, that I was under arrest—"

"They're *some* kind of cops," Joe said, "and what it's all about is they want my money."

Helen stood up. "My money," she said.

Joe smiled painfully at her. "My money, sweets. Don't be silly. It's my money. Let's don't argue in front of the neighbors. Here, let me get them settled and then we can discuss this, but we don't have a lot of time."

The colonel and Edna, like their associate next door, were passively cooperative. They were professionals. They knew better than to argue with a man with gun, especially when he seemed calm and unlikely to harm them. Joe was wary of Helen, however. He wasn't sure how far to trust her. But first he had to secure the two agents. Using their own cuffs, he shackled them to an exposed pipe in the kitchen. He stood in the doorway to the living room, where he could keep an eye on them, and he asked Helen where the money was.

"Joe, we've got to talk about this," she said.

"Sure. Later. Right now we've got to get the money and get the hell out of Dodge. These guys have had this place staked out for weeks. They're on to you. My guess is that they haven't found the money, or they deliberately didn't bother to look for it, because they knew you'd be back and they wanted to see who else was work-ing this pitch with you. But now we've got a few minutes. That's probably all we've got. So please, baby, let's take what we can take and get. You and I can discuss all the angles later. Okay?"

Helen drew herself up with a deep breath. She was on fire, he could tell, but she knew he was right. He grinned his best grin at her. She looked great. Great eyes, great spirit. "Come on, babe. Let's move it. Where's the dough?"

"Downstairs." She picked up an electronic remote device, one of two lying on top of the VCR on the shelf next to the television set. Joe followed her down the steps of the basement. At the bot-tom was a steel door with no visible lock or handle. Helen punched some buttons on the remote device and the door swung open. Inside were several identical heavy canvas shopping bags, all with Safeway logos. They were full of money.

Joe nodded, impressed. "You got it right, babe," he said. "That's very good. The Safeway thing is a good touch. Now let's get it out of here. We'll take your car."

They began to carry the bags out to the car, one of them waiting by the trunk till the other came out the door, just to avoid the awkwardness of having to lock the thing each time, so it took them longer than Joe wanted it to. But he spent his waiting time carefully scanning the street. Nothing was happening. No sirens, no cops, no unmarked government cars. He hoped against hope that there wouldn't be a sudden invasion of Tongans, especially, but so far they hadn't appeared. Still, it was making him edgy. The pro-cess was taking too long. Beyond that, he didn't trust Helen: he wasn't confident that she wouldn't decide that she could forgo a couple of bags of money, when it was his turn to go fetch, and just drive off and leave him. That moment was coming up. When Helen appeared with another two heavy bags however, he felt fairly confident that she would never be able to drive away without all the money. He dashed past her, into the house.

The colonel and Edna were still quietly languishing at their post, as it were. But when Joe came up with the last two bags, the colonel said, "I think I should tell you—"

Joe cut him short. "Save it. I don't need to hear my rights. Somebody'll be along to let you out before too long, I'm sure. In fact, I'm wondering why they haven't showed up al—" And now it was Joe's turn to stop talking.

Heather Bloom stood in the middle of the living room. She looked a bit rough. Grim, too. She had a gun in one hand and in the other, Helen. She had Helen by her hair and on her knees, looking as if she'd been dragged there. Helen was conscious, at least.

Joe threw the right-hand bag at Heather.

Heather was cool. She kicked Helen aside and ducked the other way as the bag flew past her and crashed against the wall, spilling packets of money. She held the revolver at arm's length, aimed at Joe's chest and pulled the trigger.

Joe ducked, needlessly. Nothing happened. Either the gun was not loaded or the round was defective. Joe flashed out one of the Glocks and straightened up.

"I hate this," he said. "Getting shot, I mean. Or not getting shot. It's almost as bad. Toss the gun onto the couch, sweetheart. Do it! I'll air your brains out."

Heather tossed the gun aside. Joe motioned Heather to step back to one side. Helen crawled to him and he helped her up. He handed her the Glock. "Watch her," he warned.

"What should we do?" Helen asked.

"We don't have to do anything. She can stay here. We're leaving." Joe picked up the thrown bag, squatting to reload the money that had fallen from it. "Just keep her covered and follow me."

Heather glared insanely at them, her mouth working. Joe could almost hear her hiss. They backed carefully away toward the door, Helen covering the slavering woman with the Glock held in both hands. They were almost out the door when Heather could no longer restrain herself. She sprang at them like a tiger, arms outstretched.

Helen pulled the trigger. This gun worked. It must have been on automatic fire, because half a clip stopped the woman in midair and the rest sent her tumbling to one side. Joe didn't look back. He trotted down the steps with Helen behind him.

"Hey!" he yelled. Two hulking Tongans were at the open trunk. Joe handed one bag of money to Helen and yanked out the other Glock with his free hand. He didn't fire when the Tongans hoisted their hands and backed away. "Get in the car, honey," he said to Helen. He tossed the other bags in the trunk and slammed it. Then scrambled in beside her. "Drive!"

At the end of the block he ordered her to turn right, then into the alley. He told her to pull up by his stolen vehicle.

"Joe, what the hell—" she said.

"Gotta get my toothbrush," Joe said. He hopped out, snatched his bag out of the car and jumped back in. He turned to her with a grin. "Also, my medicine. Okay, let's go."

They were at least six blocks away before Mulheisen arrived.

15

Out of Sight

Mulheisen was beginning to see this as a constant replay, a tape loop. Casting back over the years he could recall several occasions on which he had arrived at a scene with high anticipation, almost triumphant, only to find that Joe Service had been there before him and had gone, usually taking all the goodies and leaving a mess. A mess that Mulheisen had to clean up. Mulheisen was getting sick of it.

In this case he found the bullet-riddled body of Heather Bloom, tangled in a corner of the living room in a great lake of her own blood, and two enraged federal agents shackled to a waste pipe in the kitchen. If these two had been docile and quiet with Joe Service, they were not inclined to be so toward their rescuer. Fortunately, Mulheisen had come to the scene with two Salt Lake City detectives and two uniformed cops. The blue men were able to release the two agents and then dutifully headed next door to release the third.

The colonel and Edna were remarkably unforthcoming when Mulheisen and the two detectives began to question them about the events. What they wanted, it seemed, was for the cops to get out of their way so that they could pursue Joe Service and his accomplice. They seemed to think that they were in charge of the situation, rather than victims or people to be questioned. The colonel would only identify himself and Edna as federal agents and demand to use the phone.

Detective Sergeant Getulio of the Salt Lake City police was a quiet, dark man, an inch under six feet. He was a man after Mulheisen's mold. No nonsense, just a lot of sense. He listened to the colonel's raging for a while and tolerated the noncooperation for a while, then ordered the two taken to headquarters in separate cars and held separately in interrogation rooms until he and his partner, Sergeant Mabern, could talk to them. He exchanged a knowing glance with Mulheisen, who simply nodded: after the two had cooled down a bit and were given a chance to figure out their priorities, they would be able to provide some information. But for now they would be held incommunicado.

This situation changed abruptly when the third agent was brought in. His name was Adam Zazc, a Butte lad as it turned out, and he was much more cooperative. He readily identified himself as an agent of the Immigration and Naturalization Service. He said he was working on a joint task force with the Drug Enforcement Agency and the Internal Revenue Service. The leader of their group was the colonel, who was a fairly high-ranking DEA agent, Zazc explained, and Edna Swarthout, another DEA agent, was second in command. They had staked out the Helen Sedlacek house after they had been alerted by the FBI that she had been smurfing big money in the Salt Lake City area. This was all part of a project the colonel himself had helped initiate nationally, the idea being to hit the drug traffic where it would hurt the most, in the pocketbook. The plan was to seize the large amounts of money that smurfs typically possessed and hold it until its provenance could be verified—which, of course, could not be done. The drug lords did not protest—how could they?—and the money was simply confiscated and turned over to the U.S. Treasury.

Their policy was not to imprison the smurfs; they were charged with violating the Bank Secrecy Act's reporting requirements and released on bail, usually never to be seen again. Sometimes, Zazc said, they worked the "cormorant deal," a reference to a technique of certain Asian fishermen, who used cormorants with a tethered neck ring to catch fish. The smurf was turned and released to get more money and enlist more smurfs, who were then taken in by the agents. That was why they had not arrested Helen earlier.

About the dead woman, Heather, neither he nor the colonel and Edna had anything to say. They had never seen her before.

Mulheisen had seen her before, albeit in a picture taken from above the earth's atmosphere. She was a mess now, having been ripped apart by no less than ten 9mm bullets, which seemed to have been doctored to create maximum damage. He didn't know her, except as someone who had imposed on the innocent, naive Cate Yoder, in order to get close to Joe Service. And then on Grace Garland, in order to escape. That she had not simply disappeared but had continued in pursuit of Joe Service was interesting to Mulheisen. Obviously, she had still been on the contract and had intended to fulfill it. It meant that the mob had not forgiven Joe, that they had not given up on revenge for the death of Carmine. As for Heather, he supposed that now they might actually find out something about her in the files, but it was too late. He would probably never learn anything significant about her. He couldn't even tell what she had really looked like: the bullets had smashed her face and body horribly.

Sergeant Getulio said it was typical of certain gang slayings: the bullets were intended to send a big message to the other gangs. "Tongan Crips," was Getulio's terse assessment. Mulheisen had never heard of this gang. Getulio explained it as a type of the familiar Bloods and Crips gangs of South Central Los Angeles, which had spread to many other parts of the country. He aroused Mulheisen's interest by saying that, until recently, the late Clarence Woods, a.k.a. Cap'n Lite, had been associated with this gang. This man Mulheisen was familiar with.

By now the area was crawling with cops, ambulances, and forensic crews. Before long an officer reported the presence of a stolen car in the alley. It was impounded and searched carefully for prints and so forth. Shortly, a uniformed man returned with the information that Joe Service had been seen at a used-car dealership across the street. Mulheisen went over there. He talked to Bob Tyler and the secretary, both of whom gave interesting descriptions of Service wearing a wool cap and a ski jacket and sporting a beard.

"He came in here talkin' about sellin' a bunch of cars," Tyler said. "I humored him, at first, but then it began to sound like some kind of crooked deal. I didn't want no part of that, so I sent him packin'. Didn't I, honey?" he said to the secretary. She nodded with a disapproving grimace.

"He just ran out of here," she added. "And then, maybe twenty minutes later, or a half hour, we heard shooting and him and a small woman came running out of the house"—she pointed at Helen's house—"carrying tote bags and waving guns—just like Bonnie and Clyde. They jumped in a car—"

"A bran' new Pontiac Ciero, maroon," interrupted Tyler. "And whap, they were gone!"

Later, at the police station, a somewhat more cooperative Colonel Vernon Tucker, USAF (retired), and his assistant, Edna Swarthout, provided excellent descriptions of both Service and Sedlacek. Mulheisen's disappointment at not catching them at the scene was now complete, but he was not discouraged. They were in Salt Lake City, he was confident, and the nature of the place made of it a kind of trap. Unlike the large Eastern cities or the coastal cities of the West, Salt Lake did not have a lot of exit routes, at least not for a couple of outlaws on the run like Service and Sedlacek.

They were unlikely to be familiar with canyon roads, back roads, that sort of thing. But one could never be certain, especially about Service, a man who had in the past always shown a remarkable ability to elude identification, not to mention apprehension.

Service was a bold man, Mulheisen felt, even flamboyant. Helen had proven herself to be nearly as brazen in her actions: an apt pupil, evidently. It was crucial to close off the airport, the train and bus stations, and especially the interstate highway system and the trunk roads. This could be done relatively easily in this valley, but Mulheisen was interested to hear Colonel Tucker's account of how Service had eluded the task force's elaborate tracking system. The flaw there had been, of course, that a premise of the system had been that the target was unaware that he was being tracked. This would clearly not apply here. Joe Service would certainly be aware that, given the noisiness of his departure from the house on Main Street, the police would be watching very closely for any suspicious movements.

It was true, however, that a roadblock was not exactly what is depicted in popular movies. In this case it would amount to little more than some diversions or detours that had been erected in the areas around the Main Street house and already abandoned. They were not exactly legal. Nobody was actually stopped, but they were slowed down enough that the police were able to see who was inside. Police officers were also monitoring the entrances and exits of the freeway system, and an "ATL" or "attempt to locate" notice had gone to all units. Beyond that, three units had been designated as a search team, and they were currently responding to any sightings or suggestions.

No, an actual blockade wasn't possible. It interfered too much with traffic. And police personnel were hardly adequate to a long-term watch on the various train, bus, and airline terminals. If Service and Sedlacek could lie low for a few days, the chances were good that they could simply drive away. The question was, did they have a place to hide?

One of the first things to occur to Mulheisen was that Helen Sedlacek must have arrived in Salt Lake City on Humphrey DiEbola's private jet. A quick call to the airport revealed that this jet had departed Salt Lake City almost immediately after refueling on its arrival. The flight plan was filed for Detroit, with no scheduled stops enroute. Mulheisen was certain that the departure time did not allow for Service and Sedlacek to have been aboard. Nonetheless, he called Detroit and was able to get Jimmy Marshall to dispatch someone to monitor the plane's arrival.

By now the colonel had come fully on board the search operation and after a slight scuffle for control of the operation he submitted to the Salt Lake City officials who put Detective Sergeant Getulio in charge. Getulio was wholly in favor of Mulheisen being the de facto boss, an informal position that Mulheisen tended to favor. "That way," Mulheisen joked, "when it blows up in our faces, yours is the one that gets covered with pie." Getulio smiled wanly at this.

All the hotels and motels in the town and the outlying districts, including the posh ski resorts at Alta, Snowbird, and the like, were notified and given complete descriptions, including the automobile that Helen had rented. Unless they had managed to get clear somehow, or had access to a hidey-hole, it seemed unlikely that the two could evade capture. But the next twenty-four hours would probably tell the tale.

One of the nice things about money, Joe explained to Helen, was that it enhanced one's versatility. For instance, you didn't have to drive around town in a car that every cop in town was looking for. You could simply go to a used-car lot and buy, say, a fairly late-model, reliable Ford Explorer with four-wheel drive;

something in dark green, perhaps, that didn't begin to resemble a maroon Pontiac Ciero.

"Or," Helen pointed out with a little smile, "you could go to the long-term parking lot at the airport and pay the bill on your own yellow Toyota pickup."

Joe gazed at her with admiration. They were sitting in his "club," the Market Street Grill, having a celebratory cocktail. All thought of a blond Cateyo had long since fled from his mind. When it came to actually doing something with somebody, he thought, you couldn't beat someone who could actually do something, who didn't need to have the world explained to her.

"I bought that truck for you," he said, "but I never got a chance to give it to you."

"It got to me," Helen said. She didn't go into it. She wasn't sure how much he knew about what had happened after he'd been shot. The man who had shot Joe had driven the truck to the cabin and there Helen had shot him—dead. She didn't want to talk about it. "It's a great truck," she said, brightly.

"It's very handy, just now," Joe said.

There was an element of risk in driving to the airport, but not much, since they weren't going into the terminal. They had no problem recovering the truck. There were cops aplenty at the airport, besides the Airport Authority police, but they were busy on the concourses. The truck had an extended cab, which was big enough to take the money bags. They left the Pontiac in the long-term lot—which was a very good place for it, likely to encourage the police, when they found it, to think that they had escaped by air—and drove back into town.

En route, Joe explained that he had to take care of a few details. It was getting late, but he hoped that at least a couple of them could be achieved. They wouldn't be leaving town for a couple of nights, so some tasks could wait until tomorrow, but first they had to find a place to stay. This, Joe thought, could be dicey. There were a lot of motels in the Salt Lake area and the odds were fair that the police department hadn't contacted all of them, but then, you wouldn't know until you tried. Joe didn't like the odds. But it was still early. He decided to take care of a little business first.

Helen was the better dressed of them, wearing an elegant dark pantsuit that wasn't too mussed by the scuffle at the house. Joe got her to put her hair up under a fetching wool beret that would hide the all-too-memorable silver streak in her thick locks. She donned dark glasses and appeared at the funeral home that Joe had called earlier. She sadly explained the need to obtain the remains of her dearly departed uncle, Clarence Woods, from the Medical Examiner's office. The funeral home was happy to assist. They seemed a little surprised to see her, since they had talked to a man, but she explained that her brother was busy trying to secure a transit permit for the body. The funeral director pointed out that if the body were cremated they would have little difficulty in carrying a box of ashes. Why bother with the permit? This seemed an ideal solution to Helen and she agreed to it. The funeral home would pick up the body and perform the cremation, and they could come back for the ashes as early as tomorrow afternoon.

Joe wasn't so happy with her clever plans. He shook his head sadly. "Why can't you just do what I tell you? I need the coffin," he pointed out.

"Well, you should have let me in on it," Helen said. "Oh well, I can always call them back."

"No, no," Joe said. "We can get a coffin elsewhere." It proved simple enough. They just went to another funeral home and purchased a simple wooden coffin, suitable for transporting a body.

For a place to stay, Joe had decided on the apartment of Clarence Woods. He didn't know why he hadn't thought of it earlier. The only consideration he could imagine, from the viewpoint of security, was whether the police were watching the place in an attempt to get a lead on Woods's murderers. But Joe doubted it. He doubted that the police were working very hard, if at all, on this case. No doubt, like himself, they believed that Woods had been killed by his sometime associates, the Tongan gang, probably for some transgression or another. The police wouldn't really care. One dead crook is . . . well, one less crook. And, of course, the police were very busy just now with a more spectacular killing.

Along with this reasoning, Joe also felt confident that the Tongans would not be hanging around Woods's apartment, if only to avoid any contact with police. So it looked like a good, safe place. And so it proved. The building itself was modest, with only six apartments on its three floors. Joe had no idea who occupied the others, of course. Some of them might be Tongans, or allies, who would notify the gang if someone came around asking about Woods, but Joe doubted it. Anyway, it seemed worth a chance.

He and Helen waited in the little lobby after ringing the caretaker's bell. A pleasant woman of fifty or so, with graying hair in a bun and wearing an apron over a cotton print housedress, came to the door of the downstairs left apartment. She was clearly baking cookies, or cakes, from the odor wafting out the open door. She was Mrs. Homer Althing and she was so sorry to have heard about their uncle Clarence being killed that way. Salt Lake City never used to have things like that, she assured them, but nowadays. . . . She couldn't help but feel that it had something to do with the social work that Mr. Woods did—sorry, had done—among the islanders.

"They're good people," Mrs. Althing said over her shoulder as she trudged up the stairs to Mr. Woods's apartment, "but some of them get into trouble, the young ones, because they're out of their element, don't you see? I wonder if it's the right thing for the church to bring these poor people over here in the first place. And they're so *big*! Well, here we are."

She opened the door to the apartment and followed them in. "Well, this is it," she said, in a sad voice. "It's a nice little apartment and he was paid-up through the end of the month. He always paid right on time. He was a very good tenant, although some of the others complained about the islanders tromping up and down the stairs, sometimes late at night, but generally they didn't cause any problems. Mr. Woods was very strict with them." She chuckled, adding, "It was a sight to see him, so small and . . . " But then she realized that Joe and Helen were themselves not very large people, so she let the idea drop. "And you're from where, again?"

"Montana," Joe said. "We were related on our mother's side. Uncle Clarence was Ma's older brother. I'm afraid we didn't see much of Uncle Clarence, not since . . . when was it, Helen? When we were just . . . ?"

"I was ten, I think," Helen said. "I always thought he lived back east, somewhere. We didn't even know he was in Salt Lake, until the police notified us. I guess they tracked us through some letters or something he had from Ma."

"Oh, that's too bad," Mrs. Althing said, wringing her hands in pity. Then she frowned and put her finger on her lip. "Um, is it all right for you to be here . . . I mean, do the police know?"

"Oh sure," Joe assured her. "The probate court has to issue a release before we can remove any property, but I talked to them on the phone—their office is closed for the day, now, and we just drove into town—but they said it would be all right for us to come here and start packing his things up. Tomorrow morning my sister and I will get the release, but we won't remove anything until we do. I guess it'd be all right for us to stay here? Motels are so expens—"

"Oh, don't even think about it," Mrs. Althing declared. "They charge thirty, forty dollars a night! You go right ahead and do what you have to do. I've got stuff in the oven, so I can't sit around. Uh, I suppose you would get the deposit?"

"Why don't we just forget the deposit," Helen said. "We'll try not to make a mess but I suppose you would have to clean up after us anyway, so . . . "

"Unh-hunh," Mrs. Althing agreed, obviously pleased, "well, if you say so. Do you have a key?"

"No, we weren't able to claim his effects, yet," Joe said.

"Well, you stop by the apartment and I'll give you the spare, for tonight." And she hurried off.

Joe shrugged, smiling at Helen. "I guess it's all right," he said.

Helen looked around the stuffy little place and sniffed. "How did you know about this place?"

"I had some talks with Clarence, like I said," Joe replied. "I'll bring up the bags and then we've got to move on to Act Two."

After the ease of obtaining the body, it was annoying to have to deal with the Amtrak people. Helen convinced them, however, that Mr. Woods, having booked a room on the Zephyr, should be allowed to use that room although he was deceased. Room H was certainly large enough to contain a coffin, and it was conveniently located in the last sleeping car, on the bottom level. The coffin could be brought aboard with minimum fanfare and carried directly to the rear. It wouldn't disturb anyone. Woods's remains would be accompanied by her, his niece. She was happy to pay an additional fare for herself. Amtrak found it very irregular, but after considerable hassle and talking to various officials, it was agreed that the coffin could be carried in room H.

After that, Joe and Helen picked up a large pepperoni pizza and a six-pack of beer and returned to Clarence's apartment. The pizza was good. They fell upon it ravenously, laughing, between mouthfuls and while guzzling beer, at how they had pulled off their nephew-and-niece act. And suddenly, in the very midst of it, they caught each other's eyes and they leaped at each other. They tore at their clothes and only barely made it to the bed.

It was frenzied sex. Furious and passionate, their mouths bruising and bruised, their hands leaving red marks on the other's body, driving against and into each other. There was no hesitation, no doubts, no courting or care. They tore at each other with, as the poet said, rough strife.

Afterward, thrilled but sated, they lay back naked, their arms under the other's neck and stared into the dark corners of the ceiling, wondering how they could have let the other out of their sight.

"You know," Joe said, "there's just one more thing I ought to take care of." And then he told Helen about the night he had gone to the weird bar, his first night in Salt Lake City. "I can't believe, somehow, that it was all a dream," he said. "I know the two muggers weren't a dream, I'm sure of it. But what about the rest? Was it just because I had drunk some fortified wine and was unused to it? Or did I really see that weird guy, the piano player? I tell you, honey." He sat up, leaning on an elbow and looking into her face, lit by a panel of light from the other room. "He was like a bat, a freak."

"A bat out of hell," Helen said, and they laughed together.

"Let's go back down there and check it out," he said.

"No," Helen said, reaching up and drawing him down to her lean, lithe body, "let's fuck, instead."

So they did. More slowly now, but just as pleasurably. But again, when they were finished, Joe wanted to go out. This time, Helen assented.

It wasn't hard to find the place. But when they entered, an entirely different scene presented itself. Not only were there no little tables with shadowy people sitting around them sipping from paper-wrapped bottles, but there was no bar at all. Instead, perhaps two dozen people sat on folding chairs arranged in rows, facing toward the back of the room. A very large, dusky woman in a robe, clearly an islander of some sort, had just finished addressing the people, few of whom turned to see who had just entered. The large woman now took up a book, a hymnal apparently, and turned toward a skinny black man perched on a screw-type stool at an upright piano. Joe and Helen slipped into a couple of chairs at the back as this man, this piano player, spread his huge, spidery fingers and with a low, sidelong look under his right shoulder, hit a plangent blues chord.

The chord lingered on the air for a moment, then the man— it was the same tree-frog man that Joe remembered—began to slap his right foot while he blocked in several chords and nodded to the large woman. The audience, a mixed group of black people, Indians, and islanders, began to sing in a marvelous, almost shouting chorus: "Ahmmmm uh-gonna . . . *git* on mah *feets*, aftah while/ Annnn' it *won't* be looonnng!"

It was a great, loping, stomping beat and the people were enjoying it considerably, interspersing the words with whoops and yelps of rhythmical delight. The piano man was whooping too. He would cast back his head and scream, even. He wore black glasses and his spiral cone of hair was slicked with—who knows?—bear grease? His lips were wide and grimacing, usually in glee, but sometimes in agony. His fingers sped up and down the keyboard, ringing marvelous arpeggios around the thunderous blues chords.

"Ooo-yes *Jee*-ziss, you *been*/My-eye *keep*er so *loooong!*" the people roared. The player played, leaping to his feet, knocking over the stool, while the large woman waved her hands to needlessly exhort the singing crowd.

Joe got up and took Helen by the hand. "It's not him," he said and started for the door.

The door opened and two Tongans came through. They were followed by the biggest Tongan of them all. He was so huge he had to duck to get in the door and then he fully occupied the frame. The music stopped.

"You must be Joe," the big man said, extending a large forefinger.

Joe extended a large Glock and shot the man five times. The man absorbed the 9mm slugs with a succession of jolts, then fell like a tree, crashing face first onto the floor. The floor shook and dust flew up. Joe, still holding Helen's hand, waved the others aside with a gesture of his Glock and stepped on the big man's back as they went out. And then they ran.

16

Pert' Near but
Not Plumb

Mulheisen was not unhappy about the shooting at the south side social club. From what he could learn, the deceased was not a nice man. That didn't mean, of course, that it was all right for Joe Service and Helen Sedlacek to shoot him, but it did make a difference; it always does, despite one's moral qualms. Few people had bemoaned the murder of Carmine Busoni, although Mulheisen had now spent the better part of a year in hot pursuit of his slayers. This fresh shooting enabled the Salt Lake City police to keep the pressure on, and that was good. Normally, even a few hours of roadblock seemed interminable to the citizenry, even if the roadblock was little more than a slowdown, a kind of chicane at crucial points so that the police could look into slowly passing cars. Occasionally a car might be signaled out of the line of traffic and searched, but generally the traffic was kept moving. Still, the citizens didn't like it if it was kept up for more than a few hours. (One inevitable side benefit of the roadblocks was that several criminals were apprehended by the way, as it were.)

Obviously, Mulheisen thought, the outlaws (the *Salt Lake Tribune* was calling them Bonnie and Clyde) had a hidey-hole. But Mulheisen felt that there was a good chance that they would be caught. They were highly recognizable: two smallish, handsome young people whose pictures had been splashed all over the paper and television. The police had fielded several reports, none of them verifiable sightings, but obviously the public was paying attention. As the day wore on, perhaps more people would see the pictures and realize that they had seen the pair.

In the meantime, Mulheisen felt encouraged and unperturbed. He left the police department and went for a walk. He started to stroll through the grounds of the Mormon Temple, with its Gothic spires and the golden angel trumpeting from the highest one, but there was some kind of outdoor singing program going on there. He avoided the crowds and walked up the hill to the state capitol building. It was another lovely, if bracing, mountain day. The legislature wasn't in session, but the building was open and he wandered about the huge reception area, gazing with interest at the historical paintings of the Mormon pioneers. But soon he felt the need for a cigar and he set off back down the hill, pleasurably puffing on an H. Upmann petit corona.

He considered as he walked just how much he knew about Joe Service and Helen Sedlacek. He could think of at least four different cases in which Joe Service might have played a role, but he couldn't be sure. He thought that the earliest might have involved an insurance scam in which Service had managed to get away with quite a bit of money in the form of bearer bonds. Another case, he believed, was one in which Service had meddled with a gun-running scheme. What was interesting in that case, he recalled, was that an unidentified hit man had been killed by a police officer— Jimmy Marshall's fellow patrolman, Leonard Stanos—before he could make a hit. Mulheisen was fairly certain that Service had somehow managed to claim the body of the hit man (presumably a colleague). It had seemed a prankish thing, an odd example of fraternal feeling.

This thought brought Mulheisen to a dead halt, standing on the sunny sidewalk on the hillside, the city lying at his feet. For the past two or three days he had carried in the back of his mind the memory of one Clarence Woods, lately murdered in this city and sometime associate of Big Sid Sedlacek. This connection with Joe and Helen was tenuous, unclear, but it was one that he had not pursued. He hurried back to the police department and sought out Sergeant Getulio. The sergeant listened with interest, then made a phone call.

"The body was claimed by a niece," Getulio told Mulheisen. "It was released to the Goodrich and Padgett funeral home this morning."

At the funeral home they learned the bad news. Mr. Woods's body had been cremated that morning and the ashes turned over to the deceased's niece less than an hour earlier. The director identified Mulheisen's photo of Helen as the niece. She had actually shown her Michigan driver's license.

Driving back, Getulio said, "This guy sounds like some kind of sentimental dude."

"Sentimental?" Mulheisen mused. "I never thought of Joe Service as sentimental, but you may be right. Maybe he just has a peculiar sense of loyalty to the profession."

"Honor among hit men—or is it hit persons, in this case? Hit folk?" Getulio laughed. "Saints preserve us!" He nodded in the general direction of the temple, then added: "I don't think so, Mul. I've never seen it. If there was honor among these swine, Cap'n Lite wouldn't be dead."

"Still," Mulheisen pointed out, "they did avenge the little chiseler."

"Tenfold," Getulio conceded, "if we're counting pound for pound. Well, they're welcome to the ashes."

At the station, Mulheisen called Marshall. He explained everything that had happened and said, "Probably our only real chance now is with DiEbola. I don't think we've got enough to connect him to any crimes here, but if you or somebody at Rackets and Conspiracy can make a connection with this Heather Bloom, we might be able to stick something on his sorry carcass."

Marshall agreed to check it out, but he didn't seem very sanguine. "Are you coming back now?" he asked.

Mulheisen sighed. "I think I'll hang out for another day, anyway. There's a pretty good chance somebody will spot these two, but if nothing happens by tomorrow I'll head on back. There's no hurry, is there?"

"No," Marshall blandly agreed, "no hurry at all."

"I didn't think so. Maybe I'll take the train. I haven't ridden the train in a long time, and I'm sick of airports and airplanes."

"Incidentally," Marshall said, "Humphrey's plane did not return to Detroit. They filed an amended flight plan after leaving Salt Lake and landed in Denver."

This information was puzzling. Mulheisen could make nothing of it. Presumably there was just some additional corporate business in Denver that required the plane. But he advised Marshall to keep up surveillance on Humphrey and the Detroit City Airport.

Joe Service seemed disturbed. He sat in the pickup and stared at the plastic box that contained the ashes of Cap'n Lite. It was not much larger than a cigar box.

"I know he was a small man," he muttered, "but surely . . ."

"Where to?" Helen said, impatiently. She had started the engine but hadn't backed out of the parking place behind Cap'n Lite's apartment.

Joe looked at the plastic box on his lap. "If they incinerated the coffin, too . . ." He let the notion drop.

The coffin they had purchased was small and simple, made of polished pine with simple brass handles. It wasn't the child-size, but more like a youth size. They carried it in the back of the pickup, covered with a tonneau. In a downtown parking structure that housed a large mall, they found a remote corner; there they ripped out the thin padding of the coffin and Joe drilled several holes in the plywood bottom with a battery-driven drill he'd purchased. Next they stacked all the money inside and Joe crawled in. There was plenty of room. He lay in the box for a long minute with the lid down. It was not the greatest feeling, but he decided that it didn't really bother him. There seemed to be plenty of air, and he'd never been claustrophobic.

When he clambered out he stood there in the gloomy, echoing, cold space and felt nothing but warmth when he looked at Helen. She was bright-eyed, sharp, and eager. How could he ever have doubted her? How could she have ever doubted him? He took her by the arms and looked into those obsidian eyes. They kissed, a long, good, deep kiss. When they broke apart, Joe craned around the cavernous place and said, half-joking, "I wonder if we could do it here?"

Helen laughed. "In the coffin?"

"Not enough room. Alas. Anyway, here comes a bunch of Mormons. Let's cover this up." Joe threw the tonneau back over the rig. "You drive," he said. When they were a few blocks south of town, headed for the apartment, he said, "You know, I don't think we should go back there. The lady is dumb, but she can't be that dumb. Plus, some smart cop is bound to put two and two together . . . they'll connect that giant I took down with Cap'n Lite. They'll send someone to look at the apartment again."

"So what should we do?"

"Just keep driving, I'll think of something." After a few more blocks Joe said, "We've got our bags. It's at least twelve hours before that train comes. It would really make sense for us to split up until just before it gets here. They'll be looking for us as a pair."

"Yeah, I guess you're right. Where do you want me to drop you?" Helen said.

"I thought maybe I'd drop you," Joe said. "You could go to a beauty parlor, go shopping, go to a movie."

"And what would you do? Go to a movie?"

He glanced at her out of the corner of his eye, then glanced away as she caught his look. It was hopeless. She wasn't going to let him drive away with a truck full of money and he wasn't going to let her, either.

"We could both go—" they said simultaneously, then broke into laughter. In the end they went shopping. It was Joe's theory that once on the train they wouldn't want to use the dining car. It would be at least thirty-six hours to Chicago, if the passage through the Colorado Rockies wasn't delayed by snow, as it often was at this season. The route traversed some of the most dramatic ski slopes in the world—Aspen, Breckenridge, Vail. It would be wonderful to simply lay up in their compartment and eat and drink and make love, while the train climbed up through the snow country.

They found a large supermarket where they could buy plenty of fruit, some good bread, a few interesting cheeses. They bought sparkling cider, champagne, and wine. It was quite a bit of stuff. Helen bought some magazines and a road atlas, on the theory that they couldn't make love constantly and because she liked to know the country she was traveling through. They also bought a couple of heavy-duty duffel bags at an Army-Navy surplus store. Here Joe found a handy little radio scanner. He had encountered a fellow on this train before who had one; it was interesting because you could monitor the conversation of the train men and so you knew if you were running late or if there was something wrong with the heating in car 35, and so on. It was always good to know what was happening.

All of this took up time, and by attending movies downtown they found themselves only a few hours away from train time. But these were now the dangerous hours, the countdown hours. It was not a time to be sitting around a waiting room where cops came and went, nor a time to be cruising the quiet streets. There was no reason to believe that the police knew their vehicle, but a young man and a young woman driving around were bound to catch the eyes of the police. It was, in fact, a very good time to retire to the "club." The bar was crowded, there were plenty of couples about. It was the proper place to be.

They sat at the bar and Helen reminisced. "Just think, Joe: nine months ago I had my own consulting business; I had a nice apartment in Bloomfield Hills; I had a nifty little Miata, guys used to besiege me! I went out to dinner every night. Fancy places. Then I met you. Since then I've been attacked, been in jail, been on the run . . . *still* on the run. What a hot date you are!"

Joe didn't respond to this at first. He was feeling fairly tired. But at last he said, "I'm sorry you missed Christmas at your Ma's."

"I haven't missed it yet," she said. She looked pensive, however. "When do we get back?" she asked.

Joe calculated, then said, "We should get into Chicago about 4:15 in the afternoon, a day later. After that, I don't know. It depends on how we go on from there. We'll pack the money in the duffel bags and leave the box on the train. I'll have to figure out some way of getting off, maybe before we actually get into Chicago. Don't worry about it. I'll figure something out."

At two-thirty in the morning they had to leave the club. They drove around for a little while, but at last they went to the Amtrak station. This was the moment of crisis, and it didn't start out well. For one thing, there was no one to unload the coffin. The clerk at the station was aghast. He'd had no idea that a coffin would be allowed on the Zephyr. No one had informed him. He was a young black man named Daahoud. He gazed at Helen, dressed in the dark pantsuit. She looked more or less in mourning. She insisted that the coffin be put inside.

Daahoud didn't get it. The body was already cold, he reasoned to himself. Why couldn't it be left out on the big-wheeled baggage cart, across the tracks from the station? It could be more or less disguised by stacking other luggage around it and it wouldn't disturb the other passengers. Not that there were many passengers getting on here. The train was fully booked, at least through Glenwood Springs, where many of the California passengers would get off for the Aspen and Snowmass ski resorts. But it wasn't something he felt he could suggest to the young lady. If she wanted her uncle's coffin inside—he had by now found the authorization—then he supposed it could be done. Perhaps it was just as well. He could keep the coffin in the baggage room, out of sight.

Helen was tense. She went into the waiting room and sat down with a copy of *Vanity Fair*. She could not concentrate on its glitzy stories and pictures. A cop or two came in, wandered through, and left. They didn't seem to remark her, but she had no way of knowing if they did. Perhaps they had recognized her from the start and were only waiting for Joe to appear. She had her hair pushed up into a colorful woolen tam-o-shanter and she wore plain-lensed black-framed glasses. She didn't think it was much of a disguise, but it was all she could do.

She realized suddenly that this was the first time she'd been alone since encountering Joe. She decided to call Humphrey. He was a bit groggy when he finally answered. It was after six A.M. in Detroit. She explained about the train.

"Is this his idea, coming back here?" Humphrey asked.

"He hasn't actually said we're going to Detroit," she pointed out. "But it looks definite for Chicago, anyway. I don't know what he has in mind. We haven't discussed it."

"As soon as you know, call me," Humphrey said.

"It may not be that easy," Helen said. She was beginning to regret calling. Why had she called? She hadn't considered it fully. She had told him she would call, and so she had called. But now that she thought about it, she wondered if it was a good idea. Joe certainly wouldn't like it.

"Sure, sure, I understand," Humphrey soothed her. "It's all right. Joe's a cool guy. He'll do the right thing. Did he tell you he talked to me yesterday? No? He had some cockamamie scheme about dealing cars in Salt Lake. I don't know if it'll go down or not. But it was good talking to him. I think we'll work things out. Don't worry about a thing. You've done a good job, honey. I appreciate it. Everything'll work out. Just stay with Joe and we'll get it all settled. But, if you get a chance, give me a call. Okay?"

Naturally, the train was late. Fifteen minutes ticked by. She overheard another passenger inquire of Daahoud and learned that the train was entering the yard now but had been stopped while a scheduled freight departed. At last, at agonizingly last, the great silver and blue and red engines came rumbling past the doors of the station and drew to a surprisingly soft, quiet halt. It was early in the morning and very cold.

Quite a few passengers got off, looking very groggy, very hungover. Evidently, many of them had been up all night partying. They were skiers, headed for Alta and Snowbird. The resort vans were there to pick up them and their voluminous ski equipment. But just as many passengers with just as much equipment were traveling on to the Colorado resorts. Helen waited until she saw the baggage carts wheeled out, including the one carrying Joe's coffin, before she got on. She entered through the large door in the middle of the last car, pushing all her bags and Joe's on a cart. This car was located quite a ways from the station, practically out of the floodlit boarding area. Most of the new passengers were not traveling in the sleeping cars. A young black woman who seemed a little sleepy but friendly identified herself as Jessica Williams and helped Helen carry the bags into the large room at the rear of the car. It stretched completely across the car and had two beds, a bathroom with a shower, plus a table built against the left-hand window. Ms. Williams was clearly shocked that the room would be shared by a coffin.

Helen sat in the room, staring out the window, waiting. The train was all but silent, except for muffled bumps and thumps from somewhere forward, and a few quiet voices. After a very long time— she thought the train must surely be ready to depart—the baggage cart was wheeled into view and several other car men were pressed into service to pick up the coffin by its handles and quickly carry it aboard. It was not a large coffin, fortunately, and very little manhandling was required to turn it and bring it directly back into room H. The men set it down softly in the middle of the room.

They looked at Helen with something like awe. She smiled as sweetly as she could muster and gave them each five dollars. At last the door was closed. She didn't dare touch the coffin, just sat and stared at it. The train continued to sit in the station. It was unbearable! Was this the moment when the police would come, she wondered. Why didn't the train leave? Was Joe all right in the coffin? She knelt next to it and whispered, "Joe?" There was no response. Had he suffocated? Was he frozen? The cart had sat in near-zero cold on the concrete walkway for a long time. She didn't dare start unscrewing the lock-down bolts.

At last, something seemed to be happening. The lights flickered and then came a whining noise of something starting up, and the heat came back on. All of a sudden there was a slight jolt and the train began to move past the terminal and out of the light. She breathed a sigh of relief. But then, a few minutes later, the train inexplicably halted again and stood for interminable minutes. Now what? Had they discovered her presence? Were they coming for her and Joe? Just when she was about to freak out, the train hitched forward again, and now it began to move smoothly and more rapidly. Within minutes it had passed beyond the confines of the railyard and was moving swiftly along the edge of the city.

At last they were away. Ms. Williams came by to see if everything was okay and to tell her that they were beginning to climb up into the mountains. "Breakfast from seven until nine," she said. "You want me to call you?" Helen didn't, but she appreciated the offer of coffee from the pots sitting in the vestibule.

Finally it was quite dark and the train began to labor up into the hills. She locked the door and began to undo the cold butterfly nuts that kept the coffin closed. When she had freed them all she took a deep breath and lifted the lid. Joe Service popped up with a grin, brandishing a Glock in each hand. "Bang! Bang! You're dead!" he cried.

"Joe!" Helen gasped, starting back. But then her fear gave way to anger and she leapt at him, pummeling him with her fists.

"Hey, hey," he laughed, tossing the guns aside and catching her wrists. "That hurts! You're too strong. Quit!" He tussled with her and dragged her into the coffin, already trying to pull her trousers down. "Get your ass in here. You've never made love on eight million bucks. It's great!"

17

Qualities Unstrained

Mulheisen had missed the train. Or, to be exact, he had been unable to book a room, or even a seat. It didn't bother him. It had just been an idea. He had spent the evening discussing the situation with Sergeant Getulio. The Airport Authority police had located Helen's rental car in the long-term parking lot. None of the people operating the parking booths at the exit remembered her leaving, so it was assumed that somehow she, and probably Joe Service, had managed to get on a plane, or perhaps different planes. Mulheisen and others had perused the passenger lists, but nothing caught their eyes. Pictures shown at departure gates had gotten little or no response. Possibly the pair had split up—that would have been wise—and possibly they had found means to disguise themselves: a wig for her, a shave for him . . . even minor changes can be highly effective.

Getulio was apologetic. Like Mulheisen, he'd had high hopes that the pair would be intercepted. Now he conceded that they had escaped. Mulheisen wasn't too depressed. He was used to having his hopes dashed, especially when it came to Joe Service. But the scent of the trail was still in his nostrils.

"Where do you think they're headed?" Getulio asked.

Mulheisen had given a lot of thought to this. He was fairly certain, now, that Service and Helen had reunited and that they had all the money they needed. They could go anywhere. Mexico, South America . . . anywhere in the world. But he doubted it. He felt that he had a fair notion of Joe Service's style. It wasn't like Service to just run away and lie in the sun. He was too active a man, and Helen was much like him. Of course, they could go away for a while, but soon enough they would be back, eager to join the fray. Something, however, told him that they wouldn't even take a vacation. He felt that Joe would be concerned about Humphrey, about having been made a target. He had a feeling that Joe would want to resolve this, one way or another.

One thing he felt confident about: Joe would not be going back to Montana. He wondered if sweet little Cate Yoder would ever hear from her demon lover again. Not if she was lucky, he thought.

He was also interested in Helen's relationship with Humphrey. It was clear now that she was back in the fold, to some extent, at least. Humphrey had provided a plane for her to come to Salt Lake City. He realized then what he had not thought through before: Helen had been sent by Humphrey to find Joe. She had found him. And now a plane was waiting in Denver . . .

"This guy Service," Getulio said. He paused.

"Hmmm? What about him?"

"You're a little obsessed, aren't you?"

Mulheisen considered that for a moment, then said, "I don't think so. He's gotten in my way. He's a killer. I intend to take him. But I'm not obsessed with him. I figure . . . sooner or later, Joe will go down. Maybe I'll be the one to take him. I hope so."

"Nothing personal?" Getulio said.

"Nothing personal," Mulheisen assured him. "I don't think that Service ever meant *me* any harm. I doubt if he's ever even given me a thought—at least, other than as a cop who's been on a couple of cases involving him."

"That's good," Getulio said. "It never pays to get personal with these cases, you think?"

Mulheisen agreed. He pointed out to Getulio that, when you came right down to it, Joe Service had never done any real harm to his investigations, just muddled them up a bit. "He's killed people, but I was thinking about it today when I went for a walk . . . they were never exactly *innocent* people, if you see what I mean. In fact, he's practically a 'soldier of virtue,' as Guarini would say."

"Guarini? Who's he? A Detroit button man?"

Mulheisen smiled. "A poet. Died a long time ago. No, I guess you could say that, overall, Joe has done the law a few favors. Not the kind of favors you exactly want, of course. He didn't intend to help. And now that I think of it, he's in a kind of position where he could really do us a lot of good. He could bust the mob wide open, if we could get him to cooperate."

"Cut him a deal, you mean? Would you like that?" Getulio looked skeptical. "I never was too crazy about this immunity crap. Too many villains living on the taxpayer's buck."

"Yeah," Mulheisen conceded. "Still . . . if you think about it, Joe is in a closing vise-clamp. The mob on one side, the law on the other. Maybe he likes it that way, I don't know. One thing, though: he would never survive prison. He'd be dead meat there. Maybe . . . if I had a chance to talk to him . . . he'd see that cooperation was his only real option."

Getulio didn't seem convinced. "Mr. Service is free as a bird, far as I can tell. He's on the run, but he sure as hell ain't in custody. Aaah. I gotta get out of here," he said, standing up and yawning. It was late. "You got a place to stay, Mul?"

Mulheisen looked at him. Getulio was a man with a family. He could see that. If Getulio was about to invite him to stay with him it would surely be a case of invading the quiet and safety of the family home. Getulio was a good man, a generous man, but his wife wouldn't like it. Mulheisen could count on that. He decided to play the footloose bachelor role.

"I kind of thought I'd go out, catch a little of the, you know, night life," Mulheisen said.

"In Salt Lake?" Getulio laughed. "In the week between Christmas and New Year's?"

"Well . . . " Mulheisen shrugged. "Who knows, I might get lucky. I could use a drink, anyway. I'll get a room in a hotel. Any suggestions?"

Getulio suggested the Little America. It was not far. He gave Mulheisen a lift, but he declined to come in for a drink. Mulheisen checked in, had a couple of shots of whiskey in the bar, and went up to the room. Before he took a shower he called the airport and booked an early flight to Denver. Ten minutes later he was asleep.

In the morning it was still dark when he called Marshall. There had been no activity. All was quiet at DiEbola's. The plane had not returned to Detroit. Mulheisen hung up and called Denver Flight Service. The DiEbola jet was at that very moment taxiing to depart. Destination: Aspen.

There was an early flight to Aspen on a commuter line. Mulheisen booked on that and barely made it to the airport in time. Before boarding he snatched an egg-and-sausage muffin and a cup of coffee at a hurry-up shop in the air terminal. It was a very interesting flight, arcing up over the Wasatch and soon droning over some of the most craggy mountains in the world. Mulheisen was pleased. He had seen these mountains from 35,000 feet before, but they were much more interesting from lower altitudes. Some of them to the south of Aspen towered to 14,000 feet. By midmorning the pilot had cranked them into the Aspen airport.

It was a pretty busy little airport, too. Thronged with skiers. The plane Mulheisen had flown in on had been full of them, all babbling away about equipment and other places they had skied. It was not attractive to Mulheisen. "Sports-fops," he'd heard them called by a Michigan writer, and it seemed apt. His own mother, now nearly eighty years old, had more in common with these fanatical sports-fops than he did. She, too, was keen on equipment and clothing, on being "fit." Like them, she evinced a kind of moral virtue that had more to do with being outdoors and healthy than with religion, the religion he knew about, anyway. He had heard such people described as the new ascetics, and he saw that there was a kind of asexual aspect to their garb and their fervor; or at least, it was not very sensual in the old voluptuous manner. But he had little time to consider it.

He went directly to the flight service desk and found that the DiEbola plane was here but evidently ready for immediate departure. The pilots had filed for Detroit but had changed the time, now. One of the guards at the airport, part of the county sheriff's force, said that one man had gotten off, besides the pilots. He had not reboarded. He was described as average height, about forty, with a mustache. This, apparently, was the sole reason for the plane coming to Aspen, to leave this man. But he was not dressed for a holiday. He wore a sport coat, no tie, and an overcoat. He carried a single suitcase.

There was a cab service at the airport, but there was no cab available. Mulheisen called the service's phone number in the town, a few miles away. They said they would send out a cab. It would take a half hour. Cabs were not a big item at the airport; the various resorts had plenty of free shuttles constantly picking up their patrons. The cab at the airport, they told him, had taken a passenger into Glenwood Springs, which was some forty miles away.

When a cab did materialize, almost an hour later, Mulheisen asked the driver if he had taken the previous fare to Glenwood Springs. He hadn't, and he was unable to contact that driver. "He'd have to call base," the driver said. "In these mountains, the radios don't always work too good. But he oughta be back in town before long."

Mulheisen was torn. What was this man doing here? He had no way of knowing if it had anything at all to do with Service and Sedlacek. But it seemed likely. Was he meeting them, intending to bring them here to fly out on DiEbola's jet? That seemed a distinct possibility. He decided it would be foolish to leave the airport as long as the jet was standing by. He asked the cab driver to contact his base and ask them to send the driver who had carried the other fare to meet him at the airport.

After that he went for a little walk, not wanting to stray too far from the terminal. The air was clear and it was brilliantly sunny. Plenty of snow for the skiers and more was falling up on the slopes, where squalls blew off the achingly high peaks. He smoked a cigar, grateful for the opportunity. It was not often one found a place to smoke a cigar these days, and even here, in this unimaginably immense outdoors, any number of passersby glared at him with disapproval.

He took the opportunity to call Jimmy Marshall. Nothing new on that end, but Jimmy was surprised to hear he was in Aspen. He knew nothing about the passenger on DiEbola's jet. "They don't have to list passengers, Mul," he pointed out, "but the description kind of reminds me of the Fat Man's bodyguard. What's his name, Itchy they call him. About fifty, dark, has a mustache. Ezio Pinza— no, forget that. That was the singer, the opera singer. Ezio something, I can't remember. I'll ask around. He's a shooter, Mul."

By then the cabbie was back from Glenwood. He had taken the fare downtown, dropped him off in the middle of town. The description fit. "But, you know what?" the cabbie said. "I went by the Amtrak—the westbound was due in, but it turned out to be late, so I came back. Anyway, I saw the guy there. At the Amtrak counter. If he was gonna catch the train, how come he didn't have me drop him off? Would of saved a couple of blocks walking with that heavy suitcase." He shrugged.

"Take me there," Mulheisen said. In the cab as they raced down the valley, he learned that the eastbound train was due in a couple of hours. Mulheisen sat back. He felt a surge of confidence.

They had already made love twice, and fantastic sex it was, too. First in the coffin, laughing as the train pulled up the slopes of the Wasatch. Later in various postures, on the beds, off the beds, kneeling, woman on top, man on top, man behind, sixty-nine . . . they did it all. No holes barred, in fact. Later they had repacked the money in equal amounts in the two duffel bags, had drunk sparkling cider, champagne, gobbled cheese, tore at loaves of bread. . . . Joe had cleaned and oiled the two .38 Smith & Wesson revolvers. The Glocks were useless, now, as they had almost no ammunition for them. And when the train pulled out of Helper and began to rock and sway across the high plains toward Colorado, they made love again, a little more quietly but every bit as passionately, and finally they fell deeply asleep, rocking in each other's arms to the movement of the train. They missed a lot of great scenery.

Mulheisen was tempted to go to the hot springs. It was enormous, however, and that decided him against it. He had only recently discovered the delights of hot springs, but that was in Montana, and those springs were small and private. The idea of renting a bathing suit and jumping into a block-long pool with a thousand tourists, probably most of them pissing kids, didn't appeal. At any rate, the Zephyr was due into Glenwood Springs in less than an hour.

He hadn't been able to book a seat, it was that crowded. But the combination of his badge and a credit card had convinced the Amtrak people that he could ride. It was only another six hours to Denver, anyway. He could sit in the club car for that long.

In the meantime, he was tempted to contact Colonel Tucker, back in Salt Lake City. The problem was that if Joe and Helen were on this train, there wasn't a lot, legally, that Mulheisen could do. He couldn't arrest them. He had no authority here. He could, no doubt, obtain the cooperation of the local police. But he didn't know if they were getting off here. He didn't think so, which is why he had arranged to travel on to Denver. For all he knew, the mob man, Ezio "Itchy" Spinodi—Mulheisen still hadn't spotted him, but he remembered the name and was sure he would recognize him—was going to meet the pair and escort them back to Aspen. But the fact that Itchy had brought his suitcase indicated that he was planning to join them.

The real trouble with notifying the colonel, however, was that Mulheisen was afraid that the situation would get out of hand, that it would be escalated. He'd seen operators like Colonel Tucker before. They had too many resources—planes, cars, agents, satellites, money, interstate authority—and it led them into excess. Mulheisen had visions of SWAT teams boarding the train and storming the car or compartment where Joe and Helen were. They would try to get everyone out first, of course, but then there would be shooting. Maybe they'd evacuate the car and put it on a siding, then the floodlights would come on . . .

No, it was true that Joe and Helen were dangerous, but Mulheisen wasn't sure that the colonel wasn't more dangerous. As far as Mulheisen knew, they were traveling through, probably to Chicago, maybe Detroit. The Amtrak people had been able to tell him only that Ms. Woods was accompanying her uncle's remains to Chicago. They had no further information than that. They didn't know anything about Joe Service. They didn't know anything about any Ezio Spinodi, either, although a Eugene Izzi had bought a ticket to Denver. Like Mulheisen, Mr. Izzi was standing; but from Denver on he had reserved a roomette in the car next to the last dormitory car, the one where Ms. Woods and her late uncle were.

When the Zephyr swept into the station there was another rush of sports-fops, detraining and boarding. Mulheisen waited by the corner of the station and he was rewarded by seeing Itchy climb aboard. Mulheisen got on two cars forward and made his way to the lounge. It was down a semicircular stair, and he saw immediately that the place was a trap. There was no other exit. If he were down here and Itchy came down there would inevitably be a confrontation. He did not want to confront Itchy, not with so many people, so many children around.

There really were an awful lot of children aboard this train. The big cars with their rows of recliner-type seats were crawling and bubbling and scurrying with children, to say nothing of the calling and laughing and howling. He retreated to another car, and then another, working toward the back, until he nearly came face to face with Itchy. He recognized the moustache and turned into a bathroom gratefully. He heard the man tread by. After a few minutes he followed. As he had expected, Itchy descended into the lounge.

Mulheisen was content to let him go. If, as he surmised, Helen and Joe were in the last car, Itchy would have to get by him to get to them. With that he continued his passage toward the rear of the train. Glancing out the windows he saw that they had entered the Glenwood Canyon and were racing along the Colorado River, a spectacular run. The water was smashing along, sheathing rocks with ice, being funneled into frothing chutes. The train seemed at times to practically float over the water, so close to the edge were they.

They flashed into a black tunnel and quickly flashed back into the sunlight. He continued his trek rearward.

Finally he encountered the conductor, a Mr. Herman Jones. He took the man aside and showed him his identification. The conductor seemed quite unperturbed.

"You expecting any trouble?" he asked.

Mulheisen said he wasn't. He just would like to be able to keep an eye on room H.

"There's just that lady with the coffin," the conductor said. "She hasn't come out since we left Salt Lake, according to the attendant. She didn't want breakfast or even coffee. But the attendant told me that she seemed to have brought aboard quite a few provisions. A lot of people do that. They'd rather not mess with the dining car."

"Where is the dining car?" Mulheisen asked.

The conductor pointed over his shoulder at the very next car. They were talking in the noisy space between the cars. Through the glass Mulheisen could see the waiters and customers. It didn't seem very crowded.

"It's after lunch," the conductor pointed out. "Most everybody's been served."

"Mmm. Is there anyplace I could kind of hang out, back that way? Someplace unobtrusive?"

The conductor eyed him with a look of resignation. Then he nodded. "Okay," he sighed, "come on."

Mulheisen followed him back, through the diner, through a sleeper, another sleeper, and finally to the last car. They descended a semicircular stair in the middle of the car and stopped in a kind of hallway. There were doors on either side, the access doors for when they were in-station. The conductor gestured toward the rear. The very last door was labeled ROOM H. One door forward was another, smaller compartment. The conductor took out a bunch of keys on a chain and selected one. He unlocked the door and slid it open.

"This is my room," he said quietly when they had entered. There was a curtain over the door. He pulled it back slightly. "You can sit in here." he pointed at a seat that took up half of the compartment. "And if you keep the door open and the curtain drawn, you can pretty much monitor what goes on. Okay?"

"Well," Mulheisen felt embarrassed. "I don't know what to say. Thanks!"

The conductor nodded. He was a brown-skinned man of fifty, with graying hair and deep brown eyes, the very model of rectitude and responsibility. He looked almost dauntingly wise. "I'll be back in . . . " He looked at his pocket watch. "Forty minutes. Make yourself at home, Sergeant Mulheisen."

After the man had gone, Mulheisen reached down to the leather satchel that contained all his gear and hoisted it onto the seat next to him. He took out his snub-nosed .38 Chief's Special, in its hip-grip holster, and anchored it on his hip. He drew the revolver out and rotated the chamber slowly, then set it back into the holster. Then he sat back in the chair and arranged the curtain so that it gave him a narrow view of the door to room H.

He smiled to himself and was gratified to find that he didn't feel in the least nervous, despite the fact that not ten feet away, he felt certain, a heavily armed Joe Service and his equally heavily armed companion were sitting.

They were not sitting, of course. Joe had awakened first. He had left the scanner on, and a nasal voice shouting over engine noise had startled him. It was apparently a crewman asking another crewman in another part of the train if he was still not getting power to some box. Joe turned down the scanner and woke up Helen to show her the thrilling run through the Glenwood Canyon. They were both completely naked, as they had been practically since boarding. They drank from a fresh bottle of champagne, which could have done with some chilling, but they didn't really mind. And they ate some fruit and cheese. Before very long, however, they turned away from the window and began to play with each other.

Joe was very excited. He had not been this sexually aroused since . . . well, it must have been before his injury. There was no doubt that Helen's slim, hairless body aroused him like no other. She was a wicked, wicked woman and he told her so. They very quickly fell to stroking one another's genitals and in short order Joe had achieved yet another amazing erection, this one even more incredible than the last. "I feel like it's growing, or something," he gasped as Helen stroked it and licked at it. Then she turned on her hands and knees and he entered her again.

It was even more fabulous than before. He held her by the waist at first, then by the haunches as he drove into her repeatedly. He was frenzied. His head fell back and his eyes unfocused. His pelvis moved in a blur.

Helen was on fire. Joe's repeated thrusts had long since brought her to orgasm, perhaps her fifth or sixth since leaving Salt Lake City. But this was incredible. Now a kind of wave of orgasms swept over her, racking her repeatedly like sheet lightning . . . she was coming almost incessantly. Finally her legs gave way and she began to sink forward, but Joe held her up. He was still driving frenetically into her. She could not believe it. She cast a wild glance back over her shoulder and was shocked to see his head tipped back and hear his ragged gasping. It was beginning to hurt, now, to burn. But he didn't stop. He had no idea of stopping.

"Joe!" she gasped. "Stop! That's enough! Stop, damn it! You're hurting me!"

But he didn't seem to hear. He just surged on, wildly fucking her, almost like a machine run amok. She tried to wrench away, to free herself from this maniacal fucker, this mad rapist, but he seemed preternaturally strong, clutching her to his loins. His grip was itself terrifying, painful.

Suddenly the scanner crackled and a wispy voice asked, "Mr. Jones, have you got a Sergeant Mulheisen aboard? We've got a message for him."

Joe stopped in midthrust and turned his head to stare wildly at the scanner, his mouth open and his eyes blazing.

"Yeah, Ron," a voice whispered back, "I've got him, but not handy. I'll have him call you in about five minutes."

"Roger, Jonesy. Out." The scanner fell silent.

Joe looked down at Helen but did not see her, he was not focusing. His gaze slipped to the floor, and then his left foot slid off the bed and hit the floor. He tried to stand, but when his right foot reached the floor it gave way and he toppled sideways, narrowly missing the coffin, which took up so much of the center of the room. He sprawled on the floor, making odd inarticulate noises, with his left arm and leg scrabbling and contracting.

Helen shrank back onto the bed, staring, her legs drawn up. She was leaking semen but she didn't notice, and she no longer felt the tearing pain from Joe's furious thrusting. She stared at Joe, writhing on the carpeted floor.

She screamed and leaped to the door, flinging it open.

"Help!" she cried.

Mulheisen stood there, gun in hand. He pushed her aside and knelt by Joe. "Holy shit," he said. He turned to Helen. "Get back in here! You're naked, for chrissake!"

Mulheisen dashed down the hallway looking for the attendant, but then he remembered the call button in the room and stepped into Mr. Jones's open door and viciously punched the button, over and over. Then he returned to room H.

He knelt beside Joe and turned his head. The man was moving his lips, but not making much sense. "Arrgh . . . ar got arm a no . . . move it, can't move . . . ar-arm a go . . . Mulheiss!" He looked directly into Mulheisen's eyes with a wild, frightened stare.

Mulheisen looked up at Helen. She was naked, dancing on her tiptoes, as if she had to pee. Her face was twisted in concern and she wrung her hands. "Oh, oh, oh," she said, "what is it? What's wrong?"

"For chrissake, shut up and get something on," Mulheisen snapped. The thought flashed through his mind that he had seen this young woman naked far too often, considering that they had no kind of interest in each other. She was very far from his type. "What the hell happened here?" he asked impatiently.

"I don't know," Helen said. She was frantically tugging on jeans and a sweater. "He was fucking . . . I thought he was going to fuck me to death and I . . . "

Mulheisen heard someone approaching and he spun around, still kneeling. Of all people, Itchy was sidling along the corridor, craning his head, trying to look into the room. He had a hand in his overcoat pocket.

Mulheisen pointed the .38 at him. "Get the hell out of here, Itchy. Get your sorry ass back in the lounge. I'll see you later."

"Yeah, yeah, Mul," Itchy said. He showed both his hands, as if to say, Look I'm clean, and he went back the way he had come, but faster. He had scarcely disappeared when the attendant, Ms. Williams, came bounding off the stairway and down the corridor.

"What's goin' on?" she said, stopping in the doorway, taking in the disarray of the room, the naked man on the floor, the woman zipping up her jeans, the sweater only on one arm and over the head, the other arm bare and exposing a tiny breast. "Who are you?" It was addressed to Mulheisen.

"Get Jones," Mulheisen said. "This man is in bad trouble."

When the woman vanished, Mulheisen turned to Helen. "Does he have any medication? Is he supposed to take something?"

"I don't know," Helen yelped. "How the hell am I supposed to know? I'm not a nurse. He didn't say anything about medication. What's wrong? Is he all right? Is he dying?"

"M'okay," Joe gasped out, his eyes wild, "m'okay . . . med . . . med . . . " he waved his left arm.

"Look in his bag. No, wait. Here, help me get him onto the bed." Mulheisen lifted the upper torso. For a small man, Joe was surprisingly heavy, but Helen caught his legs and they soon had him on the bed. Mulheisen spread a blanket over him while Helen rummaged in Joe's travel kit. She came up with a half dozen plastic vials. Mulheisen turned them in the light from the window, trying to read their labels. They had long chemical names and instructions to take one pill at various times. He had no idea what should be done.

"Joe." He turned to the bed, then knelt by it. "Did you take any pills today?"

The conductor entered the room and asked what had happened, but Mulheisen held up a hand for silence without looking at him. Joe seemed calmer now, almost relaxed, but still mumbling.

"Joe," Mulheisen asked, "did you take your pills? Do you need to take a pill?" He held the vials in his hands, offering them to the man. Joe shook his head several times, nodded several times, then pawed at the pills, knocking them from Mulheisen's hands. Mulheisen picked them up again and, more calmly now, presented them, one by one, between finger and thumb, so that Joe could see them. Finally, Joe grabbed at one.

"Okay," Mulheisen said, "I don't know if this is the right thing to do, but here goes. Get a cup of water, Helen." He wrenched the vial open and shook out one pill. Then he held Joe by the shoulders and popped it into his mouth, followed by the cup of water. Joe gulped it down, then fell back on the bed. He stared up at the ceiling.

Mulheisen stood up. "He's had a stroke or something," he said to the conductor. "He's been recovering from a brain injury. You better call ahead. How far is it to the next stop?"

"Granby's the next stop, but there's a doctor in the next car. I'll get him."

Mulheisen sighed and squatted next to the bed. He put his hand on Joe's forehead. It was damp. He brushed the thick black hair back. "Joe, Joe, Joe," he said. Joe looked at him, blinking. He seemed calmer now. "Maybe you'll be all right, Joe." Then, "Yeah, you'll be all right." He stood up and looked about. Helen had her sweater on, at last. She looked from Joe to Mulheisen, then back again.

"Will he be all right?"

"I wouldn't doubt it," Mulheisen said. "He'll need a hospital, though." He looked thoughtful. "It'll be a lot better for him than prison. He'll have a chance in a hospital." And I can talk to him, he added to himself.

"Keep an eye on him," he told Helen. "I better go see about Itchy. The doctor will be here soon."

He had hardly left the room when Joe called out, "Hel . . . Hel . . . bags." He pointed at the duffel bags and gestured with his left arm. "Out! Out!"

Helen grasped the thought quickly. She seized the two bags full of money and lugged them down the hallway. She wrenched open the half-door at the exit and a rush of freezing air billowed into the landing area. She seized the bags and hurled them out, one after the other, then leaned out to see them tumble down the embankment. A moment later, the attendant hurtled down the stairs.

"Hey, you! What you doin'? You can't open them when we're moving!" She slammed the half-door shut. "What the hell you doing?"

"I needed air," Helen said, shrinking back against the wall. She could hear the steps of the conductor and the doctor. "Where are we?" she demanded.

The conductor and the doctor pushed by her and went on down the corridor to room H.

"Where are we?" Ms. Williams said. "We're on a train. We're almost to Granby."

"Where exactly?" Helen hissed. "I have to know."

Ms. Williams glanced out the window. "We're about ten miles. Be there in a few minutes." Then she followed the men to the room. Helen stood at the window and stared out, trying to memorize everything, the mountains, the trees, the distant ranch house.

When Mulheisen returned everything seemed in control. The doctor said Joe would be all right. There would be an ambulance waiting at Granby. Of Helen, there was no sign. The attendant said she had put on her shoes and a coat and had gone out. Mulheisen went through the train, looking for her. But he had not found her by the time the train reached Granby.

He got off there with his bag and climbed into the ambulance with Joe. Joe was sleeping. The doctor had given him something.

"Well, Joe," Mulheisen said, patting his hand, "I've got you, anyway."